THE LAST WHISTLEWILLOW
SONG OF THE ELLYDIAN
BOOK II

C.K. RIEKE

Books by C.K. Rieke

Song of the Ellydian I: The Scarred
Song of the Ellydian II: The Last Whistlewillow
Song of the Ellydian III: The Fallen Apprentice

Riders of Dark Dragons I: Mystics on the Mountain
Riders of Dark Dragons II: The Majestic Wilds
Riders of Dark Dragons III: Mages of the Arcane
Riders of Dark Dragons IV: The Fallen and the Flames
Riders of Dark Dragons V: War of the Mystics

The Dragon Sands I: Assassin Born
The Dragon Sands II: Revenge Song
The Dragon Sands III: Serpentine Risen
The Dragon Sands IV: War Dragons
The Dragon Sands V: War's End

The Path of Zaan I: The Road to Light
The Path of Zaan II: The Crooked Knight
The Path of Zaan III: The Devil King

Copyright

This novel was published by Crimson Cro Publishing
Copyright © 2024 Hierarchy LLC

All Rights Reserved.

Edited by Tiffany Shand
And Zach Ritz.

All characters and events in this book are fictitious.
Printed in the United States of America. No part of this book may be used or reproduced in any manner whatsoever without written permission except in the case of brief quotations embodied in critical articles or reviews.
This book is a work of fiction. Names, characters, businesses, organizations, places, events and incidents either are the product of the author's imagination or are used fictitiously. Any resemblance to actual persons, living or dead, events, or locales is entirely coincidental.

Please don't pirate this book.

Sign up to join the Reader's Group
CKRieke.com

ALADRAN
and its
Six Kingdoms
Arkakus
Ikarus
Celestra
Silvergale Lake
Lynthyn
The Larghos Sea
Zatan
Cascadia
Guillead
The Lyones
The Dirkwood
Myngorn
Faulker
Arnor
The Dyadric Desert
Herne Forest
Erhil
Londindam
Fae Veil Lake
Skylark
N
W
E
S
The Ambler
The Rine
Belltop
The Borderlands
Grayhaven
100 Miles
The Tibers
The Sapphire Sea

PART I
THE LADY OF CASCADIA

Chapter One

H*ope.*

A BEWILDERING BEAST, *yet it can oftentimes be the last vestige of light in the darkest caverns.*

It brims and thrives in youth. It fades and festers in the aged.

In songs it tells of tragic lovers, and triumphant feats. Yet in this world, it oft is killed more easily than anything.

It can be extinguished in the blink of an eye, or the flutter of a heartbeat, or the last note of a beautiful ballad.

It leads kings to win wars, men to ward off the shadow, and children to brave the night to see the courage of the rising sun.

Hope is human. Yet hope is divine.

Hold it close as long as you can, for nothing is as precious, and so fleeting.

. . .

-Translated from the language of the Sundar. The Scriptures of the Ancients, Book III, Chapter I.

THE WORLD WARPED. It stretched and twisted like a thin wet sheet of silk. Soren felt himself falling into an endless oblivion. As he tumbled down the foreverness, lights of gleaming, heavenly white floated through the empty air, enveloping him with the warmth of a mother's love. Yet, the further he fell, the darker it became.

A wintery landscape of rolling snow-capped hills faded, turning to a cavernous black. The red glow of the inferno he'd left behind faded as well, causing the constant pain in his stomach to lurch. His nightmarish past had returned to him, and as he fell, it cut into him like a dagger—twisting in deeper and deeper until he felt as if nothing he ever cared for again would be safe from the curse that was carved into his face.

As the blackness overwhelmed him, there was a single solace in his failure to save the city of Erhil—a hand that clung to his. It squeezed so tightly he knew it couldn't be death that was taking him, but a chance for life. It was a new path he could walk. One not so alone, so hopeless, so miserable.

It was Persephone, his niece, and his only surviving family left in this world.

Her wild black hair whipped above her head as they fell into the void. Her eyes were wide and surreally green, the color of ripe lime rinds. She looked as if she and Soren were stuck in a never-ending dream.

But it wasn't just them who fell.

"We aren't alone…" she said, as the world was still enveloped in shadow.

Soren couldn't see as the darkness overwhelmed them, but he could feel someone else tumbling in the shadow. Even in the calm chaos of falling into the oblivion, he still managed to find

Firelight fixed in his hand as he squeezed the grip, causing the leather to squeal. In the empty black, he noticed the blade of the Vellice dagger glowed that same red sheen it did under starlight. The beautifully hammered, layered steel glimmered in waves, like moonlight on the endless waves of the vast sea.

Whoever fell with them had better pray. *If you came to harm my niece, you won't draw breath much longer. I promise you that…*

As he heard Seph say the words, he felt the ground under him. He felt his body on hard ground again—he was no longer falling.

Soren was lying on his side, groggy, as a baby would be laid into its cradle by its mom. He knelt—one knee on the ground, ready to pounce once the darkness fled. He looked around, but he couldn't see Persephone. The overwhelming darkness changed then, going from complete emptiness to a swirling sphere of streaking gray clouds around him. To his right, he saw her silhouetted against the clouds.

Suddenly, the clouds burst into a fiery orange flame, causing Soren to cover his eyes with his forearm. The light was so intense it reminded him of being in Tourmielle ten years ago, and the massacre that happened there—changing his life forever.

The sunrise-orange flames glowed to a startling, chilly blue. Only for a moment, though. And just as quickly as they'd appeared—they vanished.

"Persephone," he said. "Are you all right?"

"I think so," she coughed. "And it's Seph."

"Right," Soren replied, rising.

To Soren's complete surprise, the battlefield had vanished. The king, the archpriest, the Knight Wolf… they were all gone. The innocent town of Erhil, roaring with awful flames, was but a nightmare. Soren was awake, though, and he and Seph were in a dimly lit, wide room with a dry dirt floor and old stone walls.

A torch lit the room's corner by a set of wide stairs that circled up.

"Soren," Seph said in a firm voice, with her lean arm raised, pointing at the opposite corner of the room.

His gaze followed her arm and instantly he saw what his niece was pointing at.

In the room's far corner, a tall boy lay, groaning with a hand on his brow as he lay on his side, trying to gather his wits, and rise.

I can't let him speak. He will cast a spell on us!

Soren rushed forward in the dark room. His head fogged and his legs were shaky as he ran toward the archmage's apprentice. Soren pounced on him, straddling him, and the red-haired apprentice fell onto his back, wide-eyed and terrified. Soren pressed his hand so hard over his mouth that his face instantly flushed and his eyes reddened.

Soren brought the Vellice dagger, Firelight, over the apprentice's face, angling the sharp point inches away from the center of his brow—right between the eyes.

"Soren!" Seph yelled as she ran behind, only halfway the distance Soren had covered in the same time. "Stop!"

Soren paused. *Why is she making me stop? I know this boy. I remember him from the battlefield. He's the archmage's apprentice. This boy, Kaile, was the one who followed Seph into the church in Guillead, where we both listened to her play the organ.*

And now he's here with us. Why? And how is this all possible? Last thing I remember is the great Syncron Mihelik arriving to confront the king and the archmage, and in the storm… we arrived… here… how?

"Soren, stop," Seph said as she put both of her hands on the back of his shoulders, heaving deep breaths.

Soren's hand still covered Kaile's mouth, twisting his head to the side under the pressure. Firelight's tip still hung inches away from Kaile's face, which was nearly going cross-eyed glaring up at it. Beads of sweat trickled down the boy's face.

His tan skin gleamed in the torchlight as it wetted from sweat, and his wild, reddish-auburn hair clung to his brow and cheeks.

"Why?" Soren grunted. "He's a Synth. He followed us here to kill us!"

"I don't think he did!" Seph said, gently trying to pull Soren off Kaile by grabbing the front of his shoulders, prying him back.

"You didn't see him back there when they burned the city. I did, Soren. He was scared. I think... I think he escaped..."

Escaped?

Soren moved his head close to Kaile's. He glared hard into his eyes, inspecting the intent of the young lad. He indeed saw fear—intense, deep fear.

"Listen to me, Kaile," Soren said with a grim tone from the back of his throat. "That's your name, yes?"

Kaile nodded, not taking his wide, wet, reddened eyes away from Soren's glare.

"If you try to cast a spell, if you try to hurt me, or even run... I'll kill you before you get the chance."

Kaile nodded eagerly, with Soren's hand still pressed hard on his mouth, causing his skin to crease.

"And if you even think..." Soren twisted Firelight before him. "If you even think about hurting her, I'm going to cut your head off so fast your brain won't recognize it until you see mouse droppings on the floor..." Soren looked around the dingy cellar room. "Wherever we are..."

Soren slowly withdrew his hand from the apprentice, as Kaile panted quick breaths, and his chest heaved.

"Thank... thank you..."

Soren watched his mouth move intently, and his hands, in case he decided to use any device that would cause a tone he could use to cast a spell.

"Thank you," Kaile said.

Soren stood, as he and Seph looked down at Kaile, laying back on his elbows, completely out of his depth and now devoid of any protection the king and his men would provide.

"Why are you here?" Seph asked. Her voice was deep, untrusting, and curt.

Kaile wiped the sweat from his mouth and brow with his sleeve.

Soren held Firelight out at his side, ready to strike at a split-second's notice.

"I—I don't really have an answer to that," Kaile said. His voice was youthful and cracked slightly. Soren thought he must be no older than eighteen. "I just saw a chance, and I took it."

"A chance to what?" Soren scowled down at him with his brow furrowed.

"Escape."

Seph dropped, bending her knees out and meeting him at eye level. Her forearms dangled off her thighs, and she looked mostly relaxed. Soren saw this but maintained his hesitation at their new visitor.

"Escape what?" Seph asked. "The archmage? The king?"

"All of them. All of it." Kaile shook his head, looking down at his lap. To Soren, Kaile looked more than scared. He looked traumatized, looking more like a babbling beggar than an apprentice of the archmage of Lynthyn.

"Listen to me," Seph said, putting her hand on Kaile's knee, snapping his attention to her hand, and then her face. "Do you know where we are? How we got here?"

"Here?" he asked, looking around the room. "I—I don't know this place… but yes, I know how we got here. The spell… Mihelik opened a portal. I saw you all going into it, so I ran in too. I took a chance. He's going to kill me for this."

"You bet your ass he will," Soren grumbled.

Seph glanced up at Soren and sighed.

"You said Mihelik opened a portal?" Soren put Firelight in her scabbard and folded his arms.

A portal? Soren had heard of the old archmage Mihelik using such spells long ago. Before his betrayal to the other Syncrons, burning their oldest and most treasured knowledge, the old archmage once used a portal to show Soren's lost love, Cirella, a view from the clouds. She used to say it was the most spectacular thing she could imagine. She never looked at birds the same way again—so magnificent, so free.

"Yes," Kaile said. "I've never seen him use one, but the moment he cast it, I knew what it was. And as soon as I saw you leaving with him, I couldn't help myself. I leaped through too. All that fire… All that smoke… it's still in my nostrils. I can hear their screams. I can hear them praying, begging for mercy. Why? Why did they do that?"

Soren sighed heavily. He knew the feeling all too well about what Kaile was going through. The king had slaughtered the entire town of Erhil, in the name of the plague—the Chimaera. But Soren knew that was a lie. And now his friends Bael and Alicen were dead. Soren swallowed hard.

"Because the king has gone mad," Soren said. "His lust for power has driven him insane. The only god he worships now is fire."

"But all those children…" Kaile said with quivering lips, and tears streamed down his cheeks. "They didn't do anything to any of them. They're just kids…"

Seph clapped Kaile's knee and glanced up at Soren, not knowing what to say.

"Listen," Soren said. "There's nothing we can do for them now. We don't even know where we are. You say Mihelik brought us here in a portal? Well, where is he then?"

Each of them looked around the wide, rectangular room that smelled of stale air and musty mildew.

"Let us go look," Soren said. "And remember… you try to

cast a spell... any spell... I don't care if it's to comb your hair... you won't live long enough to explain... you got it?"

Kaile nodded, his eyes still wide, wiping the tears away with his sleeve. Seph backed away from him and got up. Then Kaile stood, and as he got up, Soren saw he was over a full head taller than him.

"Real coy," Soren grumbled. "We're going to stand out like a brick of coal in a barrel of diamonds. Me, the Scarred, the giant rogue apprentice to the archmage, and well..." He stared at Seph in thought, cocking an eyebrow. "Well, as long as they didn't put together who you are... if we're lucky enough... then that would at least be one good thing in this scenario."

"We made it out alive," she said. "That's one good thing."

"You hurt the king," Kaile said. "I saw it. Your dagger cut him. He is human."

Soren smirked and looked down at the Vellice dagger resting on his hip, and then at Seph. "Thanks for bringing it back to me. I've grown attached to it, ever since it killed those Shades back on the plains. Didn't think I'd see it again."

"Don't get used to me being your errand girl," she said, somewhat in a playful voice, but her demeanor soured as her shoulders tensed and she scowled. "I'm still mad at you. Don't forget that. You still left me in that horrible place all those years. I'm not going to forgive you for that ever! Now, let's go find that Syncron and figure out where the hell we are..."

She stormed off to the room's corner with the staircase, leaving both Soren and Kaile nervous to follow.

"She's... terrifying," Kaile muttered.

"I'm starting to see that..." Soren said, as he let Kaile follow her first up the stairs.

Chapter Two

Soren stood behind, while Seph waited at the top of the staircase. All three were in line, with the wooden planks creaking under their feet. Kaile stood between them, and even two stairs below her, the top of his head leveled with hers. Soren waited at the bottom of the dark staircase, ready to draw his dagger, as he looked up at the two. The doorway that framed them was lined with amber firelight from torches beyond.

The air was still and quiet. Seph pressed her ear to the door, and seemingly assured there was nothing beyond, slowly pressed down on the door handle, unlatching it with a click. She pulled the door open with a shrill squeal of the hinges and entered the room above.

Two torches glowed their light into the room, both resting upon the far wall with a door between them. This room differed greatly from the room below. Instead of a dirt floor, their boots clapped onto stone. A wide rug of old weave rested in the middle of the square room. As Soren walked into it, he saw no windows or other doors. There was only one way out, and that was through the door ahead.

I don't like this one bit. I can't even tell if we're still underground, and there aren't any clues as to where we are. Where did the old archmage bring us? Is this a trap? If it is, goddess help whoever thinks to spring it.

Seph walked quickly to the other door.

"Hold," Soren whispered.

She halted, letting him pass her and Kaile. Soren gave the tall boy an icy glare as he went by, and Kaile looked away at the ground.

Soren pulled Firelight free and clenched her tightly. His free hand wrapped around the door's handle. He turned it, but found it locked.

He released his grip and stood back, thinking, and taking a wide stance. He was ready to shove the heel of his boot into where the door met the jamb.

"What now?" Seph asked, folding her arms.

Kaile scratched his wild red hair, which had a fresh coating of dirt and dust on one side. He didn't seem to notice it until it began flaking on his shoulder.

"Mihelik brought us here, saving us," Soren said. "There must be a reason, but to leave us in a locked cellar doesn't make sense. Why here? And where is the old, blind man?"

He stood back, taking a deep, groaning breath. "I'm not waiting to find out."

Seph and Kaile tensed as Soren prepared to kick the door in, when they heard a pop of the latch from the other side of the closed door.

Soren, still with dagger in hand, forced the other two behind him.

"Know any offensive spells?" Seph whispered to Kaile.

"Huh?" he mouthed, taking a moment to grasp the question. But then, as if a spark of inspiration had hit him, he reached his hand into his pocket and drew out a tiny tuning fork, no more than three inches long.

Seph's eyebrows raised as the door creaked open before

them. Soren spun and snatched the fork from Kaile's hand, plucking it out with ease and sliding it into his pocket. He didn't even look up at Kaile, but instead turned his attention to whoever was opening the door.

I can't trust him to cast anything…

Soren was ready to burst the door open with his shoulder, killing any with Firelight who dared to stand between him and the exit. What he feared more than anything though, was if there was a Synth in the room… He'd have to deal with that quicker than the Synth could draw breath. He heard heavy footsteps leaving the other side of the door, fading back.

"We mean no harm," the sturdy voice of an aged man said from the other side. The door swung open but stopped after only a couple of inches. The man's voice was old, but not old enough to be Mihelik. "There's no one but me and a couple of my men in here." The man spoke in a courtly manner. He was no peasant or soldier.

"Where are we?" Soren asked through the cracked open door. "Who are you?"

"Come on in," the man's voice said. "See for yourself. You can lower your weapon. There's no need for that here."

A Synth would *say that…*

Soren pressed the door open with two fingers of his free hand, still gripping the Vellice dagger with the other. The door swung open, and more torchlight filled the room, but there were also candles upon a fireplace's hearth to the left.

Once the door was open, and Soren could feel Kaile and Seph both eagerly looking over his shoulders, Soren saw the man, and the two other men at his sides.

The old man was dark of skin, bald as an egg, with an ivory white beard and robes of emerald. His veiny, wrinkled hands folded over his stomach. He held no staff or weapon and had a curious expression with his lips pursed and his eyes darting around, inspecting them. The two soldiers at his sides were fully armored and had swords sheathed on their belts. They both glowered at Soren.

"Who are you?" Soren asked in a firm tone as he entered the room. "Are you a wielder of the Ellydian?"

"If I were," the man said. "That would determine your feeling about this room greatly. Would it not?"

Soren gripped the dagger, ready to strike should the need arise.

The man unfolded his hands and held up his palms for each of them. "I am not a Syncron, no. And my men are only here for my protection. But I doubt very much they'd be able to stop the legendary Blade of Tourmielle, wouldn't they?"

Both the guards looked at the aged man and grunted.

"No, they would not," Soren said. "Now, out with it. Where are we?"

"You are in Barringstone Castle," the man said proudly. "And I am your host. Chancellor Roland Carvaise. Honor to meet you."

"Barringstone?" Soren gasped. "We're in Skylark?"

"Skylark?" Kaile muttered. "We're in the capital of Cascadia?"

"Aye," the chancellor said. "Home of Lady Drake, and you are at the heart of the capital city."

"And Mihelik?" Soren asked.

"Resting," Roland said. "The trip took a great deal out of the Syncron."

Soren glanced to the side in thought, and then stood up straight and sheathed his blade. The two soldiers loosened their postures at that.

"Is Lady Drake here?" Soren asked.

"The lady is here," Roland said. "And she wishes to see you."

"I have questions of my own," Soren said. "Lead the way."

Roland held his hand up again, causing Soren to pause in his stride.

"You are all…" Roland began. "How do I say this…? Wanted by the capital of Celestra and the king. You'll want to keep your identities hidden." The old man scanned the three; the Scarred, the runaway tall boy with the wild red hair, and the skinny girl with the frayed black hair. "And you don't exactly *blend in*…"

"Understood," Soren said. "Now, may we?"

"Certainly," the chancellor said. "Follow me, please. She's just up ahead."

Lady Drake is involved in this…? Is she secretly against King Amón? Is she one of the Silver Sparrows? And if she is—she's in great danger. The king won't be satisfied until they're all murdered, every last one of them…

They followed Chancellor Roland out of the room that led down a dim hall. Soren could most definitely smell that they were underground. The mustiness filled his nostrils, and he could feel the dew cling to his skin. He mustered his strength and resistance to the pain, but with the gash in his leg, the pain in his bruised ribs, and the swelling on his broken nose—he needed rest, but there was no time for that. He walked without a limp as best he could, but he could hear the echo of his own footsteps in the narrow hall. He did his best to correct it.

Seph was behind him. Silent yet observant, Soren knew. Kaile was behind her, and as Soren turned to look at him, he saw the apprentice had to duck his head to avoid banging it on the ceiling. Soren felt Kaile's tuning fork in his own pocket and hoped that was the only one he had carried.

If he's a Synth worth a spit, he'd have a backup… He didn't have much evidence either way…

"Just up ahead," Roland said back to Soren and the others. There was a glowing silhouette around his robes and bald head from the lights down the long hall.

Soren thought again, if this was an elaborate trap—he'd be ready. He didn't suspect Kaile would be in on an elaborate ruse with the lady of Skylark, so if things went south, he might toss the apprentice his fork back. That would be the worst-case scenario, though. And what point would a trap be after all this? Soren was at the mercy of the king, the archpriest, the archmage, the Knight Wolf, and the king's private guards—the drakoons. Up until Mihelik showed up with the single most spectacular spell of the Ellydian Soren had ever seen, he was going to be a dead man.

The tunnels turned out to be much longer than Soren anticipated. They weren't one, but a series of underground tunnels that darted in different directions in what ended up being a sort of maze-like catacombs under the great city of Skylark. He wasn't surprised the lady wouldn't be waiting in a place like this, and when they finally emerged at their destination, all worry about an ambush faded, and Soren saw Lady Drake herself.

In the underground room with many walls, many corridors leading off it, and a ceiling over twenty feet high, the lady of Skylark spoke in a ring with a dozen other men and women, all dressed in expensive cloth, save for one military man in light, fine armor.

As the chancellor moved to the side of the entryway, Soren walked in first. In the splendor of the many candles around the room, and the glowing, circular, black steel chandelier above, Soren felt the unwanted attention and spotlight on him. He wanted to be back in a forest, with the free winds, the chirping crickets, and his friend Ursa at his side.

Ursa... poor girl... I hope you managed to escape. Even if we never see each other again, I hope you lived to ride along the hills all the rest of your days.

A ring of people opened up around Lady Drake as Soren, Seph, Kaile and the chancellor's guards entered. Seph and

Kaile stood in a line beside Soren, with Kaile on the other side of her. Soren had never seen a boy so nervous. He looked as if a stiff wind would blow him right off his feet.

Seph was different, though. She, normally, would blend into a rock wall if she wanted. Unnoticeable, inconspicuous, and small. You had to get to know her to see her personality was anything but... Seph was silent, but Soren knew she was taking it all in. She'd suddenly transformed from a low orphan in Guillead to being swept off by one of the most powerful spells Soren had ever seen, to standing before the most respected woman in all of Cascadia, perhaps in all of Aladran itself.

"Soren Smythe," Lady Drake said. "Or may I call you by your true name?"

Soren growled but nodded.

"Soren Dakard Stormrose of the Knights of Tourmielle," she said, with a delicate wave of her hand outward.

Soren bowed. "My lady." He glanced over at Seph, who still stood tall, or at least upright. He yanked subtly at her elbow. She bowed, and Kaile bowed low. "Few call me by that name, but I suppose there's no use in hiding it now."

"Your secrets are safe here, in this hall," the lady said in a firm voice that filled the room all the way to the ceiling.

Lady Ellaina Drake was an Aeol, Soren knew. Being an Aeol, second strongest of the three wielders of the Ellydian, she'd pledged her power to the throne, gaining insight into the secret knowledge only those who served the king gathered.

She stood with a regal, powerful, courtly, elegant posture. She folded her arms over each other before her as she stood at the center of the long row of her followers. Her glistening, tan face and wise, coffee-colored eyes scanned the three scars down the side of Soren's face, then Persephone, and then Kaile. She wore long silver robes with ivory stitching and gold trim. She didn't wear her crown. Perhaps that was saved for above-ground meetings, Soren thought.

"Where's the old Syncron, Mihelik?" Soren asked. "Why is he not here?"

"Mihelik is being tended to," the lady said. "He will take time to recover. He's no longer the young man he once was. That spell took almost everything he had."

"And Erhil?" Soren asked, scratching his thigh, not truly wanting to know the answer.

Seph tensed beside him, and Kaile swallowed hard, wiping the sweat from his brow.

The lady lowered her head with a sigh, shaking her head slowly. "The city of Erhil is no more," she said, raising her head again, looking deep into Soren's eyes. There was a hint of sadness in hers. "There were no survivors of the attack."

"Alicen…" Soren muttered to himself. "Oh, no… not you too…"

"King Amón has again wiped a city from Aladran, and you, Soren… are the only soul alive to have witnessed both… Well, I suppose you are two now." She glanced at Persephone, who gulped.

Chapter Three

There was a draft of wind from one of the far corridors behind Lady Drake and the surrounding others. Soren smelled hints of lavender and cloves on the air. Soren folded his arms over his chest to hide the pain he felt at the lady's words that Erhil was gone. His plan hadn't worked.

He hadn't saved a soul.

Bael was dead; murdered before him with a bolt through the neck from the Knight Wolf himself. He bled to death in Soren's arms, and he could still see the pain in his dying friend's eyes, and Bael's last words echoed in his mind—*I tried... I'm sorry...*

The words bit hard at Soren. The curse that the Knight Wolf's Synth had cast on Soren was more than the scars that proclaimed him the rightful prey of the Wolf. It was also the curse that would cause vast hurt in all that Soren cared for.

He glanced to his side, to his niece next to him. All these years he'd made every effort to hide her, to protect her, and now there she was... standing before the lady of Skylark and her court. There was no hiding her now. Soren squeezed his fists at his side, but then released his grip with a futile exhale. Her stubbornness to join him had outed her to the world, and her appearance on the battlefield outside of Erhil, even more so.

"Why are we here?" Soren asked in a defeated voice, making no effort to cover his scars for all to see.

"You are here because the great Syncron brought you here," the lady said. There was an ominous tone in her voice, as if hiding something, but that didn't bother Soren. He knew there was no hiding now. They'd be coming for him. All of them. "It was his decision, and I will abide by his wishes. Not that long ago, he and I were adoring friends and comrades. So I will let him rest while I decide what to do with the lot of you."

"Let us go!" Seph said. "Those murderers are still out there!" Her voice cracked with all the pain inside her, balled up in her throat. "We can't let them get away with this. They can't keep doing this! They just can't…"

Her shoulders shook and tears rolled down her cheeks. She wasn't just talking about the attack on Erhil. She'd lost everything at the attack on their home Tourmielle ten years ago. Most of all—her parents.

"Persephone Whistlewillow," the lady said with an interested smirk on her face. She folded her arms and twisted to the side as she raised her eyebrow. "Heir to the Whistlewillows. Still alive… after all these years…"

Seph shied away, and Kaile watched intently with his mouth agape. Soren guessed this was the first time he'd put two and two together.

"I did my best to hide her from the king," Soren said. "But it was all for naught now."

"I was a friend of your parents," the lady said. "We even studied together, ages ago, that is. I have fond memories of your father Calvin and your mother Violetta."

Seph continued to cry, wiping her tears away with angry swipes. Not at the lady, but Soren felt she didn't want to cry ever again. There'd been too much of that. There was so much pain in the young woman, and Soren could relate.

"We haven't laid eyes upon each other in many years, Soren," Lady Drake said. "I've heard tales of your travels throughout Aladran since the fall of Tourmielle. My condolences for your loss. Cirella and I were also friends. I mourned her death, as I mourn so many others these days."

Soren nodded but didn't say a word.

"And you," the lady's attention shifted to the tall boy, who shuttered in nervousness as all eyes on the room fell upon him. "You must have testicles of iron." The room erupted in a brief, very brief, laughter. Soren even let out a chuckle.

Kaile feigned an anxious smile and nodded.

"Running from the archmage himself, I bet he is *fuming*..." There was a shrill delight in the lady's words.

"I'm sure he is," Kaile said, putting his arms behind his back, looking down at the floor.

"You said you were going to decide what to do with us," Soren said. "What are you planning? I'd like to know so that I can plan accordingly."

"Plan accordingly," Lady Drake said, nodding. "Very good. I suppose I'd feel the same as you. Well, you are in quite the predicament, aren't you? You can only hide in forests so long before the bastard William Wolf finally finishes what he started. He'll kill all three of you and be onto his next innocent town to destroy." She sighed. "What to do with you, indeed..."

"May I offer a suggestion, then?" Soren said, widening his stance with his shoulders back.

Murmurs scattered through the ranks of the lady.

She nodded.

"Let me go."

The murmurs increased. There were even gasps from some of the women.

"If the king," she began, "who I should mention that you sliced his face open with your blade, found out you were here and that I did such a thing... Skylark may be the next to burn."

"Hear me out," Soren said, taking a stride forward, leaving Seph and Kaile behind as the brightness of the candles seemed to grow, casting a warm veil over the high-ceiling room. "Let me go, and I'll go hunt those murderers down, one by one. I'll kill every last one of them. The king, the archpriest, Alcarond, Glasse, Garland. All of them."

The murmurs turned to a full stir of commotion and chattering.

"All of them?" Lady Drake asked with an eyebrow raised and her lips pursed. "The Knight Wolf cannot be killed by your hand. Those scars on your face control that destiny, or lack thereof."

"I'll find a way," Soren said.

Seph stepped forward to stand beside Soren. He glanced over his shoulder and groaned. He pushed her back with the back of his arm.

"Mihelik will know," Soren said. "Keep Persephone here, guarded and safe, and I'll kill every last one of them."

Lady Drake had an amused smirk on her face as she raised her chin, inspecting Soren. "I can see on your face and tell from your voice that you believe you could accomplish such a task. Yet... your actions prove otherwise."

Soren grunted, folding his arms again.

"You've had two chances against the king and his men, and two cities have fallen. Countless lives have been lost at the whim of the king's bloodlust, and here you stand, saying you won't let it happen a third time. I'm sorry, Soren Stormrose. I cannot take that chance."

"Let me go then," Seph said suddenly. "I'll be the one to do it."

A few in the room laughed, causing Seph to grit her teeth and ball her fists. Kaile seemed intrigued by her assertiveness, nearly gasping at her statement.

"I'm not just an orphan," she said with a mean hiss in her voice. "I'm more. They'd never see it coming."

"I beg to differ," the lady said. "But it won't be difficult for them to discover that you are Soren's niece, and heir to the Whistlewillow legacy. You will be captured and turned, and if you resist, you'll be tortured to your early death. Make no mistake when I say this, that this is true. I've seen it time and time again with young Syncrons. Submit or die."

"I'll do neither," Seph said.

Soren felt a strange pride well up in him, but he still turned and attempted to calm her with a push of his palm downward.

"You," the lady said, turning to face the boy. "Kaile Thorne, I'll receive quite the praise for returning you to your master. Alcarond is a spiteful man, but he certainly treasures his possessions. If I were true to the king, I'd kill you Soren, and turn Seph and Kaile over to him. I'd surely receive some of the sacred knowledge of the ancients in return. What was left from what Mihelik didn't destroy." Her eyes sparkled and she steepled her fingers before her.

"*If* you're true to the king..." Soren said in more of a question than a statement.

The lady gave a quick sigh.

"I'll require time to think about this," she said. "You three are to remain here until my decision is reached."

"My lady," Soren said. "Grant me a private session with you so that we may speak without all these ears."

"My council I trust with my life," she said in a stern tone.

"Pardon my offense," he said. "But I don't trust *anyone*."

She sighed again. "I will think about it. You will be fed and be free of chains down here in my halls. Do not make me regret this decision."

She turned to leave out of the rear of the torch-lit room. Her followers shuffled to follow, but then she stopped, seemingly deep in thought. Lady Drake looked over her shoulder at Soren, her eyes of coffee brown scanning his body as he attempted to hide the pain that ran all the way from tip to toe.

"Can I trust you?" she asked in a coy tone.

"Lady Drake," Soren said, with an eyebrow raised. "I'm not sure what you mean."

She sighed and strode toward him, her silver robes scraping on the stone floors as it glided at her ankles. Lady Drake walked all the way up to him, brushing away the shuffling soldiers as she did so. Soren had heard tales of her power. As an Ayl, she could control not only her surroundings, but had the power to manipulate her own body. Soren had no idea what sorts of contraptions she possessed to create the tune she'd need to cast a spell and had even less idea of what spells she was capable of casting.

Soren was fast with a dagger, quicker than almost anyone alive, but even if he wished to strike down the Syncron, he doubted if he'd be able to. And from the look in her wise eyes, she knew it.

Her silver hair flowed down both sides of her neck as she brushed it back with both hands, startling Seph and Kaile, as they seemed to worry she was about to cast a spell with the swift movement of her hands. Lady Drake stood taller than Soren, looking down at him as she raised her chin.

Soren looked deeply up into her eyes. There was an all-knowing wisdom locked in them—like staring into the brightest night stars. She was quite breathtaking, Soren thought, as he could feel her breath gently on his face. Her eyelashes were dark and curled like claws. She had a dark mole below her full, rosy lips. For a woman in her fifties, Soren was quite taken.

Her finger rose up his chest, caressing the buttons on his shirt, skipping over them like a stone on a glassy pond. Soren's throat caught.

"Trust," she whispered. "Do you remember it? Has it been that long?"

Soren felt frozen, as if a spell had been cast that caught him like a statue, caught in the wildness of her dark, cavernous eyes.

"I remember…" he fumbled the words as his lips hung apart.

"Can I trust you, when the time comes?" she whispered as if she and he were the only ones in the room.

"I… I don't know," he said. "Can I trust in you?"

"You're hurt," she said as her fingers caressed up his stubbly, rough cheeks, and rolled down his ragged scars.

He swallowed hard.

As she opened her mouth and her lips formed a circle, a sound left her throat that swallowed Soren into a warm, numbing feeling. His limbs felt light and free and the pain in his nose washed away. It was as if an angel had embraced him, squeezing the pain away.

A white haze like the shimmer on a misty waterfall grew on her fingertips.

She touched the tip of his nose and instantly his whole head went numb. His tired thoughts turned to a deep, relaxing focus on the freedom from pain. Her fingers moved down his neck and chest, suddenly grabbing his side with her sharp fingernails, digging into his ribs.

The stabbing pain that nagged him with his every movement was gone. Her hand then ran down his stomach, past his belt and groin, and finally onto his thigh. He felt himself gasp as she clutched onto his muscle there, squeezing as the tune from her mouth filled his ears and everything between.

The pain of the deep cut from the attack of the Shade vanished.

She pulled her hand back and closed her mouth, zipping away the tone from the air like an ending to a song from a powerful orchestra. The room snapped back to reality. He saw the rows of her followers behind her, marveling at her magic.

Lady Drake glared at him with a scowl, which left Soren stunned.

"Now, do you trust me?" she asked firmly.

He couldn't tell if there was still a spell over him, but with the renewed vigor he felt, he felt as if he could pull a great-rooted tree from the ground with his bare hands.

He nodded. "I do..."

As she smiled, she reminded him of his lost love, Cirella. She'd been gone ten years, but he felt as if at the moment he could taste her on his lips and smell her hair. Cirella had been an Aeol also, but always preferred Ayl for short. They looked nothing alike. Cirella was young, with ocean-blue eyes and chestnut hair, but the magic made him nostalgic for her. The magic made him miss her.

"Good," Lady Drake said. "That's a wise decision, Soren Stormrose."

Chapter Four

Chancellor Carvaise led them out of the underground hall and out to an exit to the side. Soren put his hood back over, but from underneath its tattering cloth, he watched Lady Drake recede into the far exit, through huge double doors capable of being barricaded from the inside. That's when he finally realized where they were—they weren't in a dungeon, they were in the tunnels of refuge, should the capital city ever come under attack.

Lady Drake didn't look back as she left the hall, and Soren felt a rare gratitude for her and her healing. No one had healed him like that in a very long time.

"This way," Roland Carvaise said, ushering Soren to follow Seph and Kaile.

Soren nodded and followed.

They went through a series of corridors with old wooden doors on both sides. It resembled some of the more rundown taverns Soren had stayed in during his meandering travels. That smell of old, musty earth was both nostalgic and reminded him a little too much of the aftermath of a battle.

There were soldiers at both the lead and rear of their line as they went deeper underground.

"You'll be staying just a bit up ahead," Roland said with a cough. "You'll have baths drawn and food ready. I'm sure you'll be wanting some rest."

"Actually," Soren said, rolling his shoulder. "I feel like a run. Haven't felt this good since I don't remember when."

"I don't get if you're jesting or not," the chancellor said. "But you'll have full access to this corner wing, but you won't be allowed to leave, or 'run,' until the lady makes her decision."

"So, we're prisoners," Seph said with a growl.

"You may look at it however you wish," Chancellor Carvaise said. "But do not make any rash decisions. It's my job to make sure you stay where you're supposed to stay, and I aim to keep it that way."

"He's a Synth," Seph said, turning to face the chancellor, pointing up at Kaile, who wore a shadowy expression on his face, dimly lit and the pupils of his eyes reflecting the torchlight. They resembled the glare of the silver bear's eyes from the deep, dark Myngorn Forest.

The soldiers' metal armor jostled as they adjusted their stances at the term, Synth.

"I—I," Kaile muttered.

Soren glowered at Kaile as he stood tall and ominous in the dark cavern hallway. "Seph…" Soren said in a drawn-out voice.

"But… he's harmless," Seph said playfully, turning and skipping down the hall, knocking Kaile's dark hood back off his head, letting the torchlight glow on his startled face.

Soren grinned as he walked past Kaile, who still stood confused as to Seph's calling him a Synth. He surely always thought of himself as a Syncron, one of the good ones, Soren thought. Synths were supposed to be the villains.

They eventually arrived at a round room with a stone ceiling and floor. There were eight doors around the dead-end hall. It had two long tables in its center, with side chairs over by the fireplace, which one soldier went over to and stoked, casting another pair of logs onto it.

The room had just been decorated, Soren thought. No dust on the table liners, nor on the floors. No cobwebs at the corners and the torches smelled of fresh oil. There was a powerful aroma of rose oil from somewhere also, perhaps from behind the closed doors.

"Please, rest," the chancellor said. "Supper will be brought in shortly. Spit ham and steelhead white fish if it pleases you."

"Supper?" Kaile asked, looking around the room, as they hadn't seen a single window in all their walking underground. "Is that what time it is?"

The chancellor smiled and nodded.

"Good. I'm famished," Kaile said, pulling out a bench to one table and sitting, pouring himself a glass of wine from one of the uncorked bottles. It was dark and thick as he poured it. He held it up before his face and twirled it. It was viscous as its long legs clung to the glass. He nodded approvingly and took a sip. It irked Soren the way the boy drank, and Seph seemed to notice it too, by the disdain on her lips that turned down at their corners.

Soren went over, poured himself a glass, and glaring at the boy, put the glass to his lips. He jerked his head back and took it down in one giant gulp. Seph went over, poured, and did the same. But it didn't go as well as she'd hoped, as she choked halfway into it, and sent the wine spilling down her chin and the sides of her face.

"It's strong," she coughed as she set the glass back on the table, wiping her mouth with the back of her hand.

Soren laughed heartily, and Kaile's face flushed. Soren assumed the boy was so regal, highborn from the capital in

Lynthyn, that he'd never been around foolhardy and rough people like Soren and his niece.

"Well," the chancellor began. "I'll leave you to it, then. You'll have an attendant down here shortly with the food, if you require anything."

He turned and left, and as the soldiers followed behind him, Soren then noticed that as they left, the door they closed behind them was not wood like the rest, but iron. It latched and locked behind them.

He poured himself and Seph another glass. She looked embarrassed, so she sat, glaring at Soren.

Soren took his hood down and rustled his hair. It smelled heavily of smoke, reminding him of where'd he just been. He caught her glare and looked down at the table, taking another gulp. A deep growl rolled in his stomach.

She's mad at me still. If I were her, I'd feel the same. But I had to do it. She should still be there, in Guillead, safe.

"Are you... are you two all right?" Kaile asked, tapping his fingers as he hunched forward on the table.

At the same moment, Soren said, "Yes."

Seph said, "No."

Soren took another gulp, knocking his head back as he finished his second glass.

Kaile didn't shy away, though, as Soren expected he would. He instead leaned in, pushing the glass away with the back of his hand. He wasn't shy, but instead itched his cheek as he looked at Persephone.

"You're a Whistlewillow?"

She leaned back in her chair, tucked her elbows into her sides as she pressed down on the seat of the chair. She pursed her lips and then sighed, not answering.

"Well, he knows now," Soren said forcefully, pouring himself another. "Everyone is going to know soon. To the nine hells Persephone, why did you follow me? It didn't do a damned thing! You should've stayed where you were."

"It's Seph." Her brow furrowed as she sat back in her chair, her face gleaming in the candlelight. Her green eyes beamed like wet spring moss.

"Fine. All that time hiding you was for nothing now."

"I didn't want to hide! Why don't you get that through your fat head?"

Kaile sat upright with his hands up, as if trying to intervene.

Soren scoffed. "Are you calling me stubborn? Because I'm sure seeing a lot of that stubborn Whistlewillow in you right now! Couldn't tell your mother to do nothin'!"

"You left me all alone!" She stood suddenly with her twiggy arms out at her sides with her fists shaking. "Why can't you understand? That was the wrong thing to do! I was just a child. You left a child alone with strangers!"

He sat back in his chair as Seph seemed twice her normal size, seething in anger. Kaile withdrew as she loomed over him with her hands out strong at her sides. He tried hard to avert his gaze at her but couldn't.

"I left you alone, so they didn't hunt you down and kill you right after they burned our home and killed our family!"

"Aren't you supposed to be the best in all of Aladran? You couldn't protect me? So you dumped me on the stoop of an orphanage in the dirtiest, meanest, most awful city you could think of? Thanks! Thanks a lot for your forethought and concern. It was great. I loved being there."

Soren folded his arms, unsure of what to say. He itched his elbow and sighed.

"And one more thing," she said. "You better get used to this, and right now! I'm not going to put up with your grumpy, mopey, 'I want to die' attitude while I'm here. I'm here and I'm not going back. I'm not going away. You're stuck with me. It's your penance. You messed up and now you've got to do whatever you can to make it right. And I'm not talking about just with me, with everything."

"What do you mean, everything?" Soren couldn't help the tinge in his voice that he unintentionally thought resembled spitefulness.

"You want me to bring it up in front of him?"

"Yeah, I do." Soren rose from his chair with his knuckles on the table. "Go on."

"You didn't do enough. You could've done more. You could've saved more people."

He was pressing down so hard; Soren just about drove his knuckles through the table.

"I'm not saying you could've saved everyone, but you were the only one who could've done anything, and nothing is perfect in this world. In fact, I'm seeing evil wins more often than not."

"You might want to apologize," Kaile said. "That's not quite—"

"Hush!" Both Soren and Seph said coldly to the boy at the same time.

"What're you saying?" Soren growled.

"The same thing you told Lady Drake. It's on you to make this right. All of it. You got the king, but not enough. You've got to go and kill every last one of those murderous bastards. And you're going to take me with you. I'm going to help you do it. Because… you can't do it alone."

There was a knock from the other side of the door, and the latch unlocked.

Soren swallowed his anger, and Seph glowered at him.

"We'll finish this later," Soren said.

"You better believe we will…" she replied.

As the door creaked open on thick iron hinges, a woman appeared. She was up in her years but had kind eyes and a soothing presence. Soren's shoulders relaxed, and he sat with his back against the chair. Seph still scowled as she withdrew from the argument. Soren knew it was going to take more than an apology and reason to get the girl to forgive him for what he'd done.

But I know I was right. She'd be dead if I hadn't had hidden her. She'd be dead or turned to their will. I did the right thing. I know I did…

The old woman brought with her a young boy, a boy with curly blond locks no older than ten, and Soren remembered the boy in Erhil who took care of his horse, Ursa, every time Soren rode into town. The boy's name was Magnus, and Soren let out a deep sigh as he thought of the boy laying murdered in the town, burned asunder. He took a long gulp of wine, but he knew numbing this kind of pain again was only so very temporary. These scars were going to be with him forever.

I don't want to hear it, but I know Seph is right. It was my fault I didn't do more. So many are dead because I couldn't stop it.

My master Landran would be so disappointed in me. I was the best he produced, and look at me now. Washed up, powerless to stop the king, sitting here getting drunk in a cellar while a lord thinks about whether to kill me or turn me over to the ones who ruined every part of my life.

He sighed and drank again.

The boy brought a large tray behind the old woman. She tidied up the table as he laid out food on the runner she pressed the wrinkles from. He laid out fresh, salty bread that smelled as if it just came straight out of an oven. Beside it he put green, murky olive oil, creamy butter and purple and orange sweet jams. Finally, he put out a jar of chocolates. Seph grabbed the jar with hasty fingers and plunged the chocolates into her mouth, chomping down onto them eagerly. Kaile grabbed and broke the bread. The old woman gave Soren a curious glare, as if inspecting him.

He just glared right back, not in a mean way, just acknowledging her interest.

"You're him, ain't ya?" she finally asked.

He nodded.

"I knew they'd have someone down here, special…" She finished straightening the runner and collecting the empty bottles. "Didn't think it would be you, though."

"Why do you say that?" Soren said, folding his arms and leaning back.

"I shouldn't say nothin'," she said. "Come, boy."

"Do you get visitors down here often?" Soren asked. "Is this a prison the lady brings them too often?"

In his mind, while he looked at the old woman, Soren thought, why was Lady Drake so adamant that he trust her? She healed him like no medic in all Aladran could. Was that worthy of her trust? And why was it so important that someone like him trust her at all?

He had so many questions about the leader of Cascadia. He tried to remember them all in case he got his private conversation with her.

"No, not often," the old woman said with a forced smile. "But when we do, they're usually… special."

Kaile swallowed a bite of bread with jam, and asked, "What do you mean by special? Who else do you see down here? What kinds of guests?"

The woman gave Kaile a paled expression, pulling her lips tight, not responding and ushering the young boy with the tray back toward the door.

"I'll be back shortly with your full dinner, and to make sure you're all getting whatever you require for the night. Warm baths will be drawn shortly after dinner."

She left promptly with the boy, quickly latching the door behind her.

Kaile's mouth was agape, and he was frozen in place.

"Not used to being viewed as the villain?" Seph smirked.

Kaile just slowly shook his head, closing his mouth and swallowing hard. "I—I didn't do anything…"

"Gotta be careful who you associate with," Soren said in a gruff tone. "You may not have murdered those people, but the archmage sure did, and you're his apprentice. With the world the way it is, you can't be too naive about how people are going to stare at you with fear."

Chapter Five

They ate and drank that night, but no mirth found its way into the dingy room. A heavy somberness covered them like a thick wool blanket, weighing them down but giving none of the comfort. Kaile mostly looked down at the table, dinging his fork against the plate dusted with crumbs.

Persephone seemed to be off in a distant place, her eyes glossed over and twirling her hair with her finger. She glared up at the ceiling, to the one cobweb the cleaner had missed. It hung loosely, swaying when a breath caught it. She looked on the brink of tears, but none came.

Soren drank.

Glass after glass, he downed the dark wine until he couldn't feel the tannins on his tongue. He swallowed them down spitefully. He couldn't drink away the clear vision of his friend dying at the hands of the Knight Wolf. Over and over his mind went through the thoughts of regret he had for all his failures. So many were dead, and it was all on his conscience. He gulped down another.

Without realizing it far past the meal, he found Kaile looking at him with fear in his eyes. He looked like a street dog backed into an alley corner by angry men.

Soren looked down and saw the Vellice dagger was in his hand, as he was twisting its tip into the table. He didn't know for how long he'd been twisting the blade, but it was a full inch deep into the cone he'd unintentionally cut in the hardwood. The blade stopped twisting once Soren caught Kaile and Seph's glares.

He laid it flat on the table, taking his hands back and putting them on his thighs.

Suddenly, Soren wished he was far away with his horse. He wished he was deep in the woods, alone, perhaps with Bael, but mostly just wanted to be alone where only the stars could judge him. Hell, he'd rather be killing more Shades than sitting there in the depths of the castle of Barringstone, at the heart of the capital of Cascadia.

He abruptly stood, knocking the table hard enough that the glasses jostled. He snatched Firelight and went to one of the rooms, slamming the door behind him. But then he burst back out of the room to the table. Kaile stood and stepped back with his arms up. Soren went straight to an unopened bottle of wine and grabbed it. He returned to his room, closing the door behind him, gentler this time. There he waited for the attendants to return with the bath water—alone.

He sat with his back against the door, hunched over to the bottle.

He felt trapped. Not just in the castle by the order of the lady, but in himself. There was no escaping his own failures. They haunted him like the scars. Seph wanted redemption, as he did, but it was like trying to leap across a mile-wide ravine. No matter how far you stepped back, or how hard you ran, there was no point. Soren knew he could kill anyone—anyone

—but against the Knight Wolf and Zertaan, his red-eyed Synth and her spell upon him, there was no hope. His own body failed him before he even sensed the Wolf was around. He tipped back the bottle and gulped.

He tossed Firelight, still in its sheath, across the room. It slid until it knocked against the far wall. He sighed. Soren was angry Persephone had gotten what she wanted, too. She wanted to be a part of this madness. She shouldn't be here. Kaile, however, while Soren thought about the archmage's apprentice here with him, he thought about all the information he could gather. The boy lived in Celestra. He knew the capital city. He knew the king. If Soren was to stage an attack, then the boy might be the key. The problem truly was, he didn't know whose side he was on.

Lady Drake seemed wise enough. Soren figured he'd leave that for her to uncover, at least at first. But Seph had a little of the Ellydian in her, and it was untrained. Only from the book Seph had somehow managed to get out of the king's attack ten years ago, had she learned to use her magic. She'd had Cirella's book on everything—all that time.

Another swill went down.

Soren decided something at that moment. Something he promised himself he'd make happen.

You're going to do whatever Lady Drake asks of you. No matter what it is. Under one contingency, though: the lady has to put Persephone back into hiding. Somewhere, anywhere, but far from here. She's all that I have left in this world. She's my only blood. I can't fail her. I just can't.

If the lady asks me to turn myself over to the king... I will. If that's what she wishes... then I'll do it. I'd rather be put to whatever torture they can imagine than to lose her. I'd rather die knowing she's safe. She deserves better. She deserves to start a family of her own—something I was never able to do.

That promise gave him enough of a sense of relief that the

sore tenseness in his shoulders abated. He relaxed with a deep exhale.

"As long as she's protected. That's all that matters…"

⁓

From the other side of the door, utensils clanked together, brooms scraped upon the floor, and the older woman whispered orders to whoever else was in the room. Soren counted three sets of footsteps.

He sat in the rocking chair in his room with his back to the room's corner. The bed was still pristine, with sheets tucked in neatly at squared angles. Firelight lay on his lap as he glared at the door. He was unwashed, devoid of rest, and thought possibly on the brink of insanity.

He'd lost too much.

Losing Bael and Alicen were losses that overwhelmed him. The image of the young boy's face, Magnus, was burned into his mind. Over and over he vividly imagined the boy feeding Ursa with his bare hands, stroking her mane with a brush, and taking down the saddle with his little arms. He remembered so many faces and names from the town, all dead now, lying in the snow, or burnt to death in their homes.

Sleep was a phantom to Soren, anyway. The only escape Soren may get from his grief was out in the wilds. But he was stuck, trapped, and imprisoned. He worried about his ability to think clearly and make decisions. He was nervous about meeting with the lady again, worried about what he might say or how he might behave. He hoped breakfast would help slow his mind.

A knock came at the door from dainty knuckles.

"Master Soren?" the squeaky boy's voice said from the other side of the wooden door. "Good morning, er… um… Would you like me to prepare a bath?"

"Yes," Soren said, the word coming out far gruffer than he intended.

The boy scampered off.

Soren yawned and wiped his eyes, wet with fatigue.

An hour later, he was washed and in fresh clothes they'd given to him to wear. It was a white linen shirt, cuffed at the wrists, that he rolled up. The pants were a dark cotton, with fresh, warm new socks and black leather shoes. He asked for a hood and cloak, which they provided. It was a burgundy with a black stitching. After drying his hair, he pulled the hood up over his head.

There were times in his life where he was genuinely shocked how much a hot bath and clean clothes could make him feel like a new man. Even after the most trying events.

He returned to his room, where a plate of food was brought to him by the young boy again. The boy's glances were those of pure intrigue and wonder. Perhaps the boy had heard of the Scarred who roamed Cascadia, or maybe he was just curious about them escaping the slaughter at Erhil. Soren tried his best to smile at him through the cracked door as he accepted the food. His stomach was in knots, but he ate half the plate, which made his eyelids heavy.

Another knock came to the door another hour later, this time harder and with a man's knuckles.

"Pardon," said the chancellor. "But the lady requests your audience."

Soren was startled awake from his brief nap in the chair. He hadn't even realized he'd dozed off. His hand clapped his sheath instinctively. He set the half-eaten plate on the bed and walked over to the door. He opened it and saw Chancellor Carvaise waiting with the same two soldiers behind him. "Follow me, please."

Soren left the room with the clean clothes gliding softly on his skin. The chancellor led the way, and the two soldiers followed behind Soren.

At the room's center were Seph and Kaile. They were also both dressed in new clothes. Seph wore a loose-fitting pair of white linen pants and a tan vest tied up the front, over a long-sleeved dark shirt. Kaile wore black from head to toe; a tunic too, from his hood to his heels, leather boots up almost to the knees, and a button-down shirt.

Part of Soren thought, *That's more like it. That's what a proper Synth should look like.*

"It's quite a walk," Chancellor Roland Carvaise said. His brow wrinkled deeply as his bald head glistened in the candle-light. "I assume you don't mind." He smiled as he turned back to admire Soren in his new clothes. "I hope all has been to your liking."

Soren nodded with a grunt.

The chancellor seemed pleased enough and continued toward the iron door. The attendants all watched Soren, but he was used to the prying eyes. What was more interesting to him, though, was the way they avoided looking at Kaile. *What a fall from grace he must be feeling*, Soren thought. *One moment you're training under one of the most revered hierarchs in all the lands, and the next—to those who know what really happened—you're a pupil of a mass murderer.*

Seph came up to Soren's side, but slightly behind his shoulder, as they followed Roland.

Soren groaned, not at her, but at himself.

He turned. "Listen Seph…"

She looked up at him, but with tired, sad eyes.

"If I did anything last night, to—" he said, not knowing what words to say to follow.

"I don't care," she said, her words filled with sorrow and her gaze down at her feet.

"I'm sorry if I upset you," Soren said. "Sometimes I'm not myself. In fact, I'm not entirely sure who myself is anymore."

"I know the feeling," she said. The words startled him. His fingers spread and he felt as if he wanted to embrace her. She, too, had been through so much.

"I'm here for you," he said. He wasn't sure if he meant to say that or if it just came out from impulse, perhaps from his fatigue or brain fog. But he realized, yes, he did mean it.

She didn't answer, but continued looking down at the floor as they walked out into the dark, cavernous hallway.

The roaring of the torches echoed through the hall as they walked. Kaile walked behind Seph, occasionally having to duck through the parts where rock cut through the worked stone.

"What are you going to say to her?" Seph finally asked after a couple of minutes.

"I don't know exactly. I'll figure it out."

"Be nice," Seph said. "More flies with honey, got it?"

He nodded. "Maybe I should let you do the talking?" He smirked. She smirked back.

"I'm not so bad at talking my way out of… *prickly* situations," she said.

"Prickly?" Soren asked with piqued curiosity.

"Yeah, that's what I said."

Soren found a renewed vigor in his step then. He was quickly becoming proud of the young woman she was growing up to be.

Kaile didn't say a word until they approached the room that hummed with a warm glow, like sunlight seeping its way through the darkness.

His voice was timid, almost afraid as he spoke. "Do you think they're going to kill me?"

Soren didn't know how to respond. But Seph sure seemed to.

"Don't speak unless spoken to," she said. "Let us do the talking. Be polite and honest. She'll know if you're lying." She suddenly spun to face him. "If you don't have anything to hide, you'll do fine. You aren't hiding anything, are ya?"

She was far smaller than him, but he was stopped in his tracks and looked like a puppy cornered by the Black Fog.

"Well, don't bring that part up then," she said, spinning back to continue toward the room ahead. "But you better believe that you're going to tell me, and soon."

Soren puffed his chest out as he chuckled.

Chapter Six

As they entered the room, a dormant fire in Soren sparked alive. His nostrils filled with the smell of old oak and lush flowers. The sunlight that filled the room through the tall windows warmed his skin. It wasn't only those things that made him brim with energy. Those helped, but it was a feeling he hadn't felt in a long time. He could feel the raw power in the room, and from the two seated before them, he absolutely knew it to be true.

He'd grown accustomed to that feeling, as he approached Lady Drake, sitting beside the great Lyrian master, Mihelik Starshadow. Soren used to feel it in those late nights he spent with Cirella and with Seph's parents, the Whistlewillows. He embraced the power. It made him feel strong, as if he could move mountains, especially when he had his love wrapped in his arms, or as they lay in bed together under the silvery moon and divine starlight.

The feeling was so enamoring that Soren didn't notice the door close behind him until he turned to see the last bit of the chancellor's hand pulling the latch from the other side. The door closed with a puckering seal. Soren felt it wasn't only the two in the room that were magical. There was something different about this place…

The room had a wide row of windows overlooking the edge of the lower cliffs of the city. Beyond the clear windows was the vast beyond of the southern reaches of Cascadia. As the city of Skylark was perched upon the cliffs of Blackstone, its southern borders beheld a breathtaking view of the Tibers, a mountain range of sharp tips, and the southern ocean, the Sapphire Sea. Only a sliver of the sea was seen at the tip of the horizon from that distance, but the beautiful, snowy white lands of their country sprawled all the way to its glimmering waves.

Within the wide room with only three doors, one on each wall, were only the five of them: Lady Drake, Mihelik, Seph, Kaile, and Soren.

I suppose she took me up on my request. Need to be on my toes, and on my regal behavior. Our lives depend on it…

Lady Drake, in her midlife years, was quite striking to Soren for her age. Her silver hair was braided and flowed down her chest and down to her lap. Her tan skin was youthful and free of wrinkles in the warmth of the morning sunlight. She didn't smile but looked… uneasy in her chair. Her legs were crossed under her dress of dark crimson red, and her fingers tapped on the armchair as her wise eyes inspected the three of them.

Mihelik slumped. He looked nothing like the man who rode into the battle in Erhil upon the huge horse, casting the most magnificent spell Soren had ever seen. He wrought the anger of the heavens and gods upon the king and his men there! Now he sat wearing spectacles with lenses of black, his beard frazzled and frayed down his thin chest. His hand rested at the side of his chair, with his thin fingers wrapped around his staff—a dazzling, powerful staff of tightly wrapped dark wood with its tip decorated with dozens of gleaming white jewels Soren didn't recognize. Around the old Lyrian Syncron's neck hung the necklace of tuning forks—dozens of them, ready to strike upon the wrapped metal around sections of his staff. His long white hair fell behind his back. He stroked his white beard with his free hand as his gaze angled down at his lap.

Seph and Kaile were tense. Soren could feel it. As they should be, he thought. The old archmage and Lady Drake, the leader of Cascadia, were two of the most powerful beings in existence, at least that Soren knew of. Seph and Kaile, both young Aeols, could learn so much from these two, seated before them, if given the opportunity.

Mihelik stirred as if to speak, but ended up muttering something to himself.

"Good morning," the lady said. She spoke from deep within her chest. "I hope you've been treated well."

Soren nodded. The other two did the same.

"Where do we begin?" Lady Drake asked, glaring at the three of them standing before her, bathed in wonderful sunlight.

"What have you decided?" Soren asked abruptly, partially regretting his decision. He was supposed to lay charm on her, not end the conversation before it even began. He swallowed hard as Lady Drake looked at him, squinting her wise eyes.

Seph suddenly spoke. "I have a question, if it pleases the lady." She cleared her throat as Mihelik's ears perked up at her youthful voice. "Why have you brought us here? And why did you save us? Why did you risk your life and your seclusion out in the open against the king and the archmage just to bring us here?"

Lady Drake wore no expression on her face or in her posture. She instead turned her head to look at the old man beside her as he stirred in his chair.

He moaned slightly as he shifted his sitting position to his other side.

"Persephone Whistlewillow," he said in a cracked voice that sounded nothing like the booming voice of thunderous words from the battlefield. "I know much about this world. Many things that ought not be known. But you… you were a true surprise to these old ears. I thought you were lost to time and sorrow, yet here you stand—a young woman. And an impressive spell you wield. Amazing really."

Soren saw Seph's cheek flush.

"Would you like to go down the line?" Lady Drake asked Mihelik, who nodded with a murmur.

"You are the heir to a great family," Mihelik said. "I knew your grandparents. I respected them with reverence and held them dear to my heart as friends. The Ellydian's vibrations run deep into you. I can feel them pulling at you." He leaned forward in his seat. "Tell me, girl, do you feel them? Do you feel them even without the sound of your fork? When you lay awake at night, what do you feel?"

Soren looked curiously at her, awaiting her answer as she scratched her cheek. Her eyes gleamed as if his question had stirred deep in her.

"I feel… I feel the world pulling me. It's hard to describe." She shook her head. "Sometimes I feel like I'm goin' crazy, like I'm being pulled apart in my own body. I always thought it was grief. I thought it was because I didn't have no one."

"It's the opposite of that, child," the old archmage said. "That's no weakness. That's your greatest strength. But it's gripping you like spiders fighting over a fly. But you're not the fly. You're the spider."

"You've surpassed the Doren magics and moved already onto the Aeolien," Lady Drake said. "How have you managed what most never accomplish? Or take many years to learn? And on your own?"

"I took a book with me from Tourmielle," Seph said bashfully.

"A book? What book?" Lady Drake asked, leaning forward in her chair as Mihelik steepled his fingers before him. His staff wondrously remained standing straight up at his side.

"It was Cirella's," Seph said. "It was her diary, with a lot of notes about other things, like the Ellydian…"

Lady Drake smiled widely. "Excellent."

"Tell me Persephone," Mihelik said.

"It's Seph, actually," Soren interrupted, winking at her.

Mihelik seemed thrown off by that, but cleared his throat and continued. "Persephone is such a beautiful name, but Seph it is. Tell me then, what do you desire in this life most?"

She staggered back a slight step, fiddling with her fingers in front of her stomach. She muttered the question to herself. Clearing her throat strongly, she replied, "Revenge."

"Ah," Mihelik said with a high-pitched voice. "Revenge. That's a dangerous road to travel. Most times, it has no end, only a steep cliff with no bottom. You sure that's where you want to walk?"

"Yes," she said in a firm tone. "I want to kill the ones who killed my family. All those that were there at Erhil deserve to die."

Lady Drake grabbed Mihelik's hand and squeezed.

"We know the desire for revenge greatly," she said. "Perhaps more than you would guess."

Who are they talking about? After Mihelik's betrayal and burning of the old scriptures, who would he want to get revenge on?

"Take care to guard that book, young lady," Mihelik said. "Can't have that fall into the wrong hands. If the late Cirella Misthaven caused you to become the Aeol that stands before us with no training, then that book must be safeguarded."

Soren had the feeling the old archmage was speaking to him, and not Seph.

"He did right to send you there," Lady Drake said, and Soren could feel Seph tense up beside him. Her fists clenched and her shoulders hunched. "You would not have lived this long, had he not. But the praise is not only upon him for his actions; the fact that you stand before us now, the child of the Whistlewillows, is no trifle accomplishment. You've survived. I fear I can't say the same of many who would've been placed in your shoes."

Seph didn't respond, but she heard the words, nonetheless.

"Now," Lady Drake said, shifting in her seat, switching her crossed legs which slid under the fine crimson velvety dress. "Soren Smythe. What do you we do with you?"

"The lady said you requested a private meeting with her," Mihelik said. "So here we are."

"I had planned on things to say," Soren said, pushing his words out past the fatigue and pain in his throat. "Over and over throughout the night, I changed my mind about what I may ask of you. But now I stand here, and I can't think of a single thing to ask, except for this… why was it so important that I trust you?"

The room fell silent. Lady Drake glared at him, and then the other two, and then finally, turned in her seat and looked back out behind her, out into the vast open beautiful white fields of Cascadia—their home.

"Do you?" she asked, still twisted, looking out into the great beyond.

"I don't trust anyone," he said, and then took a deep inhale and exhale. "But… something tells me I can. I don't know what it is, but I've learned to trust my instinct over time, and it tells me that, for some reason, yes, I can."

She snapped her gaze back to him. "Good."

A rare smile crept across Mihelik's thin lips, causing his white beard to shift.

"I asked because you and I are going to become a sort of business partners."

"M'lady?" Soren asked, with a cocked eyebrow.

"If I release you to go on your hunt, which will take an insurmountable amount of information, time, and luck—then we're going to have to work together."

If *she releases me…*

"Much of what we are going to speak about in this room," the lady said, "will also depend upon what happens with the boy who stands at your other side."

"We will come back to you," Mihelik said, while his smile faded.

"Kaile Thorne," Lady Drake said. "Apprentice to the Archmage Alcarond Riberia himself. Lives in the halls of towers of Celestra. Born to a fisherman in Ikarus, rising from rags to one of the most prestigious institutions in all of Aladran. You've had quite the journey for a man your age."

Kaile, trying hard not to shuffle his feet, eventually nodded. "Yes. That's true."

"Let's get right to it then," Lady Drake said, leaning forward in her seat, as her silver hair fell from her chest and hung down to her thighs. "Why did you go into the portal to follow Mihelik and the others? Why did you abandon the greatest post a boy your age could hold? You must have known what you risked by doing so."

He shifted in his stance, swaying at the hip, glancing down at the floor.

"Answer!"

All gazes were heavily on him, waiting to hear the answer all of them very much wanted to hear.

"I—I don't know."

"Yes, you do," the lady said forcefully. "Out with it. The truth!"

"I—I don't know. I just got so scared. I didn't know what

they were going to do once we got there." He was still looking at the floor. "They told me we were going to end the rebellion. All my years, I'd learned to hate the Silver Sparrows. They were the reason for all the bad in the world. I hated them for hating us. But… when we got there, and I saw what they were doing… that wasn't an insane lot of bandits with magic. Those were just innocent people. There were kids in there. They weren't evil. They weren't conspiring. They were just kids. I was with them, too. I was with the ones who caused all that. There was no Chimaera outbreak there. Even if there was, the king didn't need to burn the whole town and everyone in there. I saw the look in his eyes. There was a darkness there. He enjoyed it… he enjoyed the destruction and death. At that moment, I knew what I was doing wasn't right. History would tell that moment was a glorious victory for the king, but I was just so scared I couldn't move. And then Mihelik came, who betrayed us all, and who I was told to hate more than anyone. But he wasn't coming for evil, he was coming to stop it. So, I don't know what happened at the end, but when I saw all of you escaping, I took a leap of faith… I guess."

"And what do you think of that leap of faith now?" Lady Drake asked, all ears eager for his answer.

"I think I may have made a mistake."

"Why?" she asked quickly and with a sharpness that cut through the tenseness in the air.

"Not because I should have stayed with them…" He swallowed hard. "Because you're the Silver Sparrows, aren't you? I either have to join you now, or you're going to kill me…"

Lady Drake glanced over at Mihelik, grabbing him by the hand and squeezing. Mihelik exhaled hard.

"Yes," she said. "We are the Silver Sparrows."

Chapter Seven

"And also, yes, you cannot leave this place with that knowledge," Lady Drake said, leaning back and folding her arms. She lowered her chin and scowled at the boy as she watched him like a lioness stalking her injured prey.

Mihelik sat as still as the windless night.

"I don't know what to do. I'm so confused," Kaile said. "I don't know anything is true. What they told me was lies. How do I know what you're telling me now, isn't?"

Mihelik sat forward, moaning in his old years as his knuckles popped as they gripped the armrests.

"Truth," he drawled. "An interesting concept, truth. In fact, I believe that rests entirely in between the ears of the listener. The past is the past. What happens in this very moment is true, but what happens to this moment as time passes? Memories change and fade, distortions become reality, and what is left is a mangled mess of what truly was. But do you know one truth that is uncorruptible by time and lies and hate?"

Kaile scratched his chin, searching for the answer.

"C'mon, boy. Alcarond taught you this, because I taught him!"

"The... the Ellydian?"

"Yes!" Mihelik roared. "So pure that even those with the most greed spilling out of their ears can't touch it. It is as pure as sunlight, as wretched as the seas, and as powerful as the stars themselves."

Kaile nodded. Soren could tell the boy was in a whirlwind of utter turmoil in his mind. Here he was, standing before the mightiest Syncron in the whole world. Kaile had been told the old man was also the evilest, but now he looked at the old Syncron wizard with a sort of admiration; a pupil thirsting for knowledge, and Soren knew there was no one with more knowledge of the Ellydian than him.

"The king is evil," Soren said bluntly to Kaile. "Lady Drake is not lying. Trust me, I'd be able to tell. The king did the same to Tourmielle ten years ago, and took everything from me, giving me these scars and cursing me to be an outcast. Seph is all I have left."

"They told me that town burned to end the rebellion of the Silver Sparrows. I never knew they killed everyone in it."

"Fire," Soren said. "Wicked fire. That's what King Amón loves more than most anything. More than land, more than gold, more than lust. He thirsts for fire. He wants to watch the world burn."

"I saw that," Kaile murmured as he looked down at the room's corner. "I saw that look in his eyes. It was... an obsession. Even Solemn didn't watch the way the king did. The archpriest seemed to enjoy it for necessity, not pleasure."

"The archpriest," Lady Drake said. "What's he like?"

"Pardon, m'lady, but you don't know him?" Kaile asked. "I've seen you in the capital with him."

"I want to hear it from your mouth," she said. "What sort of man is he?"

He cleared his throat. "Why would I tell you anything if you're just going to kill me?"

She paused. "I won't lie when I tell you that you cannot leave my kingdom with the knowledge of what we are now. It's far too much risk for my people. The king cannot come here with his army. We would fight tooth and nail, but we would eventually succumb to the army of Lynthyn. I am no fool. I know this to be true. But… death is not the only means of silencing you, should you choose not to abide by our wishes."

"Your demands…" Kaile added, causing Soren and Seph to stir.

"Easy," Soren said with a hush.

Kaile breathed deeply through his nose and exhaled.

"Sorry. The archpriest is a kind, eerily wise man for his age. I don't think he's all that much older than me, but he's one of those people that when they speak, the entire room listens. I don't know if you thought that about him. He appeared maybe seven years ago? I'd say yes, because it was 1285 when Silvergale Lake flooded. It was all the way up above the tree line. I've never seen it like that. He came into King Amón's court just around then."

"What else?" Lady Drake asked.

"He's the seventh of his name. Devotees to the goddess Shirava. Solemn came down from the north all those years ago. From across the sea, he sailed. Hails from Eldra. Same place as where the drakoons are trained. I don't know much about Eldra except what Alcarond taught me. The Roane family is a renowned, prestigious name there. He was famous."

"Why do you think he came here?" Lady Drake asked.

"To help."

"Help with what?" she asked.

"Everything."

Lady Drake looked at Mihelik, who seemed to sense it, as he angled his gaze toward her lap.

"King Amón wants total, absolute control of Aladran," Soren said. "He must control the church too to do that. Solemn is revered by the clergy in all six kingdoms. I heard the king summoned him and he came. Makes sense from the king's perspective. Unify the dioceses of the six kingdoms and crush all opposition."

"He's awfully young to be so revered," Seph said. "I wouldn't trust him."

Soren smirked.

"Any other questions?" Kaile asked.

"What do you think his intentions are?" the lady asked.

"I always thought they were good," Kaile said. "He wants to figure out why the Black Fog and Demons of Dusk are here. He speaks about them constantly. I think he's scared they're going to kill everyone and everything if he doesn't figure out where they came from and how to destroy them. In my opinion, I think he needs to figure it out and get rid of them. I've lost friends to the Shades. I hope they all die."

"Yes," Mihelik said. "That mystery has kept me awake for many sleepless nights. Where indeed did the Demons of Dusk come from?"

"I killed three Shades," Soren said.

Kaile gasped with his fingers spread.

"You did what?" Mihelik asked forcefully.

"They attacked, saw through Seph's spell. I had to fight them. Would've died, both of us, had it not been for this…"

He pulled Firelight free from its sheath. The sunlight reflected off the layered, rippling steel like a sunrise on the sea. It was an inch wide and ten long. Its crossguard were three twisting metals of white, dark gray, and silver, which curved up to two sharp quillons. At its pommel was the black stone of infinite darkness, which no light reflected off.

"What is it?" Mihelik asked.

Lady Drake groaned. "It's a dagger of Vellice."

"Oh," he muttered. "Which one?"

Which one? Does he know every weapon of Vellice in Aladran? If so, how many are there?

"I don't recognize it," the lady said, squinting. "Bring it here."

Soren looked at Seph, who shrugged.

Soren walked forward and handed her the blade, with the pommel and grip out for her to take, which she did delicately. He stepped back as she held the blade up to the light that shone in from the windows behind.

"May I?" Mihelik asked with his thin, bony fingers extended over the armrest. She gently laid it in his hand. He held it up before him with the tip of the dagger pointed up as he held it with one hand and traced its lines and curves with his other.

"What do you think?" she asked.

"I—I don't recognize this weapon. Where and how did it come into your possession?"

"Garland Messemire of Faulker gave it to me, in exchange for what he thought would be a bargaining tool to let him scurry back into his rat's nest."

"Messemire," Mihelik said. "How did he get it, then?"

"From a lord in Zatan," Soren said. "He didn't say who, but I aim to find out someday."

"That is as rare as a lizard with two heads," the old Syncron said.

"You asked which one it was," Soren said. "What did you mean by that? Do you know all the weapons forged in Vellice that came to Aladran?"

"Your mentor knew them too," Mihelik said. "I'm surprised he didn't teach you. Yes, there are five known Vellice weapons in Aladran. Almost all of them reside in the capital. Yours here is the sixth."

"What makes them so special?" Seph asked. "I've never

heard of them. But I've heard of Vellice, just like I've heard of Eldra."

"Their forging techniques remain a mystery," Lady Drake said. "But it's said that one weapon takes a master a lifetime of training to produce only a handful in his or her later years. That dagger is worth more than you could imagine."

"Garland said he was planning on trading it for favors," Soren said.

"He's a fool," Lady Drake said. "He could've gotten half a kingdom's riches for such a weapon."

"Or one great favor," Mihelik said. "Sometimes those are worth far more than gold and land."

"True," she said.

Mihelik handed the dagger back to Soren, then folded his veiny hands over his lap as Soren returned to the far end of the room.

"So, Kaile Thorne," the lady said. "You have a decision to make, but you will have time to decide it, and perhaps our next conversation will push your decision one way or the other."

"What's that?" Kaile asked.

"Finally," Lady Drake said, "we arrive back to you, Soren Stormrose of Tourmielle."

Soren squared his stance at shoulder distance. With Firelight firmly nestled into her sheath at his side, he pulled down his hood, letting the sunlight pour onto his skin. He put his hands behind his back and perked his chest out. If this was the moment of his reckoning, then he'd do it proudly—as a soldier—no matter the outcome.

But what came was not at all what he would've expected.

"Archmage," Lady Drake said, ushering her colleague to proceed.

The old Syncron leaned in, shaking his finger in Soren's direction. His brow furrowed and his mouth flattened. Soren could tell he was perturbed about something.

"Soren... now this curse upon you, I've pondered it many days and nights."

The hairs on the back of Soren's neck prickled into his shirt and sent a shiver down his back.

Mihelik, the greatest wizard alive, has been thinking about what happened to me? But why? Why do I matter? There are so many more important things in the world the Syncron could be thinking about. Why me?

"Zertaan of Arkakus," Mihelik said with a hiss. "The woman in black creates far more questions than answers, even for me. I've wondered about the spell she cast upon you and William Wolf as he cut the scars into your face. The bond between him and you is a fascinating, terrible one."

Lady Drake nodded as she listened to the old man, while Seph and Kaile hung on his every word.

"Not only is the pale Synth ghoulish in her albino complexion, but nightmarish in her casting. Though she's only but an Aeol, I fear she may attempt the test to become a Lyrian. Although if she failed and died a fiery death attempting the Black Sacrament, I would not shed tears for the Synth, that much is certain."

Soren hadn't thought of that. He knew the danger of the test to transition to the most powerful of the Syncrons, and the dangers if you failed. But he rarely thought about the decision that those must make, and assumed most at the level of Aeol were there for a reason—be it the capacity of skill, or complacency. Should Zertaan attain the level of Lyre, becoming one of the true elites of Aladran... well, that thought alone sent beads of sweat trickling down Soren's brow.

"She uses a flavor of magic, which is unfamiliar to me," Mihelik said, stroking his beard. "Although I greatly desire to understand it. Arkakus is a land of many mysteries. It's a pity the great floods didn't wipe them from our world completely."

"So, you're saying there's no cure for him?" Seph asked suddenly. She hid her fidgeting fingers behind her back.

"I didn't say that," Mihelik said. "And with the tenacity in which our world is changing, that insight may be right around the corner… or…"

"Or what?" Lady Drake pressed.

"Or… we kill her," the old Syncron said.

I like the sound of that! Soren grinned.

"What…" Kaile began. "What do we know about the spell she used?"

Mihelik sat back in his chair and exhaled, folding his arms and crossing his legs under his robes. "The Knight Wolf wields the Ember Edge, as we surely all know. He used the blade of Vellice to cut you. Zertaan used a B note to cast."

"B?" Kaile asked, with his eyebrow cocked. "Unusual. The B is difficult to sustain, and usually draws from a less pure energy from the Ellydian. It requires a massive amount of concentration and practice. Not usually worth the effort. Safer to use a C or an E. Even G would require less energy."

Mihelik hunched over with a grin. "You've done your homework. I can see the sparkle in your eyes when you speak of the Ellydian." Mihelik's words were directed then to Seph. "I can feel the unease in your posture and the hamper in your breathing. You will learn these things too, child. But you must have a teacher. The book will only take you so far."

Seph's mouth fell agape. She seemed to have no idea the old Syncron could read her the way he did, and without his vision.

"We will figure something out for you, should that prove to be advantageous," Lady Drake said. Her words were equally optimistic and ominous.

Seph was brimming. Her thin legs couldn't twist far enough around each other as she couldn't help her excitement. She tucked her chin to her chest and raised her shoulders to her ears as she gushed.

"I hope Lady Drake teaches me," she whispered to Soren.

"We'll see… if we get out of this…" he breathed back.

"May I ask a question?" Kaile asked. Lady Drake nodded. "And I mean no disrespect in any form when I ask this. In fact, I hold you in very high regard, Lady of Skylark. To you, former archmage, you were my idol until your fall from grace, which I'm still quite confused about…"

"What is your question, lad?" Mihelik pressed.

"Erhil…" Kaile began. "You rode in like a hurricane. You risked your life to save Soren, and I don't want this to come off disrespectful to him either, but why? Why risk your life to save one man? Why not bring an army to stop the king and his men from doing what they did?"

"A worthy question," Mihelik said, "and one that deserves an answer. But I will not answer it yet. First, we must decide as to what happens next, and depending on that conclusion, then I will give you an answer." The old man listened for a response from the boy, but seemed to hear nothing. "Not the answer you wanted, but the answer you get…"

"Soren," the lady said, turning their attention back to him.

"Yes," he said, squaring his shoulders.

"Our numbers are dwindling," she said. "And King Amón and his wrath spreads like the Chimaera. Helena, Amara, and Gregor were our friends and comrades. They were passionate, fierce, powerful, and brave. Their lights were forever extinguished when the flames destroyed Erhil. King Amón and his men won't stop until every last one of us is dead. But we are fighting the good fight, the hard fight. If we don't continue, then his hate will spread, and a darkness will take over our world for generations to come. You were once part of this brave rebellion, and you lost more than most because of it."

"Are you asking me to join the Sparrows?" he asked

politely. "I refused their offer when they presented it to me in Erhil. And now they're all dead, my friends and comrades included."

Lady Drake leaned forward with her wise gaze heavily on him. "I'm asking you to do more than simply join us. I'm asking you to avenge us."

Soren was taken aback, looking down at Seph to his side, who scratched her thigh and shrugged at him.

"I want nothing more than to kill the king and all his men," Soren said. "Is that what you're asking me?"

"You were once a soldier," she said. "You fought with honor, with pride, for family and home. I ask you to return to that service you once swore an oath to."

Soren's mouth twisted, and he crossed his arms.

"I don't ask you to pledge allegiance to me," she said. "At least not specifically."

"Then who?" he asked.

"To the three who you watched be murdered in Erhil," Lady Drake said with hate thick in her voice. "For Cirella, for Seph's parents, and for every last Syncron who dared to fight against the tyranny and genocide we witness in our fair lands."

Soren was irked when he heard Cirella's name. "You think I don't want to avenge her? Out with it!" He was growing impatient with the lady's regal manner. "You want me to lead an army? You want me to become a Silver Sparrow? I'm not in the mood to be toyed with."

Lady Drake smirked at that, which surprised them all.

"There's a rat," she said, crossing her legs and touching her lips with her fingernails. "A mutual disgust we share."

"Go on..." Soren said.

"Edward Glasse," she said. "He came from Londindam for more than to protect Garland Messemire in Faulker."

Soren hung on her words, eager to hear more.

"Glasse is a high lord in Londindam, and it takes more

than a morsel of cheese to lure him out of his hiding hole. He was tempted by power. He got word of the Sparrows in Erhil, and knew that giving the king that information would reward him with knowledge from the ancient texts so that he may increase his magic. We all know the more you suck the king's toes, the stronger you are allowed to become. And there is no greater hatred of the king's than the Silver Sparrows."

"How?" Soren asked. "How did Glasse learn of them in Erhil?"

"He had a spy, of course," the lady said.

"Who?" asked Soren.

"We don't know."

"Because I have another mystery from Erhil that needs answering," he said. "When we left Erhil the first time, after Garland sent his goons in, throwing a damned digger bomb into my room, nearly killing me and my friend Alicen… Bael and I camped. But there was something he carried with him, something he didn't know… and in the middle of the night… the Black Fog came for us…"

Mihelik and Lady Drake both leaned forward in their chairs as dark clouds rolled over from the top of Skylark, casting dark shadows over the infinite lands beyond.

"Yes, go on, lad…" Mihelik said.

"We nearly died, as all do to those monsters. But Bael was given something, or something was planted in his purse. A coin. It lured the Black Fog to us. They wanted us dead, and whether or not it was Garland, I do not know. I have my doubts, but would he really try to kill us two different ways on the same night? And who has the capability, and the evil, to be able to control the Demons of Dusk? I can't think but it may be the same person who ratted to Garland about the Sparrows, that may have been the same person who gave Bael that coin."

Mihelik sat back, stroking his beard. His gaze was pointed up at the ceiling, and Lady Drake steepled her fingers.

"You killed a Shade," the lady said.

"Three, actually," Seph added quickly.

"You killed three Shades, and evaded the Black Fog…" Lady Drake said, puzzled, yet intrigued. "You are most definitely the right man for the job, then."

"Job?" Soren asked.

"The question of who had the ability to weaponize the Black Fog will need to be answered," Lady Drake said. "We will investigate such an act, for I fear that won't be the last time that ability will be used against us. But yes, I have a task for you."

"You want me to kill Glasse, don't you?" Soren asked, in a grim tone.

Lady Drake nodded. "He needs to die for us to live."

"He's grown too powerful," Mihelik said. "I fear he will attempt the Black Sacrament. And should he succeed in attaining the rank of Lyre, then I may be the only one to stop him, but I fear I may not be strong enough in my years."

"Then no one could stop him," Kaile said. "It would only be he and Alcarond as Lyrians… and you, of course."

"The King may give him access to the ancient texts for his reward," Lady Drake said.

"What is left of them, after you destroyed them," Kaile said to Mihelik. His words were lined with spite, but the spite he really had to push past the reverence Soren could tell he had for the old Syncron.

In that moment, Soren remembered that indeed there were only two Lyrians in all of Aladran at that moment: Alcarond and his master, Mihelik.

"I will do it," Soren said. "If he's in Londindam, then I will pursue him and kill him. I already injured him. He fears me."

"He won't be easy to kill," Lady Drake said. "And you won't get a shot like you did last time at him. He'll be ready and protected."

"I like those odds," Soren said, as his eyes narrowed.

"You'll need the Ellydian against him," Lady Drake said, causing Soren's eyes to widen.

"I—" he began to say.

"I don't mean you," the lady said, glancing at both Seph and Kaile.

"You don't mean…" Soren gasped.

"I'll do it!" Seph said excitedly.

Kaile didn't respond, but by his wondering glares, Soren thought the boy realized what Lady Drake meant by Kaile would have a decision to make, and that this was it. Turn on your own for us, or you go no further…

"Soren can't go hunting Synths without help," Mihelik said.

"So that's why you came to Erhil?" Kaile asked. "You came to fetch your killer so that you could release the hound?" Kaile seemed to grow dark as the thick clouds rolled out onto the horizon. A shadow grew over him, as he was already draped in black.

"M'boy," Mihelik said. "I did not ride to Erhil for him. I came to Erhil for you."

"Me?"

PART II
MIHELIK AND THE DEMONS OF DUSK

Chapter Eight

❦

T*he Connection of all things.*

THE CONNECTION *of all things has been researched in no shortage of time and energy. Generations have puzzled over the source of the Ellydian, and the potential for its power.*

Those that can tap into the connection of all things, can feel the tenseness with which this wonderful chaos maintains balance. It pulls and shoves at your core as others slip through it like walking through air.

Many texts have been written about the Ellydian, but the oldest of those believe it was created by the old gods to hold everything in place—to maintain the order that surrounds us.

It is what hangs the stars in the sky, keeping them from colliding into one another and keeping their light forever glowing. It's what swings the golden orb of life around our world, and what causes trees and crops to grow straight out of the ground so they may grow us food to eat.

It is not known why certain people and families can tap into this connection, but for those that can harness it through the power of music, a great responsibility follows.

For it is often those that can control the connection of all things are the ones who change it the most, causing the greatest prosperity the world has ever known… or break it entirely.

-Translated from the language of the Sundar. The Connection of all Things, Book 1, Chapter I.

Soren Smythe stood between the archmage's apprentice and his own niece, the last Whistlewillow. He now knew they were the new generation of Syncrons, and how valuable they were.

At the revelation that the great former archmage had risked his own life to ride against the army of the king, including the Archpriest Solemn, the Archmage Alcarond, the Knight Wolf, the legendary drakoons, and even Glasse—Soren felt a bit foolish.

He'd assumed Mihelik had ridden there for him, as the old archmage didn't even know Persephone was still alive at the time, and he made no effort to try to save the people of Erhil, but what one person could stop that kind of ruthless attack by such a powerful foe and his army?

Kaile? How did Mihelik know Kaile would follow of his own free will through the portal? How could he possibly predict that? The Ellydian surely is a wondrous and head-scratching thing…

"Me? Why would you come for me? I'm a nobody," Kaile said, facing the lady of Skylark and the most powerful Syncron in the world.

Mihelik groaned, shifting in his seat. He almost seemed… annoyed, as he scratched his elbow. Lady Drake seemed to scowl at the boy.

"Come now. You don't really believe that, do you?" the old Syncron wizard asked him.

"I come from nothing," Kaile said.

"That's one reason for your importance," Mihelik said. "Do you think Alcarond Riberia would handpick you from the shores of Ikarus out of a whim?"

"No." Kaile's shoulders slacked. "No, I don't think he would at all. He's a stickler for highborns."

"There's not a trace in your family of connection to all things," Mihelik said. "And you've moved from Dor to Ayl in only a few short years. We may have two of the most promising prospects for the next generation of Lyres."

"If we live," Seph added bluntly.

"Yes," Mihelik said with a nod and a stroke of his beard. "Indeed, that is the case."

"How did you know I would just follow you?" Kaile said, shaking his head. "That's impossible."

Soren knew better than to assume anything was impossible from the old legend sitting before them.

"Call it a hunch," Mihelik said.

"He would have pulled you through," Lady Drake added. "Had you not had the… *inclination*, you did."

"Oh," Kaile mouthed the word.

"There's time to train you on the right path," Mihelik said. "Alcarond is a truly magnificent wielder of the power of the Ellydian, one of the greatest in a hundred years. But there's a darkness in him. It was a darkness I thought I could tame… but I was wrong in my confidence."

"What happened between you and my master?" Kaile asked, before Soren had a chance to ask the same.

Mihelik sighed and fell casually back into the chair as the dark clouds trickled raindrops onto the glass behind them. The vast lands of Cascadia fell into darkness. Thunder clapped overhead, shaking the glass. Soren felt it in his chest.

"We were once close," Mihelik said in a defeated voice. "But that cord was long severed."

"He said you two fought, and he won," Kaile said. "He saved what scriptures he could in the halls below the capital from you and cast you out. He told the king he thought you'd die of your wounds, and that he saved the ancient texts that you once revered so. The king then made him the archmage. I was so new in Celestra, I didn't know what was going on. But I was glad he saved what he could. It sounded like you'd gone mad." Kaile scratched his chin as he glared at the old man. To Kaile, the man before him, and the man who'd conjured the immense lightning storm to crash into the attackers of Erhil, didn't seem to add up to the madman his mentor had warned him of. "And now you want to steal me from him, to train me?"

"Our relationship grew complicated," the old archmage said. "His thirst for the ancient knowledge of the Sundar drove him down a dark path. He sought to control things I didn't deem appropriate... his heart was corrupted by greed."

"What kinds of things?" Soren asked.

"I'm going to keep that secret with me, for the time being," Mihelik said. "And I have my reasons for doing so."

Soren's mouth flattened. He didn't like not knowing the true strength of the archmage—should they meet again, and by the goddess, Soren hoped they would.

"What are you thinking?" Seph finally asked Kaile after a long pause. Thunder boomed again as the storm intensified, casting down sheets of heavy rain. "It sounds like we're going with my uncle to Londindam."

"Absolutely not," Soren said, almost out of reflex. "The apprentice and I will travel together to hunt down Glasse. You're moving somewhere safe, away from all this. You need to hone your magic first, anyway."

"Don't tell me what I can and can't do..."

"The plan is for you three to travel together," Lady Drake said. "And you will be escorted by another."

"No, and no," Soren said flatly, waving his hands out at hip level, palms facing the floor.

"Who's the other?" Seph asked.

"And pardon my hesitation," Kaile said, "but we three are surely the most sought out three in all the kingdoms, and we don't exactly blend in. We wouldn't make it to the border."

"You certainly will look different without your red hair," Lady Drake said with a smirk. Mihelik gave a raspy chuckle at her side. "The more difficult measure will be concealing Soren's scars. Which is part of the reason for your extra companion."

Soren growled. *I work alone...*

"What reason do you have to make me take my niece with me? She's untrained and young." He could feel her scowl heavy on him, even without turning to see it.

"Yes," Mihelik agreed. "The young Ayl is untrained. But Kaile has had years of training under my former pupil. The knowledge he can pass on while you travel will be a sufficient place to start."

"When you return," Lady Drake said, "then, her formal training will begin. Not in my kingdom, though. We cannot draw the attention of the king here."

Soren's lips twisted, and he gritted his teeth. It wasn't since he spent time in the court of Tourmielle that he'd been given orders he had no say in. It was perhaps the one nice thing that came with his loneliness.

"Where, then?" Soren asked.

"The forest," Mihelik said. "Myngorn is a fine place to rest when one doesn't care to have visitors or distractions." His thick gray eyebrows dropped on his brow. "You didn't notice me there."

"No, I did not..." Soren snorted. "I suppose I owe you a

thanks for calling those silver bears off. I can handle my own in a sword fight, but those were about the most ferocious things I've ever seen."

Mihelik gave a raspy laugh. "Those two? They're sweethearts, you just need to get to know them is all. Love a good belly scratch, they do!"

Soren remembered his horse Ursa tumbling down the tree-covered trench as they fought to escape the beasts, and didn't think tickling their stomachs would've been the best defense against that.

"So you want us to kill Glasse, somewhere in Londindam, probably in his fortress," Soren said. "Then you want us to return here, all the while hauling someone else with us? And your plan is to dye our hair and put paint on my face? I'm not meaning to insult, but that is the gist of the plan, yes?"

"Yes," Mihelik said.

At the same time, Lady Drake shook her head *no*.

"You will be given weapons, and this isn't just anyone aiding you on the way. There will be a stop on your journey. That is part of the reason for the necessity of all of your abilities. There's an item we will require in our ultimate battle against evil."

"What?" Kaile blurted.

"You'll be told once on your journey," the lady said. "If you accept your role on this path…"

Kaile's lips pressed together, as he scratched his cheek.

"Well, you have my attention," Soren said. "Seems like you've thought this through in the one night we've been here."

Lady Drake leaned forward in her chair, glowering at Soren.

"This is no fool's errand," she said in a mean tone. "This is the battle for the heart of the world. There is something behind the power of the king. Something is feeding his hate, spreading it like a disease. Until we figure out what that is, and stomp it out, we need to proceed very cautiously. We need to be pinpoint precise with our tactics. I must remain completely hidden, and Mihelik needs to recover before he can resume his operations. You three have become a key piece in the war. It's an honor and a duty, and to be completely blunt—your very best shot at revenge."

Soren rubbed his chin, and Seph crossed her legs and swayed her head, deep in thought.

"I'll do it," she said.

"At the risk of my life," Kaile said. "I'll do what I can to aid Soren and the Silver Sparrows. I may regret it, but after seeing the look in the king's eyes as he burned that town full of children, I can't not try to fight that kind of evil. Standing here before you, I don't sense malice in your words. And when you say Alcarond sought something else in the Ellydian, I believe you. I've seen it, but don't know how to express it. He's obsessed with his search. His hatred for you has grown, sir. He thinks you're his only chance to become so powerful that only Shivara herself could be his equal."

Mihelik and Lady Drake both watched Soren, standing between Kaile and Seph. He grunted as his chin hit his chest. He thought long and hard, for what seemed like ten minutes, but was more like a half of one.

"I want to meet this person before we go. They either need to be keen with a sword, a deadeye with a bow, or as knowledgeable about the Ellydian as I, at the least."

"Is it the chancellor?" Seph asked. "No, that would be too obvious."

"He is none of those that you mentioned, Soren," Lady Drake said. "But worry not. His abilities will still be quite useful out on the plains and in the forests."

"So, who is this man? And what is this thing you wish us to get for the war?" Soren asked.

As the rain poured beyond the mighty glass windows

beyond the two powerful Syncrons, a ray of light slid through the dark clouds, shining down onto the plains as if the finger of Shivara had pushed through, sending her golden light into the darkness.

Lady Drake simply smiled at Soren's request. Soren cocked an eyebrow, not expecting that reaction.

In the room's corner he sensed movement, as if the stones of the wall themselves shifted. Soren had as keen of eyesight as anyone he'd met, and his instinct almost never steered him wrong. Yet, behind Lady Drake, in the right corner of the room, a man emerged.

"Huh?" Kaile muttered.

Soren blinked his eyes hard, staring at the man. He hadn't been there a moment ago, and there he was, walking forward with short legs. He had a cloak on, which covered his brow, but Soren saw the beady eyes of the short man as he made his way to Lady Drake's side.

"This, Soren, is Davin Mosser," the lady said.

The half-height man bowed his head.

This is the man I'm to trust with mine and Seph's life? Him?

Chapter Nine

Davin Mosser stood beside the lady of Cascadia, yet Soren didn't know what to think of the man. Perhaps he was so thrown off that he hadn't sensed him all that time during their conversation.

The dwarf stood with a sense of pride and apprehension himself. He stood with his short arms out at his sides, with thick fingers curled, ready to make fists. His feet were shoulder width, and he held a certain kind of balance Soren sensed rarely in men. Davin looked as sturdy as a boulder.

Davin scanned the three of them with a hawk's eyes. He was intelligent, Soren could quickly tell. His pale violet eyes screamed that much about him. He had dusty blond hair that peaked out from under the hood that fell nearly to his collar, and Soren thought he caught a faint glimmer of a thin chain that wrapped around his neck and fell under his shirt.

"Pleased to meet you," Davin said. His words were pronounced well, almost in a forced courtly speak. But his accent seemed distant, to a region Soren didn't recognize. "I hope to be a great service on our journey."

Soren couldn't stop the twisting he felt on his lips and the scowl on his brow.

Seph nodded to the dwarf, but glanced up at Soren to see his reaction, which caused hers to remain cold.

Kaile didn't seem to know what to do with himself as he stood with his long arms dangling and his fingers rubbing.

"Davin has certain abilities that will prove advantageous to you as you travel," Lady Drake said.

"Another Syncron?" Seph asked.

"No." Lady Drake brushed a loose strand of hair behind her ear. "But he is educated on the principles of the Ellydian, so he may have wisdom to share with you about your own abilities. He will help to conceal your identities from those who are surely looking for you."

"Seph's magic should be enough," Soren said coldly. "Thanks, but no thanks."

Lady Drake sighed, looking away at the ceiling as the dark clouds rolled out toward the distant sea behind.

"Persephone can hide yourselves from the world," Mihelik intervened. "But she must remain focused, and the spell can break should something interrupt that concentration and focus. Your fight with the Shades is a reminder of such truths. Davin will *mask* you. You will be able to hold full conversations with those who hunt for the king, and that in itself is a rare gift you should be grateful for— Scarred."

Soren grunted to himself, but tried to swallow his pride. He knew the great Syncron wizard was correct. Seph couldn't cast her spell constantly, day and night.

"What is the source of such magic?" Kaile asked, as a student would ask a teacher in class.

Davin smirked. "You wouldn't recognize the name if I told ya. And I ain't tellin' you yet. We all have our secrets, don't we, apprentice to the archmage?"

Kaile shied away as he turned his head, letting his red hair cover half his face.

There was a thick pause of heavy silence in the room. Soren felt an unease as he and the dwarf exchanged glares.

"I've heard of you over the years," Davin said. "Even before the king's attack on you. Unparalleled with a blade, honorable and courageous."

"I've never heard of you," Soren replied.

"I haven't been in Cascadia long," Davin said. "I've been riding the better part of a week since Lady Drake's summons. I've only been in Skylark since yesterday."

How does she trust a man who, it seems, isn't from her court, or her kingdom?

"Where did you ride from?" Seph asked.

"We'll have plenty of time to catch up about where we're from on the road," he replied.

"Listen, Soren," Lady Drake said. "I know you have your apprehensions about this party that we're insisting on, but that is part of the trust that we need to hold in one another. We are going to war. And you're going to need strong allies. This mission is too important for you to be stubborn about. The Silver Sparrows need you, and you need them."

"I don't need the Sparrows," Soren said. "I could kill Glasse on my own."

Lady Drake paused and looked to Mihelik, who nodded.

"Perhaps, and perhaps not," the old man said with the knowledge of nearly a century of years within him. "But you have your own sort of apprentice now. If you wish to protect the girl, you'll need her trained. More than with a dagger, mind you, she'll need to learn to wield that Whistlewillow Ellydian that stirs inside her. Kaile Thorne has ample knowledge to begin that training, and Davin, I trust with my life. He will safeguard you as you make your journey through Aladran."

Soren sucked up his pride as best he could. Protecting Seph

was the most important thing, and with how stubborn she was proving to be, he knew that training her powers would be vital.

"If you trust him," Soren said, crossing his arms over his chest. "Then I will trust your judgement."

"Excellent," Mihelik said with a brilliant grin as he clapped his hands. "You see. I told you he'd agree."

Lady Drake smirked and laughed. "You were right."

Soren grimaced, instantly regretting his words. But it was too late. He'd have to stick with the plan laid out for them.

"As for your first mission…" Lady Drake began. "Your ultimate goal is Glasse in Grayhaven. He's on his way back there now, with the king's praise shining upon him. Your first task will be on the border between our two lands. My informants have only gotten us so close to the location of the object I seek. You four will find it, procure it, and bring it back to me once Glasse is dead."

"On the border? Where?" Soren asked. "What object?"

"Davin will fill you in on your journey," the lady said.

The dwarf huffed and nodded.

"When do we leave?" Seph asked.

"With everyone on board," Davin said. "Before first light tomorrow. There's a hidden entrance at the base of the Blackstone, behind one of the waterfalls. We'll head west, once I've done my job to conceal the three of you."

"What about you?" Soren asked, scratching the top of his head. "Don't you stand out too?"

"I'm not a wanted man," Davin said. "And as for my height you're referring to, I blend in far more than you may expect…"

"To Grayhaven then," Kaile said. "And… master Mihelik, I don't think that I'm quite qualified to be training anyone on the Ellydian. I'm still a student myself… hardly with enough…"

"Hush," Mihelik said abruptly with a sideways chop of his hand. "I'll not have it. You may be an apprentice, but you have far more insight into the connection of all things than her. She's had a book, and you've had one of the most powerful Synths ever as your master. What you think is insignificant will prove to be a gushing fountain to her."

"I would like to learn," Seph said in a sweet voice.

"I'll try until we return and Mihelik can teach you," Kaile said with a slight bow.

The room turned to silence as the thunderstorm beyond the glass darkened the lands, and lightning crashed in the clouds. An eerie feeling rose in Soren. His stomach tightened, his thigh itched, and the hairs on his neck straightened. Even though he'd decided to allow this makeshift group to travel all together for the sake of this mission—he didn't like it—not one bit. He knew nothing about this Davin, but if it came to Seph's safety, then the dwarf was going to be in for an eye-opening revelation about who made the decisions in this quest, and who was in charge!

"This will be the last time we meet," Lady Drake broke the silence. "Until you return, that is."

Soren bowed and Kaile bowed, and Seph quickly followed after noticing them.

"Whatever you need before your trip, please let Chancellor Carvaise know."

"Thank you, m'lady," Soren said.

"Yes," Kaile said. "Thank you for everything. I'll do my best."

Seph fidgeted with her fingers, unsure of what to say.

"We will meet again," Lady Drake said to her. "You will become a strong heir to your name. Just stay alive long enough for that prophecy to come true."

Lady Drake stood. Davin backed away as the folds of her dress loosened to flow down her long legs. Mihelik stood too, as Davin rushed over to help him.

"Thank you, my lad," the old man said. "Soren, I wish to

meet with you before you go, after I've had time to rest these old bones."

Soren nodded, but then kicked himself. Internally, that is. "Yes, of course."

Mihelik grunted, stepping away from the chair. Davin led him to the far side of the room as he and Lady Drake made their leave through the door, and once it closed, it was just the three of them left in the room.

"Well," Seph said, "I've never been out of Cascadia. So, I guess that's something to look forward to."

Soren groaned.

"Are you going to groan at everything I say? Or everything that involves me?"

He groaned again as the door behind squealed open.

"Fine, be like that," Seph said. "But I'm not some child you need to look out for all the time. I had to raise myself, remember? I can take care of myself."

Soren didn't respond as the chancellor stood in the doorframe, ushering them to follow back.

"Good talk, I gather?" Roland asked.

Soren turned and walked through the doorway. "You know damned well it wasn't."

Roland swallowed hard as Soren walked past him, toward the soldiers that held torches further down the tunnel.

"Forgive him," Seph said. "He's grumpy when he's sleepy."

Roland chuckled, nearly letting spit fly from his lips as he covered his mouth quickly.

Soren turned back to glare at her as she shrugged. He spun back and trudged down the hall.

"This is going to be an interesting journey..." Kaile muttered to Roland.

"I believe it will be," the chancellor said, wiping his lips with a kerchief from his breast pocket. "I trust it will be something to remember the rest of your life."

"If I live to remember it," Kaile murmured as they walked down the torch-lit hall, back to their rooms. Food had been laid out on the table and covered, with bottles of wine and pitchers of water. Seph and Kaile went to the table, poking their noses under the coverings to smell what savory morsels had been cooked for their lunch.

Soren went straight to his room and slammed the door behind him.

Chapter Ten

Every time he closed his eyes, he could see the flames. They were so ingrained in his mind it was truly a waking nightmare. His heart ached when he saw memories of Cirella's face shining with warm sunlight and knew he'd never see it again.

He wanted to talk to her, he wanted to hold her, he wanted to just say goodbye.

And now Bael and Alicen were burned away to nothing. They couldn't even have a proper funeral. The king and his men just left the town as a trophy in their war against the Chimaera. They'd be hailed as heroes while Soren was left to remember the truth of his isolation.

But now Soren wasn't alone.

They wanted him to join the Silver Sparrows, a rebellion he left long ago. A rebellion he had joined by default—because of his love for Cirella.

He said he'd go. He said he'd fight their war. But there was only one reason he was going to war—well, perhaps two…

Revenge. He'd kill Edward Glasse, and Garland, and the Knight Wolf. Then he gave himself permission to die. He'd want to kill the king and every last soldier under him, but he didn't think that the opportunity to get that close to the king would ever arise again. Those three… those three with their heads cut from their shoulders would be enough… it would have to be enough.

The second reason he'd go was because he didn't know what else to do with Persephone. She knew too much now and wanted her own revenge as much as he did. He didn't know how to stop her from the mission laid out for them. Soren knew she was an adamant recruit, and no pressure from him was going to change that. Even if he walked away completely, he knew Lady Drake had her claws sunk in too deep. The reward was too enticing.

Soren sat in his room as his thoughts burned like a forge. Every time his eyelids were too heavy to keep open, the bellows blew hot air onto the coals, surging the inferno is his mind. Images raced through of screams of pain, cries for help, and the brutal, painful deaths that followed.

Eventually, a knock at the door jolted him awake. He was laying in bed, boots on and fully clothed. He had no idea how long he'd been out or what time of day it was. But as he sat up in bed, swinging his boots to the floor, his stomach grumbled.

"What?" he moaned, wiping the sleep from his eyes.

There was a short burning candle on the nightstand with wax pooling at the bottom of the candelabra. He slid his finger into it and lit a candle beside it, doubling the light in the dim room.

"Beg your pardon," the old woman's scratchy throat said, as she cleared it. "You're beckoned. No rush, but you may want to get ready."

He hunched over, rubbing the top of his nose. "Beckoned," he murmured. "How long was I asleep?" He stood up with a deep groan. "I'll be right out."

Soren walked over and opened the door and saw the old

woman and the young boy attendants waiting with their arms draped low below their stomachs.

Seph and Kaile both sat at the table beyond the attendants. Seph had her shoes off and her feet up on the bench, with her hands clasped before her shins. Kaile shied his gaze away, making Soren wonder if he was scowling.

"Well?" Soren pressed.

The old woman, not impressed, straightening her back and shoving her shoulders back, said, "The other guest of Lady Drake wishes to speak with you within the hour. Perhaps you'd like some supper before you go off to meet him?"

"Supper?" Soren asked, scratching his temple.

"You've been in your room all day," Seph said. She didn't seem annoyed. More like bored, Soren thought. Her knees bobbed as she waited for a response. Kaile was using his fingernail to pick at something on the wooden table.

"I see," he said, clearing his throat. "Yes, perhaps I'll have something to eat and then go and meet with him." He glanced around the room, as the attendant and the young boy still stood there. "Yes?"

The old woman turned to the young boy, who bashfully put his hands behind his back and swayed from side to side. "Go on," she pressed.

"I—I was wondering, sir… sorry sir, I don't mean to pry, but… I heard a tale that maybe…"

"Go on," the old woman said in a pleasant tone. "It's all right…"

The boy gulped. "I heard that you killed one. One of the Demons of Dusk."

Soren folded his arms and nodded.

"They scare me," the boy said, scratching his elbow. "I've seen them at night from the towers." His eyes were wide and full of dread.

"Just stick to the sunlight and you'll be just fine," Soren said.

"That's it though," the boy said. "What if there's a day when the sun doesn't come back? What do we do if they ever get into the city? I want to know how to fight them. I don't want them to hurt my sister…"

Soren unfolded his arms and knelt. He looked straight into the startled boy's eyes. "They aren't going to come into your city. You're safe here."

"You… promise?"

"I promise," Soren said, patting the boy's shoulder.

The old woman grabbed the boy as Soren stood up. "There, now you've been reassured. Now run off and grab this man something to eat."

The boy ran off through the heavy door.

"Wine?" she asked.

"Yes," he replied.

Soren sat at the end of the long table as the attendant poured him a glass of deep red wine that smelled floral, like violets. She then poured a glass of water beside it as he sipped the wine. As she walked away, he leaned back in his chair, swirling the wine in the glass. Seph continued bobbing her knees and Kaile continued picking at the table.

"What?" Soren asked.

"Nothin'," she replied quickly.

He groaned and took another sip.

"Out with it," he said.

Seph leaped from her seat and ran over to sit beside Soren. "Kaile's been telling me all about the Ellydian, and the capital, and the things the archpriest did, and…"

"Happy for you," Soren said. "There's going to be a lot for you to learn from the boy." Soren glowered at him from over the top of the glass. "As long as he is teaching you the right things…"

"Yessir," Kaile blurted. "Only things that will help her. I think, from what she said, that she's a natural, and teaching her the wave patterns of the notes will help her to control their rhythms quickly."

"Just take it easy at first," Soren said. "Don't need any explosions in the middle of the night because you taught her some spell too soon for her to control."

Kaile nodded. "Yes, of course."

"I want to know all of it, everything," Seph said excitedly, bouncing up and down.

"I'm sure you do," Soren said. "Got that Whistlewillow blood in you."

The old woman opened the door from the inside and the boy walked in, carrying a wide copper platter with a domed lid. He looked as if he was about to collapse under the weight of the vessel that looked nearly half his size. He set it on the table with a sigh of relief and backed away with his hands behind his back.

Soren pulled it forward, and the woman grabbed the lid by the handle at its top and removed it. The steam rushed into his face as his nostrils filled with the pungent gamey smell of roasted lamb. It was wrapped in twine, slathered with butter and rosemary. There were boiled, buttered potatoes and root vegetables surrounding it. The boy came rushing over with a thin loaf of fresh bread with more butter and some baked pastries with pistachios swirled within.

Soren nodded and grabbed the knife and fork, cutting into the meat. His mouth watered immediately.

"I don't think I've ever had food this good my whole life," Seph said. "I didn't know it could be so good…"

Soren cut a piece of the roast and put it in his mouth, sitting back with a deep moan, chewing the tender meat as the fatty juices gushed.

"Aye," he said between chews. "A master works here in these kitchens."

He continued eating his meal, while Seph and Kaile remained mostly silent. The eeriness and emptiness made it abundantly clear there was something else on their minds. Whether or not it had to do with him, Soren didn't know.

The answer came once Soren had put the last bite of potatoes into his mouth and swallowed.

"I want to go with you to meet the Syncron master," Seph said, sitting on her hands but leaning her chest over the table.

"No."

"Why not?"

"Because."

"Because why?" she asked, squinching her brow and nose.

"Because I said so," he responded quickly, folding his legs as he leaned back. He pulled a pipe from the round side table and began packing it with musty, earthy tobacco from a pouch.

"Why not?"

"Because, Persephone, there are things I need to discuss with him, alone."

"It's Seph."

He nodded. "Sorry."

"There are things I need to ask him too," she said. "We're leaving in the morning, and he knows so much… about everything! He knew my parents. I want to hear more about them."

"I understand," Soren said, holding a burn stick above a candle to let the flames lick into it. "He summoned me, and me alone. You'll have time to talk to him when we return and he begins your training."

"I can't wait till then," she said.

"Then don't go."

"You're infuriating," she said, leaning back with pouted lips and folding her arms. "Say something!" She scowled at Kaile, who sent his gaze to a far corner of the room, scratching his cheek. "I don't know how I'm going to survive just you two. You're going to drive me mad!"

Soren sparked the pipe, taking a deep inhale from the curved pipe of rosy, dark wood. After he pulled the pipe away, the thick smoke plumed from his lips to the ceiling.

"No answer?" she asked with a mad frown.

"You need to have patience, and get used to the word *no*."

Apparently, that was not the right thing to say, as she burst up, smacking the pipe from his hand as it flung to the floor, spilling the burning tobacco onto the stone. She loomed over him as he sat back with his mouth agape, legs still crossed. She shoved her finger right between his eyes.

"You listen to me. We may be family. But you're gonna have to earn my respect. You've done nothing but speak to me like a child since I escaped that hellhole you put me in. I'm not a fucking child anymore! You're the one who left me in that prison. You left me under the care of those awful women. You should be the one working on this relationship. Not me!"

She sat in fury. Arms folded, legs crossed and held angled down and away. Her knee bobbed wildly.

"She's got a point," the old woman suddenly broke the silence with a raised eyebrow as she swept on the other side of the room.

The agreement of the old attendant irked Soren, but he couldn't help the feeling that Seph was right. He was in the wrong and needed to be the one to work on repairing what trust still dwindled by torn threads. He was just so used to being alone that he didn't know how to act like he truly cared for someone.

"I did save your life," Soren said, causing Seph to sigh, still gazing away. "From the Shades. That should prove something."

Tears welled up in Seph's eyes, still not looking at him. Before she needed to wipe them away, she ran from her seat to her room, sniffling, holding in her choking tears until she could close the door behind her.

"Damn it," Soren mumbled.

"Stop trying to be right all the time," the old woman said. "None of my business though…" She continued sweeping. "Stick with 'I'm sorry' for a while. That might help…"

Soren poured a fresh glass of wine and drank it down in two gulps. He stood, picked up the pipe and kicked the ashes into where the wall and floor met.

"I'm ready to meet with Mihelik," he said to the old woman.

Chapter Eleven

While Soren was led down the dim tunnel into higher parts of the underground complex beneath the castle of Barringstone, he knew he should be thinking about what to ask the legendary Syncron wizard, but instead, he concerned himself more for the road that lay ahead, and how he was going to protect Seph.

"This is the one," the soldier that led Soren said as he knocked on the wooden door, hinged heavily with iron brackets.

"Come," Mihelik's raspy voice said from the inside with a cough.

The soldier popped the latch and opened the door inward, moving back for Soren to step past into the wizard's quarters. The soldier closed the door behind him quickly. Soren stood at the entrance, examining the room. Curtains were drawn back to two wide windows of old drooping glass which faced south. The western skies were filled with ribbons of crimson clouds, cutting through the apricot-colored sky like claws raking through skin. To the east, the sky darkened to a dark sea color. Cold winter winds howled from the outside of the windows as Soren stepped into the center of the room.

Mihelik sat with his back to Soren, who could see the bony frame of the wizard through his robes. His shoulder blades popped like sharp mountains from the earth, and his spine protruded like a ridgeline that carved between them.

"Come, sit beside me," Mihelik said, not turning but waving his hand. The old man was sitting in a cushioned chair before a wide table, before the windows, which was strewn with tomb-like books and loose scrolls.

Soren approached and sat in a creaky chair beside him.

"Wine?" Mihelik said, trailing the spine of a three-inch wide book before him with his finger.

Soren nodded and Mihelik placed a glass before him, and Soren poured himself one from the carafe between them. Soren sipped the wine as he scanned the books and papers on the table and gazed around the room. It smelled like an old person, and Soren wondered how long the Syncron wizard had used the room. He knew he was in the Myngorn Forest, but was this where he'd been hiding all these years? Right under the king's most trusted in Cascadia? The bed in the far corner was disheveled, with blankets draping to the floor and socks scattered around the bed. On a cupboard by the door rested a plate of food half-eaten, ready for an attendant to pick up, surely.

Neither spoke for several minutes. Soren had the feeling the old man either had nothing to say or was about to start a conversation he didn't want to.

So, Soren waited, finishing his glass, and poured another. He knew that where he was going, there would not be fine wines and soft beds. There was going to be wet mud, wintry nights, and hungry stomachs.

"Let me see the dagger," Mihelik finally said. "If you don't mind."

Is that why he brought me? Just to see the dagger that I used to kill the Shades?

Soren pulled it from its sheath at his hip and placed it before the Syncron.

Mihelik sat up straight, pressing his shoulders back and staring hard at the blade.

One inch wide and ten inches long, the rippling layers of Damascus steel held a powerful essence in front of the wizard. He glared down onto the blade, not able to see it, but with his long nose nearly touching the steel. His fingers glided down the blade, inspecting the three different colored metals of its crossguard, past the leather grip, and finally down to the black-jeweled pommel.

"Interesting," he said, almost in awe.

"What?"

"The stone at the bottom… it doesn't reflect any light at all."

How can he tell that? Perhaps he can sense magic from it? The wizard is full of little mysteries.

"Yes," Soren said. "I assumed its magic, or some mineral I've never heard of."

"Both, perhaps," Mihelik said. "There are rare gems down in the southern lands. In Garrehad, specifically."

"Yes, I've heard," Soren said. "Garrehad has many volcanic regions that produce the rare gems, and the blacksmiths in Vellice to forge them."

"Mhmm," the wizard breathed.

"I did see the gem flash briefly," Soren said. "When I killed the Shades. It was faint, but I saw the light from within glow."

Mihelik drew his head up and took a gulp of wine. Soren did the same.

"What does it mean?" Soren asked.

"I don't know, but that may give a clue to not only what the dagger is, but—"

Soren interrupted, "But what the Shades are!"

"Correct," Mihelik said. "With all the mysteries of this world, and the trying times we are in, that question perplexes me the most. I admit, I deeply desire to understand why the Demons of Dusk, and specifically the Black Fog, are doing in our world."

"What have you discovered?" Soren asked.

"Little, I'm afraid to admit. That's why I'm so fascinated by this dagger, and by the coin you mentioned that lured the fog to you and your companion. That was what Alcarond and I were working on in our last years as teacher and pupil—what caused the darkness to come to Aladran?"

"And you didn't find *anything*?"

"I believe they are a mix of both a virus and some perverted form of purification."

"What?" Soren said, with his brow furrowed, gripping the table with both hands.

"It came to devour, kill, cleanse, whatever you may call it. Like bottom feeders on the sea floor. They feed to purify in their own sense. The Shades and the Black Fog are connected, as you'd guess. But there's more than just that they are bound to the shadow, and appear black to the eye. The Black Fog consumes, and it seems to transform that which it devours into Shades."

Soren's jaw dropped. The revelation hit him like a punch to the gut.

"The Shades that I fought, the ones that discovered Seph in her spell. I heard Alcarond say that they'd lost some of their soldiers in the night, ones that risked the road under the night sky. It must have been a fog that killed them. That might have been them!"

Mihelik nodded.

Soren cradled his head in his hands, sinking to his seat.

I'd assumed the Black Fog ate what it destroyed, but the idea that they make the Shades...

Soren had a vision then, a glimpse of what might become. This wasn't just monsters stirring in the night. If the Black Fog had its way, everyone would roam the night lands as Shades. There wouldn't be anyone left... and he'd seen both up close. There was no escaping the fog, and no fighting off the Shades without a Vellice blade. The gravity of the moment filled Soren, and the overwhelming odds of his retribution and saving his home felt impossible.

"Something about this blade was able to kill those Shades," Mihelik said. "And I aim to find out what, so that we may replicate it."

Soren stirred, but didn't say what was on his mind.

"I don't mean to ask to keep it," Mihelik said. "Just for the night. I'd like to have some people inspect it, diagram it, paint it and sculpt a replica."

Soren didn't agree verbally.

"I'll return it in the morning," Mihelik said. "This is a prime part of the research I've been searching for years."

"Fine," Soren said. "Back in the morning, though. I feel naked without it."

Mihelik didn't laugh, but continued feeling the cold steel with the tips of his fingers.

"Can I ask you something, master Mihelik?" Soren said, staring at the side of the old man's head with his silver hair flowing down in strands.

"You want to know about my *betrayal?*"

Soren nodded, but then said, "Yes. I, myself, believed you'd gone mad, betraying what you loved most. I assumed you'd gone off and died in your madness and possible self-loathing for burning such important texts. After the floods, it was a miracle they'd survived, anyway."

Mihelik had a sort of half-cocked grin on his face, an

amusement that Soren didn't expect.

"Those two are connected more than you might imagine," the old Syncron said.

"Tell me," Soren said.

"I don't have time for all of it, and I don't trust you enough with half of it," Mihelik said, irking Soren.

But Soren knew that he wasn't a Syncron, and the knowledge that Mihelik held between his ears was only known by the archmage and the king. Soren swallowed his pride.

"What can you tell me? Persephone's parents and Cirella were devastated by your betrayal."

Mihelik sighed, sitting back, putting his hands into the pockets at the front of his robes, over his stomach. The candlelight of the room glowed a warm amber, glistening its light off the paintings of figures of old or rustic landscapes. The sky before them darkened as the old man grumbled.

"The Demons of Dusk arrived slowly over the years, first being fables, rare sightings of mysterious monsters. Many thought they were tall tales parents told their children to keep them in their beds. But over time, I had to know the truth as too many were going missing in the moon's light. The first time I saw them with my own eyes, I knew something about our world had changed."

"Go on…"

"There are ancient texts from the Sundar that talk about a world not unlike ours. It existed many lifetimes ago, a world that was ruled by an evil that took a flood to wash away. These lands of Aladran were under water for thousands of years. That was what it took to wipe away the evil that overtook good. But I fear the floods weren't enough. The evil lived on, and it's returning…"

Mihelik slumped in his chair, sliding back so the folds of the back of his robes creased at the chair's top.

"You discovered this? So you destroyed it?"

"No," Mihelik said. "That tale has been known by the kings and their archmages for generations."

"Well, what caused you to do what you did?"

Mihelik sighed. "Alcarond Riberia."

"The archmage? He caused it?"

"He was such a promising apprentice. So much thirst for knowledge. Such raw power. I remember when he attempted the Black Sacrament. I was so proud. I don't think I've ever been prouder in my whole life."

"Go on…"

"We researched the Demons of Dusk together. He poured all of his time and effort into discovering what they were and how to defeat them. Even more so than I, he became obsessed. As the years went on, we worked together to figure out the mystery. We had to be careful, though. As you found out, the Shades aren't affected by the Ellydian. It doesn't work on them. Nothing has… until you killed them."

Soren glared heavily at the blade with the infinite black pommel. He watched the candlelight glow off the wavy ridges of the Damascus pattern. "Firelight."

"That's your name for her?" Mihelik asked.

Soren nodded. "Aye."

"I'd like to see what you see when you look at the blade," Mihelik said. Soren didn't answer.

"How'd you lose your sight? If I may ask."

"Another question with the same answer I gave you before…"

Soren thought for a moment. "Alcarond?"

Mihelik nodded.

"I see…" Soren said, pulling the pipe from his pocket and stuffing it with tobacco leaves. As he lit the pipe, he sensed the Syncron's mind whirling. Mihelik sat motionless, breathing wheezy breaths through his hairy nostrils, with his gaze angled down at the table.

"I suppose there's no foul in telling you," the old man said futilely, feeling for his own pipe on the table to the right, which Soren helped him find by guiding the pipe to his fingers. He stuffed it and lit the earthy leaves, inhaling, and deeply exhaling with a moan. The smoke wafted up to the rafters above, gliding along the glass of the windows and the night sky beyond. "I don't expect either of us to live that much longer, anyway. Does it trouble you that I say that in all seriousness?"

"No."

"Good, I suppose. It's probably best you know your opponent's potential, if you're going to war with them."

"Tell me. What happened between you and Alcarond?"

"We were together nearly two full decades. I found him in a village near Sarcasus. Still in Lynthyn, but only by the grace of the goddess and by only a couple of miles. In the capital we'd heard stories of his power, so the king sent me to find him, and when I did—my life was never the same…"

"Go on…" Soren puffed at his pipe.

"The boy was mean, in his midtwenties with a temper that could move mountains. He wasn't cruel. Thank the heavens for that. No matter how hard that bastard William Wolf pressed him, Alcarond didn't enjoy the pain of others, but his temper flare-ups would have him fuming with uncontrollable, powerful magic."

"So, what happened between you two? Twenty years in, and you fought over the Demons of Dusk? The scriptures of the Sundar?"

"It was that and more…" Mihelik said, taking the glass of wine from the table and drinking it down.

"A woman?"

Mihelik nodded. "Not just any woman, though. And let me be very clear about this, it wasn't just about romance or sex…"

Soren withdrew slightly. He wasn't sure he knew where this was going, and he worried what the answer would be.

"It doesn't really matter who it was over, but we started to drift apart. I would teach him, but he began to pull away. He still wanted to learn the lessons of the Ellydian, but he was upset I wasn't teaching him more—faster."

"Who was the girl?" Soren asked.

"It doesn't matter."

"Is she still alive?" Soren asked, putting his pipe on the table, turning his chair to face Mihelik, and resting his elbows on his thighs.

"Yes."

"Sophia?" Soren asked.

Mihelik sighed and took another sip of wine, polishing off the glass, putting it back on the table and waving for more. Soren poured.

"She's so much younger than you," Soren said, as Mihelik took the glass and swirled the dark contents as the bottom of the glass glided in circles upon the wood.

"The heart wants what the heart wants," the old man said.

"Very true," Soren said, sitting back up and smoking his pipe. "So that's what started the feud, and then he grew impatient with training, and then what?"

"Sophia became another student of mine, and I'll spare you the details, but her affection drove Alcarond and I apart. So after a year of that, our investigation into the Demons of Dusk had grown to all-consuming. We, especially Alcarond, were growing obsessed with them. He wanted to know how to defeat them. He thought he could become the savior of our world, and curry the favor of the king, and her, if he were able to destroy them."

"This is where the burning of the ancient tomes came in to play, I take it?"

Mihelik sighed. "Not a part of the story I relish telling."

"I need to know... Cirella idolized you. You were her hero before you did that. You destroyed irreplaceable knowledge.

You destroyed the last scripts of the old world pertaining to the Ellydian. How could you?"

"Because they didn't only speak about the Ellydian!" the Syncron blurted, knocking his hand into his glass, rocking it on the table as wine flew from its ring onto the wood.

"What do you mean? What else was in there?" Soren pressed.

"The fifth and final book in the Scriptures of the Ancients alludes to something else. Something that the Ellydian doesn't control. There's another force in this world, one not based on the rhythm of the world, but harnesses the rhythms of something else, not from this world."

Soren's head slunk as he looked down at his hands as he interlocked his fingers.

There's another magic foretold in the ancient texts? How have I never known this? Is it possible they kept that secret away from even the Whistlewillows?

"Alcarond found out about this and wanted to use it against them?" Soren asked.

Mihelik gave a frustrated shrug. "The texts don't say what the rhythm is or where it comes from. It doesn't say how to use it or what in the nine hells it is, anyway! He was obsessing over a fairy tale! Even if it was true, the texts say it was a destructive magic far more dangerous than even the Ellydian. Can you imagine? More destructive? That would put all of Aladran in danger. Hell, the whole world might break if such a magic existed, and if it fell into the wrong hands…"

"That is a worrying thought…" Soren said.

"Worrying?" Mihelik said. "I think you fail to comprehend the magnitude of what a reckoning force like that would unleash upon the world. No army of men, nor covenant of Syncrons, would easily defeat such a force. If it were to exist, then no one could be trusted with such magic."

"So you burned it."

"So I burned it…"

"Alcarond found out…" Soren said.

"Because I told him, even before I told the king," Mihelik said, in forced words, pushing them out past the slight crack in his voice.

"It was difficult for you, I'd imagine. To be the one to destroy something you cherish, something so special—divine even—to your people."

"You have no idea, Soren."

"I want to hear about you and Alcarond," Soren said.

"It took me a full day and restless night to figure out how to tell him, and when it happened, I instantly regretted it. I've never seen rage in a man like that, and I've seen sickening battles and the fiercest tempests on the seas. When I told him, just before we were scheduled a lesson, and before Sophia was to have her lesson, he erupted into a mad rage."

"What did you tell him, exactly?"

"I told him I burned the texts, for fear that one with a heart of darkness would seek to learn the unnamed power, and wreak utter havoc upon this world. I told him none of us could be trusted with such destructive power." Mihelik sighed. "Then he lost his mind. Not in the sort of way when you get into a fight, or argue over politics. It was like he grieved the loss of someone truly dear to him—yet never met. He was so infatuated with the lust for power, and how to drive the Demons of Dusk from our lands, that I became the focus of his hatred. I never wish for anyone to be on the receiving end of such madness and hate."

"He attacked you?"

"Aye," Mihelik said. "I think he'd decided long ago how to attack me, if he was ever going to. He must've known there was no going back if he fought me, and even after successful passing and surviving the Black Sacrament, his power was no match for mine. But he learned a spell that I didn't expect, one that is rarely used, and one I never taught him. He learned it somewhere else, and used it on me."

"What was the spell?"

"It's called the Wraithfire spell. I wasn't able to put up a spell to deflect it. He used the keys of D flat minor and B major. The combination of the notes made for an unusual rhythm that I didn't have time to instinctually defend. I wasn't quick enough, and I felt the heat immediately. I felt it burning on the underside of my skin. I could feel the unbearable burning and could smell the horrible stench in my nose. It was a pain I can't describe, and as it coursed throughout my entire body, it eventually went up into my neck and head. I nearly died, but it took my eyes and burned every hair off my body. He left me to die. I remember laying there, on my back, unable to move my body as I lay broken and burned to the bone. It felt like a horrible eternity of unrelenting pain and sadness. But after what felt like a full day of inexplicable pain, I felt the most beautiful thing. It was like my body was doused in cool spring water. It cleansed my body and soul, freeing me of the misery. I felt in that moment that I probably died, and the Golden Kingdom was welcoming me to the halls of my ancestors—but that wasn't the case. I felt the tender touch of soft skin on my face, and heard the most wonderful voice a man could ever hear. It was her. She did what she could to heal me as she cast the Ellydian into my body, healing what she could."

"Sophia…"

"Yes," Mihelik breathed. "She was my angel that day."

Soren shook his head, looking down at his lap. "Well, I'm glad she was there to save you. But I won't lie that it troubles me that he was able to defeat you. I knew he was strong, but you were the strongest of them all."

"Yes. There are many mistakes I've made in my life, and hindsight has been a curse that keeps me awake many nights."

"I can relate to that," Soren said somberly.

"I'm sure you can."

"So, you destroyed everything, right?" Soren asked. "There's no existing mention of this old magic that could destroy everything?"

Mihelik raised his hand and pulled it up to the side of his head, extending his finger and pressing it to his temple. "This is the only place it lives now."

"Good," Soren nodded.

Mihelik took a slow sip of wine, grabbing the pipe after, lighting it, and smoking the musty tobacco.

"I have another question," Soren said. "The portal spell you used. How did you do that? And could you do it again? How far does it go?"

"You mean to ask if I could transport you far, so that you could drop into a room with the king and kill him? Well, it doesn't work like that."

"You read my mind," Soren said.

"No, that spell takes an incredible amount of energy, time, and focus. I've only used it a handful of times in my life. And that time warranted it. I don't feel that I may ever use it again. I'm not getting any younger, as you well know."

Soren nodded.

"But you used it to get Kaile. Why?"

Mihelik leaned back, put one thin leg over the other, and smoked his pipe with a look on his aged, wrinkled face. He held a curious thought but kept it to himself.

"The boy has great potential," the old archmage said. "And he didn't need to be under the wings of Alcarond any longer. The boy needs to learn to fly."

"And you're going to be the one to teach him?" Soren asked.

"I will, for as long as Shirava gives me life. Lady Drake too, perhaps, although she must live her secret life with the Sparrows in the shadow. Ellaina is a good woman. I hope you can find it in your heart to trust her, because she's entrusted you with the knowledge that, if found out by the king, would spell the end of all of Skylark. Everything she's built, and everything she's ever loved, would die in fire."

Soren grabbed the old man's forearm and squeezed. "I'm trying. It doesn't come easy to me, though."

"You can trust your niece. That much is certain."

Soren squeezed once again and slapped his forearm once. "I believe I can. It's just that age. She's a bit… too emotional and unpredictable. I haven't been around children much in my solitude."

"It'll come back to you. Just remember, Soren, what you went through—she also did, and she didn't have a grown man's years and experience to push through like you did. She not only lost her family, but she was abandoned… by you. Even if what you did was right, you're going to have to work to repair what was broken."

"Aye," Soren said, sitting back up straight and taking a gulp of his wine. "That's why I never had kids. Didn't know how I'd figure out how to raise them."

"Well, in a sense, you've got two now," Mihelik said with a chuckle. "I don't envy you for that. Those two are going to bring trouble. I don't need to be able to see the future to know that."

Soren laughed. "They're not the only ones."

Mihelik leaned toward Soren and patted his knee. "Soren, if you don't find a way to lead those two and shape them into the Syncrons they need to become, I fear Synths like Glasse, Zertaan, and Alcarond will continue morphing this world into a place that none of us will want to live in."

"I'll do my best," Soren said.

"I know you will," Mihelik said. "For if you fail, everything you love about our world will die."

PART III
THE JOURNEY TO LONDINDAM

Chapter Twelve

❦

T*rust.*

EARNED, praised, and coveted. Unspoiled trust is as rare as the most valued gemstones from deep underground.

Often it is placed without merit, and a soul crumbles and festers once betrayed. It has the privilege of holding strongest in youth and pulling out to sea with the tides in those last years.

Place it with caution. Hold it true to your heart. For once given, it forms a deep bond that, once broken, is seldom repaired.

In our world of infinite sorrow, yet triumph, it is a gift to give, one that builds our humanity. Cherish it, for it is one thing that keeps broken hearts from the shadows.

-Translated from the language of the Sundar. The Scriptures of the Ancients, Book II, Chapter XXI.

. . .

Their boots plodded through puddles of cold water in the dark tunnel beneath the city. The tunnel was straight, and seemed to go on for miles, with every inch forward growing colder, with wisps of frost on the vapors of their breath. The air was fresher, however. Roland led the way, with a full dozen soldiers in tow. Six in front, and six behind. The chancellor was leading them to their journey beyond the city of Skylark, and their new companion, Davin, walked just in front of Soren, with Seph and Kaile behind him.

Soren didn't sleep, at least he didn't think he did. In the realm of insomnia where he dwelled, sometimes he couldn't tell the difference between the waking world and the dream one. There were too many things on his mind.

What if Alcarond would have found the information about this forgotten magic? Would the world be worse off? Is that even possible?

He thought about Sophia there back in Guillead, traveling with the archmage. *Did she know about the fighting between the archmage and his master over her? How much of all this did she know?* Mostly, he thought about Seph and the road ahead, though. He considered the best ways to kill Glasse. He was slow, slow enough that Soren had a chance to fling his dagger into his shoulder before he could cast a spell, the first time they met. But Glasse wouldn't be slow next time, especially if he knew Soren was coming for him. Stealth would be their only advantage, and Soren desperately wished to know what Davin the dwarf had to offer.

Eventually, down the forever-long tunnel, the white light of an early morning snow-capped sunrise peaked its rays in an upright rectangular shape, signaling a door ahead. Soren was eager to be free of the underworld of the castle and the city, but he could sense the tenseness from Kaile as he hunched his way through the tunnel, embedded within stone walls.

Once the sunlight was at its brightest, the chancellor stopped. He stood before a thick door of iron ahead, and

Soren heard the key as it inserted into the heavy lock. The door opened inward as a spectacular blinding light filled the tunnel—the purest of white and the crispest of air.

The soldiers stepped to the right, and Soren, through his squinted eyes, saw the white landscape beyond. They were facing west, in the direction of Londindam.

Roland exited the tunnel, bowing, ushering them to join him outside the city. Davin walked forward with powerful strides on his short legs. Soren followed. Davin exited first, inhaling deeply through his nostrils, letting out a delighted sigh. Soren pulled his hood down low as he exited. Whatever the dwarf had planned to conceal their appearances from the world had yet to be revealed, and the scars on Soren's face were an invitation for a great reward from the king, and a hard, grueling death for himself.

Even before the blinding white faded from his sight, Soren could hear the horses, and as his eyes adjusted, he saw them down the hill in the trees. Four of them.

"This is where we part," Chancellor Roland said, with his hands behind his back.

"Thank you," Seph said, pulling her collar up to fight off the drafty air.

He smiled and nodded. "May we see each other again. May the goddess protect you on your travels."

Soren watched as the chancellor seemed to wait for anyone to speak, but no one did, so he flattened his mouth into a half smile, nodded his head, and fell back into the tunnel, closing the door with a muted pop of a locking latch behind.

Soren, Seph, and Kaile stood there, looking up at the outside of the great city of Skylark. Perched upon the crest of the lake behind, Skylark towered toward the sky like a golden palace erected for the goddess herself. The city rose in increasingly tall towers until it reached the main keep at its center. The city wasn't made of gold, but mostly a white stone that held the golden warmth of the rising sun, causing it to glow like a dragon's most treasured horde.

They were standing on its western border, far below the outer walls of the city. They stood before a rocky cliff, that would be a difficult climb in itself, to even reach the kingdom. The door that had shut before them was nearly invisible to the unassuming eye. Rocks from the cliff had been built into the backside of the door, and only when inspecting close enough, could one see a single keyhole.

"Well, first things first," Davin said, setting his pack down and dusting his hands off. "Let's get you all concealed and be on our way."

Each of them looked at him wearily. Soren crossed his arms and shifted his weight to his right side.

"I thought you didn't wield the Ellydian..." Seph said. "And they didn't color our hair or anything."

"The Ellydian isn't the only magic in this world," Davin said with a wink. "That dagger on Soren's hip is evidence of that, no?"

"What kind of magic is it?" Seph asked, and Kaile was keenly interested in the answer as well by the sparkle in his eyes.

Davin pulled his leather pack before him and knelt, digging into it. He pulled a rectangular pouch from it, bound in thick leather, and opened it by unsnapping its front rivet. He stood, pulling from it three necklaces, each unrolling from their thin chains. The bottom of each was a pearly metal with a stone inlaid in their centers. He handed one to Seph, then Kaile, and then walked over to Soren and held it out to Soren, who took it skeptically.

"These pendants you'll need to keep with ya at all times," Davin said in a gruff voice. "They won't work if they're not within about six feet o' ya. And keep them under your clothes. No one would recognize them as anything other than jewelry, but the ones who would, well… you definitely don't want them knowing you have 'em."

"Okay," Seph said, nodding and putting the necklace around her neck, tucking it under her shirt. Kaile did the same, after quickly inspecting the stone, but seeming not to notice anything different about the stone.

Soren, however, held it up before him, fully scanning it in the sunlight. The deep, violet stone was cut like a teardrop, with dozens of sharp sides cut into it. The metal it was on was a whitish pearl with a sort of milky hue and sheen.

"What is it? How does it work?" Soren asked.

"It's drixen," Davin said.

"Drixen?" Kaile muttered, mouthing the word as if he recalled it from a distant memory.

Soren knew what drixen was but had never seen it.

"We call it pixiestone here," Soren said.

"Oh! Pixiestone," Seph said. "I've heard about it in songs. It can protect you when you sleep, help you find your way when lost…"

"It doesn't do any of those things," Davin said. "But… it will respond to this…"

Davin slid his thick fingers under his collar and pulled a chain of the same hue out. Pulling it up, a pendant fell out from the front of his shirt. It was a similar size to theirs, but the stone in its center wasn't purple, but a rich shade of deep-sea blue. It was the kind of blue one might imagine being at the center of an ancient glacier, pure and hidden from all impurities for ages. Soren was entranced by the white sparkle the blue stone held as it dangled from Davin's hand, twirling and glimmering in the early morning's rays.

"What is it?" Seph asked.

"This is eldrite. Rarer than diamonds, it puts rubies and sapphires to shame. It's one of the sacred three of my people.

More desired than a palace or a prince. It has the power to disguise you three from the world, anyway I wish."

"Wow," Kaile said, rubbing his chin with wide eyes.

"It's gorgeous," Seph said.

"What is anyway you wish?" Soren asked.

"Let me show you," Davin said. He took the pendant and slipped it back under his shirt. He closed his eyes, stood with his back straight and shoulder blades pressed close together. His lips moved, and he mouthed words inaudibly to them.

For the first time, Soren felt as if he got a true good look at the dwarf. Before, he'd gazed at him with a weariness, a glaring scan to decipher the intentions of the man who Mihelik believed in with his life. His sandy blond hair rustled at the tops of his shoulders, scars marked his face in small cuts healed long ago, and his bushy eyebrows twitched as he muttered. The cracks at the corners of his eyes showed his age, as he seemed older than Soren, but then again, Soren hadn't met many dwarves in his life. They mostly stayed in their homelands to the east.

As Davin's lips moved, a glow emanated from his chest, beneath his thick wool shirt. It was a soft, dark blue at first, but it gleamed to a pale white. Soren felt a humming coming from the pendant, and then he looked down at his own chest to see the violet pixiestone, or drixen rather, glow.

Soren's gaze darted to his left, at first in shock, and then in amazement, as he watched the black, frazzled hairs on Seph's head grow long, turning from their ebony wildness to auburn strands of straight hair that rolled down her chest to her naval and nearly down to her rear. Her pale face darkened to a tan complexion and her dark green eyes faded to tree-trunk brown.

Kaile shrunk what looked like three inches, and his red hair darkened as it retreated to a length only the length of his brow. His chestnut skin lightened to a pale color like Seph's normally was. His dark eyes lightened to a warm hazel, and he looked nothing like his old self—save for his clothes, that were now slightly too big and hung past his ankles.

Soren looked down at his own hands, which the backs of turned shades darker, to a deep oak brown. He reached up to his face, expecting to feel the scars washed away from his face, but to his dismay, he felt the three gnarled scars still cut down his brow and cheek.

"The spell is a disguise," Davin said, with his eyes open, watching Soren. "It'll shield ya from unwanted glares from those who work for the king, but you're still who you are. No magic can change that."

"How does the spell work? What's the magic's name? Where does the eldrite come from? How did you come to acquire it?" Kaile spat the questions off unconsciously.

Soren wished to know the answers to the questions, and Seph hung on Kaile's words as he asked them.

Davin laughed a single, hearty laugh. "We'll have plenty of time to get to know one another in the days ahead. But for now we should be gettin' on our way." Davin spun to walk down the hill toward the forest ridge with the four waiting horses and the man that held them.

"What about you?" Seph asked.

"What about me, lass?" Davin asked, spinning back.

"You're uh… you're the same…"

"Ah, yes," he said. "Suppose I should change me appearance, too. Not that the king has a price on my head like he does yours. But can't be too cautious now, can we?"

He turned back around, facing down the hill as he lowered his head. Moments later, the backs of his shoulders rose and grew slenderer. His thick hair extended down his back and his stocky frame was graceful and elegant. He was Kaile's height, as he turned his head to the side with a smirk. His lips were full and his eyelashes long. Soren even saw the tips of his breasts as he turned to the side. Soren's jaw slacked.

"Better?" Davin asked, blowing a kiss to Seph.

Soren looked over and saw Seph's jaw hanging with her mouth agape.

"He's beautiful," Kaile muttered.

"All right," Davin said, turning back and walking with long legs down the hill.

Soren scratched his head, but simply shook his head with a snicker, and followed.

"Did I just see what I think I did?" Kaile asked.

"I think we did," Seph said, shrugging her shoulders. "And Kaile. Don't stare, women don't like that."

Kaile swallowed hard as Seph followed after Soren. Kaile cleared his throat and ran down after her.

Chapter Thirteen

Decimbre 9, 1292

The four approached the horses as the wind stirred the bare limbs above. They scraped above like chefs sharpening their knives. The wilds called. Soren heard and grinned as he turned back to send one last farewell to the high rising towers of Skylark, cast in its glimmering golden glow of the morning sun beaming over the trees.

"We'll take it from here," Davin said in a firm woman's voice.

The attendant held the reins of the lead horse, a magnificent black steed with a shimmering ebon coat and lustrous silky hairs falling down its neck from its mane.

"Anything else?" the attendant asked. He was a stocky, years-worn man with beady eyes.

"That'll be all," Davin said, taking the reins and putting his pack into the saddlebags.

The attendant gave a curious glare at Davin as the woman put her boot in the stirrups and straddled the horse quickly. The stocky man scratched his temple but bowed and meandered back into the forest along a dirt path, trampled with horse hoofprints in the snow.

Kaile walked up to a horse with a deep brown coat. Seph approached a tan one, leaving Soren with a milky white steed.

Kaile got up with ease, petting the horse's neck. Soren put his foot in the stirrup as Seph got atop her horse, but Soren pulled his boot back to the ground and walked over to Davin.

Soren gripped the reins halfway between the horse's mouth and where Davin held them. He glared into the woman's eyes but saw Davin still deep in them.

"Where are we going and what are we after?" Soren asked bluntly.

"We'll discuss on the road. We need to separate ourself from the city."

Davin pulled the reins, but Soren yanked them back in place, causing the horse to stir and neigh.

"Where?" Soren grumbled.

Davin growled. "The borderlands. Along the Rine. We're after something that was taken from the lady."

"What? Who has it?" Soren pressed.

Kaile and Seph both leaned forward on their horses to hear the muted conversation.

"A thief has it. She's hiding out where Cascadia and Londindam meet," Davin said in an annoyed tone.

"Why are we going after it now? Who is the thief? What is it?" Soren said in a stern voice.

"I'll answer your questions on the road," Davin said. "But we need to make it to Belltop by dusk. As you're well aware, I'm sure."

"Don't keep me in the dark," Soren said. "You may hold the key to the secrets you keep, but this is my duty. You all are along, but I'm here to protect and keep you all safe. Don't get that the other way around. I'm in charge."

"Aye," Davin said. His elegant face and flowing hair hid whatever demeanor the dwarf held when he said that. "Now, we must be going. If that's all right with you…"

Soren released his grip, and Davin kicked his horse with his heels.

Soren looked at Seph, with her straight auburn hair nearly reaching the saddle. It was a strange feeling to not recognize the girl, and for a moment, he wondered what he looked like.

"Think o' names fer yourselves," Davin said, trotting down the trail into the forest. "Nothing fancy…"

Soren mounted his steed and dug his heels in. He was behind Seph, who rode behind Kaile. Soren wanted to be the last in their pack, so he could see everything.

"I—I was told we'd have weapons?" Kaile asked Davin.

"You don't have your forks?" Davin said, turning in the saddle to look back at the boy.

"I—" Kaile mumbled but didn't fully respond.

Davin dug into his breast pocket and threw one to Kaile, and then one high over him to Seph, which she snatched from the air.

"There's more in Belltop," Davin said. "Can't just be giving you staffs right after leaving Skylark and changing your appearances. There's watching eyes… everywhere."

"Staffs?" Seph said excitedly, spinning to look at Soren with wide eyes and a brilliant grin.

Soren forced a smirk and nodded. He truly despised not being in control of the expedition. *What gives a dwarf from another land authority over me, in my home? Once we get to where we're going, I'm not going to let this outsider do more than stand aside while I do what I need to do.*

They rode west, trudging over the wet snow along the forest path, until twenty minutes later, when they emerged on the backside of the wood. Soren watched the steam from his mouth as it blew thickly in front of his face. The frost bit at the tip of his nose and eyes.

Once the trail opened up, Seph rode up beside Kaile, as they rode side by side.

Soren was curious, but let it go. He knew he was going to have to get used to the idea of the two becoming sort of… friends.

They talked amongst themselves quietly, and Soren distracted himself by scanning the vast, flowing plains of white. To their right was the immense lake of Fae Veil. It went on so endlessly, Soren couldn't see the other side. It may as well be a sea in the middle of Cascadia, he thought. Belltop was rideable within the daylight hours, Soren knew, but they'd indeed have to ride all day through the snow to get there, and out on the open plains. He refused the idea of them not making it by dusk.

Hours later, as the sun hung just past overhead as it began its slow descent before them, Davin turned, ushering the other two to continue riding, as he rode back, to ride beside Soren.

Seph and Kaile both turned their heads to look back, but continued their slow trot through the snowy plains.

"This thief," Davin said, perking Soren's interest. Soren shifted in his saddle. "She's not an easy one to find."

"Thieves usually aren't," Soren said.

Davin groaned, but nodded.

"It's Ravelle," Davin said, looking forward at the pillowy, thick clouds floating low in the sky ahead.

"I know of her," Soren said. "What about her?"

"The relic she stole," Davin said, clearing his throat. "Causes her to blend into the shadow."

"What do you mean?" Soren asked. "Be more specific."

"Once the wearer enters a shadow, of any sort, any time of day, they blend into it. Making them nearly impossible to spot."

Soren scratched his chin.

"That does sound like something I'd want back, if it were stolen…" Soren said.

"So, we'll need a fair amount of luck to find her," Davin said. "The lady's spies say Ravelle's been hiding out in a cave system in the borderlands. That's where we're heading after Belltop, on our way to Grayhaven."

Seems like a desperate attempt to get back this item. Sending us out, like this… It's most likely because she needs me to hunt it down. Ravelle could really be anywhere, even if the lady's spies said she was west. I guess there's no refusing Lady Drake now though… and she did make me feel better than I have in years!

"What do you think?" Kaile asked Soren. Soren was alarmed by the question by the boy. He always thought the boy was brave, in a sense, from asking him direct questions. Soren had intentionally given him an inkling that he liked the boy.

Seph and Davin both seemed curious about the answer, as they all waited on their horses, which grazed the grass that poked through the snow.

"Ravelle is a thief, yes," Soren said. "That much is absolutely true, but she's also hardened. *If* we find her, I'll be the one to confront her. And that's a big *if*."

"Let's be clear about one thing," Davin said, his harsh voice creeping through the elegant voice of the tall woman who sat beside them, speaking the words. "This mission is too important for you to decide to go rogue. We will work together to accomplish all our goals."

Soren scowled at him.

"Next to you sits the archmage's personal apprentice," Davin said. "Few wouldn't want him on their side."

Soren was about to speak, but pressed his lips shut.

"This is that part where he says he works better alone," Seph said, pressing her palms to her horse's back with her elbows in.

Soren wanted to be mad, but instead huffed a brief laugh. "Let's move while we have the sun. Belltop isn't far."

He rode off, and the others followed. As Soren rode at the lead, Davin slowly dipped back to ride between Seph and Kaile.

He whispered to them, "He's going to need you. He may not know it yet. But he can't do all this alone, on his own. There's a reason he's kept failing in his pursuits. Don't let him bully you around. He can't do all this on his own, whether he thinks it, or not…"

Chapter Fourteen

Belltop, with early dusk tendrils of smoke snaking their way up into the indigo sky, lay at the bottom of the hill before them. It was a squashed town, sprawling out between two hills, and a single road running from east to west. Towers dotted the hills at its sides, surely later additions for defenses, but the city itself was nearly as flat on the plains, save for the defining bell tower at its center.

Soren and the others were mounted side by side at the top of the hill before Belltop. They were on the outskirts of a patch of woods before the ride that would lead them to the town through the plains. The horses neighed and were catching their breath from the long day's ride. Soren scanned the area with keen eyes. He couldn't help the pit in his stomach about leading Seph, now known, out into the open world.

The spell of disguises would work, because if Mihelik said he trusted Davin, then Soren would trust him—as best he could.

"Remember to stick close together," Soren said. "Can't have the spell wearing off in town. It only takes one person to spot us, and who knows who the king would send out after us.

The plan is to take them out one by one, not get killed before we even make it to Londindam."

"Couldn't have said it better myself," Davin said. "Now, shall we? I could use a soft seat under my ass after today."

He dug his heels in and flicked the reins, and they were all on their way, out of the woods, and into the plains. Soren gazed hard out into the surrounding landscape. He saw some caravan pulling in from the northwest and saw a man riding in from the south. They were all pulling into the city before night. This was the way of Aladran now, Soren thought. If you wanted to live, you found shelter. If you wanted to die, then walk under the stars.

The rider and the caravan worried Soren naught, because they were dressed in civilian clothing and the rider was an aged farmer. Soren, again, inspected Seph, who appeared with long auburn hair and tan skin. Kaile was pale with short midnight black hair, and Davin, well—was gorgeous.

So they rode into town, with a pair of soldiers inspecting them, but not paying much mind to four travelers who were surely going to spend coin in their shanty city. After they entered, with the caravan and the rider safely inside, the two soldiers swung the thick wood doors of stacked logs inward. Soren, Seph, and Kaile watched as the two turned-handled wheels that pulled the doors shut with thick chains. The doors closed with a powerful thud, and then they barricaded the gate with a wooden beam—not only locking the Demons of Dusk out... but locking them in...

"There's an inn just up the road that we'll stay the night," Davin said, leaping down off his horse with his long legs.

Soren noticed Seph's eyes were wide as she glared all around the city, still teaming with life.

They were at the front gate, and a vast square that was lined with merchant shops decorated with their wares out front —colorful flours, pungent spices, sturdy leatherwork, baskets overflowing with candy, and so many other sorts. Many vendors were just beginning to put their wares away for the night, even though around a hundred people were still meandering around the square.

"Do you have any money?" she asked Soren.

He shook his head. "It was all with Ursa."

"Come, lass," Davin said, a weird term to be coming from a grown-looking woman. "Let's get a proper supper in you, and then we can talk about shopping in the morning."

"C'mon," she pleaded. "Please... I've never been anywhere, ever... I just want something for late night... something sweet..."

They all got down from their steeds.

Kaile handed the reins of his horse to Davin and walked over to Seph. He pulled his purse from his pocket and handed her a bronze ten torren coin.

She gave a brilliant, wide grin.

Soren knew they all needed to stay near each other, so they followed her, each leading their horse behind them. At first he was annoyed, as he wanted to get her safely behind shaded windows and a locked door, but her mention of never being anywhere plucked his heartstrings. He rather enjoyed watching her skip toward the candy vendor on the side of the market.

"Which ones? Which ones?" she said, letting her fingers dance over the taffies, hard, tart candies, and chocolates. "You know I normally wouldn't take money from someone like that." She was speaking to Kaile without taking her eyes off the mouth-watering confections before her. "Usually there's a price to pay for taking it from someone like you."

"Someone like me?" he said, standing back with his fingers spread.

"A rich brat," she said, with snark heavy in the words.

"Brat?" The insult on his face turned sour.

"Oh, you're not from Lynthyn? You don't live in a castle?"

she said, grabbing a dozen chocolates in her hand, as the weathered, old man behind watched.

"I'm from Ikarus, born and raised," he said, with his hands on his hips.

"That's enough about that," Soren said. "It doesn't matter where you're born. You two bicker like brother and sister."

"Ew," Seph said, snatching another cherry-colored candy. "How much for all this?"

"Two torrens, fifty," the old man with the scratchy throat said.

"How about two?" she asked, in a high-pitched, cute voice.

The old man thought, and then nodded.

She handed him the coin, and he gave her four back. She reached back and offered them to Kaile, who waved them away. She shrugged and drove the coins deep into her own pocket.

"Follow me," Davin said.

They led the horses around the outside of the market, perusing the wares of the merchants as they tucked away their stands for the night. Soren continued eyeing the surrounding crowd as Seph inspected the many things that were being stored. Many around the market watched them with the corners of their peering glances. It made Soren want to get them out of there quickly, but he trusted the spell enough to not rush them out of the square.

Davin led them out of the market and down a wide stone road with signs that designated it was Tanterbaan Road. Up ahead, as the night sky darkened and the lights of the torches that lit the road blossomed, the bell tower of Belltop grew. It stood six stories high, with a massive bell towering above the city. The tower was carved of fascinating, old design. Gargoyles hung over the top corners, and spires lined with circular bases, needling up like a fine comb. The bell itself was a deep, murky black, perhaps iron, Soren thought.

Along the road were single-story buildings, some stone, some of wood, and some even painted white. Above, the two hills loomed high on both sides, with the city's towers capping each, making Belltop seem like a formidable city, more than a couple hundred-year-old town of merchants and castaways.

They tied their horses up to a long post with a trough outside the tavern. The tavern stood two stories tall, making it stand out like a welcoming invitation to weary travelers. Soren dusted his pants off, but slowly, the smells of the interior of the tavern beckoned at his very core. He could smell the musty pipe tobacco, the tang of wine and strong spirits, and the awful aroma of men with scraggly beards soaked with old ale. This was exactly what he desired after a full day's ride.

Davin handed a coin to the boy who ran out of the tavern's doors to them.

"Food and a warm place for them to rest," Davin said to the wide-eyed, shivering boy. "We'll be taking them back out in the morning."

The boy pocketed the coin and petted the horses, readying them for a stable.

Davin held the door open and ushered Seph to enter first. It was another thing unusual for a tall woman like Davin to do. Usually, she'd be the one having doors held open for her. Soren rushed past Kaile and entered with Seph. He inspected each person within the smoky tavern. Mostly men, mostly in stupors, mostly calm.

It was a long rectangular room with a huge bar at its center. Two chandeliers hung on the sides of the room, on either side of the wide bar. Tables were strewn throughout, with some groups of men playing cards, talking low, or others snoring with their faces plastered to them.

"I'll get the rooms," Davin said. "Then we'll get cleaned up and settled in."

He went off to the innkeeper while Soren was left with the other two.

"You have enough for a few?" Soren asked Kaile begrudgingly.

Kaile nodded eagerly, excited that Soren had asked him for a sort of favor.

Kaile darted to the bar, sitting on a barstool with one on either side.

He took the middle seat. Of course he did...

Soren and Seph sat on either side of him as the barkeep came over. He was a stout man with bushy black eyebrows and a shiny white freckled head. He wiped his hands with a towel and tucked it into his red apron.

"What can I do for ya?" the bushy-browed man asked.

Kaile, with his shoulders back and chest out, looked to Seph.

"White wine, please," she asked.

Kaile then turned to look over at Soren.

"Ale and something strong." He looked at the bottles behind the barkeep. "That." He pointed to a green bottle with a thick amber liquid inside.

"Same for me," Kaile said with a wide grin.

The barkeep went to gather their order.

"Well, we made it," Kaile said.

Soren glared over his shoulder to make sure Davin was close. He was only at the other side of the bar, and the spell continued to conceal Kaile and Seph's identities.

"I like this place," Seph said, putting her hands under her legs on the barstool. "I like the name too. It's so much more alive than Guillead."

"We probably should not mention the places we're from. Disguises, remember?" Kaile whispered.

"What about names?" Seph asked. "Did you decide?"

"I haven't," Kaile said. "Been thinking about other things, I suppose."

Soren didn't answer.

The barkeep placed their drinks in front of them, and they each took them up. Soren and Kaile took up the small glasses of the amber, honey-smelling liquor first.

"Au Saluda," the three exclaimed as they clinked the glasses.

They drank, with Soren licking his lips after, and chasing down the sharp spirits with cool ale.

"Well, maybe we should name each other," Seph said. "That will be fun!"

"Sure," Soren said. "You're going to be Candy."

"No, no, no," Seph said. "I hate that. Come on. You can do better than that. What do I look like?"

Seph pursed her lips, flicked her eyelashes, and waved her long hair behind her back, pulling it over her right shoulder as she posed. "C'mon! Who do I look like?"

Kaile scrunched his nose in thought. "You look like a Pricilla. Is that a good one? It's just the first one that came to mind."

"I love it," Seph said. "Do you like it, uncle?"

"Yeah, that'll do," Soren said with a smirk.

"What?" Seph said, shoving her hand in front of Kaile and pushing Soren's shoulder. "Out with it!"

"No, nothing," he said. "It fits you just fine. Regal, yet pushy."

"Okay, your turn," Seph said to Soren. "Do you have one for him?"

Kaile scratched his chin while glaring Soren up and down. "Not really. Dark, moody, scary…"

"How about Michael?" Seph asked.

"Michael?" Soren said, shaking his head. "No. You've got to do better than that."

"How about Victor?" Kaile asked. "I knew a Victor once. Kind of broody. I think it fits."

"Victor…" Seph said. "Uncle Vic. Has a nice ring to it. That's it, and there's nothing you can do about it, sorry." She winked at Soren.

"Well, you both came up with those, so I get to pick the last one, and no complaining about it," Soren said. Kaile pulled his lips in, nervously awaiting his new destiny.

"Careless, awkward, and brash," Soren said, winking at Seph. "You're a… Alfred."

Kaile said, "I knew something like that was coming. You sure I can't complain about it?"

"It's nice," Seph said, nudging him in the arm with her elbow. "Al. Yeah, I think that fits. Al, Vic, and Pricilla."

Suddenly, something leaped onto the bar top on the other side of Seph. She spun to find a cat with golden hunter eyes and midnight black fur purring beside her, brushing up against her glass.

"Hey there," Seph said. "What're you doing up here?" She stroked the cat's back as it purred thickly. "You live here, or just visiting like us?"

The cat strolled under Seph's arm, curling her tail up around it. She nuzzled into Seph's side. Seph put her cheek to the side of the cat's head as she purred.

"I wouldn't do that," Kaile said. "Might be sick."

"Aw, she's not sick," Seph said.

"Hey! Get off'a there!" the barkeep shouted, running down the backside of the bar. He swung his towel in a wide arc at the cat, with its damp cloth splashing next to Seph, while the cat nimbly dodged to the side. "Get outta here, ya mangy thing!"

"Hey," Seph said. "She's not doing nothin'."

"Get outta here," the barkeep said, ignoring Seph, swinging the towel again at the cat.

"Stop," Seph said. "She's fine!"

The cat leaped again, dodging the barkeep's attacks.

"Stop!" Seph said, standing up, and moving to get her arm between the two.

Soren watched in dread as the tips of her fingers transformed from a tan to a pale white skin. Her arm continued to reach, but Seph didn't notice yet, as the further she pushed her arm toward the fight, the more of her skin transformed colors.

The barkeep was so busy in his assault, he didn't seem to know.

"Grab her," Soren whispered forcefully to Kaile, who grabbed her by the upper arm and yanked her back onto her stool.

"Aye," she protested, but Kaile held her firmly down. "What's that for?"

The barkeep continued his attack until the cat leaped down off the tall bar top and ran off into the room's corner.

"Mangy, nasty thing," he muttered.

Soren and Kaile both saw Seph's arm had returned to her disguised shade.

"You need to be careful," Kaile said to her.

"Don't tell me what to do," she rebutted.

"Seph," Soren said, but was cut short by her sharp words.

"*Don't* tell me what to do," she said through clenched teeth.

Chapter Fifteen

"These will be your rooms," the innkeeper said in the upstairs hallway of the tavern. The dim hall was thick with wafting smoke that glowed from candlelight. "One for the ladies, and the other for the boys."

The thin old man gave Davin, a tall woman with a kind smile, one key, and Soren the other.

"You're all paid for, so just leave the beds for us to tend to in the morning. Baths can be drawn down the hall. They're a bit small for the big lad, but you could at least fit a pair of legs in there, I'd wager," the innkeeper chuckled.

"Thank you," Davin said, taking the key and unlocking the door on the left.

"I'll take my leave," the old innkeeper said, turning and walking down the creaky stairs, back into the warm light of the bar below.

"Will *it* work on us through the rooms?" Kaile asked, intentionally being vague enough so prying ears wouldn't recognize what he spoke of.

"Yes," Davin said. "Now who's sleeping where? Suppose you and I, Soren, should…"

"Seph and I will share a room," Soren said, glaring at Kaile, who quickly shied away.

"Very well," Davin said. "Now, if we're going to bathe, should we all meet in twenty, back here?"

"I—" Seph squeaked. "I'd like to see more of the city, if you all don't mind. I know we need to stay close, but…"

"I don't think that's a good idea, Seph," Soren said, tapping his fingers on the outer door handle.

"Please…" she begged. "I've never been anywhere in my life. I know we're leaving tomorrow. But… I've been so cramped up and crowded in Mormond that I never got to see anything except when I snuck out at night. But here we are, in this new wonderful city, and there are people out there enjoying the night. I want to watch people sing and play. I want to go dancing. The thing about being here… with you all… is that we can go anywhere and do anything. When I was back at the orphanage, I couldn't do anything…"

Davin looked to Soren for the answer.

Soren thought. But it really didn't take long. The two things that helped him make up his mind, other than his sympathy for Seph's imprisonment in the orphanage back in Guillead, where —the fact that the spell disguised them, and also that there wasn't an inkling of tiredness in his mind or body. They may as well go entertain her, and he'd be there to watch over her. If anything happened, he had Firelight at his hip.

"Okay," Soren said, and Seph brimmed instantly with glee, leaping onto him and wrapping her arms around the back of his neck.

"I'd like to take a quick bath," she said. "But we all need to—"

"We can wash up before," Soren said. "Let's get settled in first, and then meet for baths, back out here."

Seph burst into the room, claiming a bed and setting her pack down, which was filled with almost exclusively clothes, a comb, and a brush for her teeth. The saddlebags were filled with supplies, but Soren didn't have the time or care to go through it all while they were on the road. He was more concentrated on the vast, snowy plains.

They met back outside minutes later and made their way down the hall together, entering the bathroom. To their luck, there were four baths in a row with partitions between each. On either side of the room were wood-burning stoves with huge barrels of water simmering on top. There were more barrels on the room's sides, and Soren and Davin went to mixing the hot and cold waters to find a warm mix for each wooden tub.

Soon they were all in their own, each letting out soothing sighs.

Soren lay with his head back and his hands down deep in the warm water, warming his bones from the cold.

Kaile suddenly asked from the far end of the line. "Davin, so, when you wash, do you... I mean, what do you feel?"

Davin didn't respond, but Seph giggled.

"What are you asking, exactly?" Davin finally responded from the other end in a grumpy tone.

"Oh, I meant, uh," Kaile muttered. "Do your legs feel sort of long, or... not long..."

"Oh, hell, Kaile," Seph laughed.

"What? I'm just curious," he responded.

"It was starting to sound as if you were gonna ask about some other body parts," Seph said.

"I, uh... no, I wasn't..." Kaile stammered.

"I'm kind of curious how it works," Soren said with a smirk.

"I'm a man, you dimwits," Davin said. "It's a spell, not a knife."

"Oh," Kaile breathed audibly.

Seph giggled wildly from her tub, and Soren laughed

heartily. Davin chuckled after, but Kaile seemed too embarrassed for any of that.

Soren was the first out of the tub, and wrapping a towel around his waist, he walked to the room's corner. Through the wafting steam, he stood before a basin with a comb in a green liquid and a bar of soap. In front of his face was a mirror, just wide enough for his face. He wiped it with his bare hand. It squeaked as he did so.

He peered at the mirror, and what he saw, he couldn't believe was real.

Soren knew it was an illusion, but it was powerful.

He'd seen the changed faces on his companions that day, but to see his own face—scarless, took his breath away.

I... I look... normal...

It made him remember the days back in Tourmielle, before he was forced to live a rogue life as a Scarred. He remembered going out in the daylight, shopping for food and drinks with his love. No one batted an eye or fought to avert their curious glares at the hard-cut lines on his face. It made him remember he used to be normal. And to his surprise, Davin's spell had changed him little. He still had the same face with his dark hair falling down both sides of his face. The scars were all that he needed to change.

That is all that defines me now, isn't it? That is the only thing that matters about me to this world... my curse...

He turned in disgust from the mirror to see Kaile standing behind him, patiently, quietly waiting for the mirror and for the washbasin.

"Oh, I... I didn't mean to—"

"Just wash up," Soren said. "You could use a shave too."

Soren walked past and put his clothes on. Seph was out of her tub and seemed to see the brief encounter between the two.

They were washed up and out on the streets of Belltop

shortly after. They'd purchased a couple of bottles of wine from the bar, as well as some bread, soft cheese, and dried meat.

"Where do ya want to go?" Davin asked. "I'm not totally familiar with the city."

"We should start at the bell tower," Soren said. "It's a pleasant view."

Seph nodded eagerly. They made their way deep into town. The further they went, the blacker the night sky grew gloomier overhead. Torches roared in the winds as they walked down the jutting roads of Belltop. Drunkards meandered and hustlers perched on corners. Women in long fur coats waited with the men on corners, but they paid little mind of the pack of four that moved through the city.

Soren was astounded at the lack of soldiers he saw as they walked for twenty minutes toward the gothic bell tower that loomed high. They emerged from a narrow alley, opening into a splendid courtyard that sparkled with torch-light. It was a long courtyard, which during the spring would be a majestic, lush city brimming with shades of green and rainbows of flowers growing in the gardens. But here, in the dead of winter, with a fresh covering of white snow, it was serene.

Soldiers were stationed at the entrance to the bell tower, which caused Seph to scratch her thigh.

"We can't go up it?" she asked.

"Doesn't look like it," Kaile said.

"Oh, no?" Soren asked, who cocked his head at Kaile.

Kaile raised a suspicious eyebrow.

"How'd you get into the cathedral in Guillead?" Soren asked. "When you wanted to see Seph play the organ. Those doors had been locked a long time, by the state of the church."

Seph smirked, nudging Kaile with the point of her elbow.

"C'mon," Kaile said, puffing out his chest as if realizing

what they'd asked him to do, even if he was the last to realize it. Davin followed.

They walked around to the backside of the tower, whose vast base wound far around the center of the courtyard. There was an iron gate that surrounded the tower, and a few doors, but no windows.

Kaile led them to the shadowed side of a small building that perhaps held tools for the gardeners in the warmer months. He knelt and reached into his boot, fishing out a tuning fork that held a warm copper hue.

"We won't look any different," he said. "And it doesn't last long, but it'll be long enough for us to get into the tower from here."

Davin frowned. "What happens if the spell runs out before we get *through* the wall?"

"I don't know," Kaile said. "Never meant to try it. Just be quick, and you'll be fine."

Kaile struck the fork against the backside of the wall. Soren instantly felt his senses heighten, as nowadays that same sound usually meant something very bad was about to happen. An E note vibrated from the fork. It was low and subtle.

Soren felt a strange, warm sensation in his fingers and hands. It tingled up his arms, down his stomach and legs, and up into his ears and made his follicles stiffen.

"All right," Kaile said. "Let's move."

They left the shadows and went straight toward the immense tower, while the fork still hummed low in his hand. As they approached the wrought-iron gate, Kaile didn't pause, sliding through it as if the metal was no more than a veil of mist. He emerged on the other side, paused, turned, and waved for them to follow.

Seph was next, pressing her slender fingers through the metal bars first, and then sliding her entire body through with ease.

Davin was next, gliding through, and spinning back to Soren, waving for him to follow.

Soren approached the bars and watched with a marveling splendor as his strong fingers glided through the bars before them. He took a single, powerful stride through, and was quickly on the other side.

"Come," Kaile said. The four of them dashed to the tower. Soren watched for any prying eyes, for he knew if they were spotted using magic, then there'd be a storm of soldiers coming for them. If there were any Dors or Ayls in Belltop in the king's service, they'd surely be en route as well. "It should only be a couple feet thick, so just walk all the way through until you're sure you're on the other side. Follow me."

Kaile strode into the murky stone wall, completely disappearing from view.

"Here goes nothin'," Seph said. "See ya on the other side."

She walked through with her hands back, face and chest first. Her fingers were the last things to slide into the stone, and then she was gone.

"You know," Davin said. "If he wanted to kill either of us, this would be a very easy way to do it."

Soren clenched his teeth and groaned. The thought had occurred to him.

"Or with the fork he had hidden, he could'a cast any sort of spell upon us on the plains today. He is the apprentice to the archmage, who knows what spells he knows. Suppose this bodes well for the boy."

Davin turned to the wall, took a deep breath, and walked through.

Soren, swallowing hard, knew if Kaile was there to infiltrate and kill them, perhaps taking the last Whistlewillow with him back to Lynthyn, this would be the time. He clenched his fists, breathing in deep through his nostrils, and with his breath held, plunged himself through the wall.

Chapter Sixteen

⚜

The inside of the bell tower of Belltop was a cramped room, dark and cluttered. Brooms clacked along the walls as they bumped them with their knees.

"Where are we?" Seph asked, rubbing shoulders with Soren.

"Hold on," Davin said. "I'm lookin' for the knob."

A latch popped and torchlight poured into the room.

Kaile's shoulders slumped.

"Can't know where you end up," Seph said. As Davin left the closet, Kaile went to follow, but Seph stopped him suddenly as she grabbed his wrist. "Can you teach me how to do this?"

"I believe I can," he said. The words made him seem much older, more mature than the nervous child he appeared to be often.

She smiled and released her grip.

I wonder what else he can show her? How many spells and tricks has Alcarond taught him over their years together?

Davin looked down both sides of the short hall outside the closet, before making his way to the stair at the left. Soren heard footsteps above, but as they made their way to the foot of the circular stairs, he assured himself they were in the center of the tower, around which the stairs spiraled up.

They climbed up the bell tower, ascending to the highest parts of the spire. Exiting the door at its top, a bitter wind rushed into the stairwell. Soren clamped down onto his hood as they emerged into the room where the great bell rested. It rose fifteen feet high and hung from great beams above. Chains clattered together in the winds above.

The winds howled as they stepped to the waist-high wall. The vast lands beyond sprawled out to the east and west, with the hills on its other sides nearly level with them.

"It's beautiful," Seph said.

"Aye," Davin said. "Nothing like that of Skylark, but it's not without its own charm."

They all stood for a long moment, watching the clouds slowly roll past the crescent moon, the leafless trees bend and crack, and in the far distance—the Black Fog scoured the white-capped lands.

There were dozens of them out in the western lands. Elongated like maggots, but huge like ogres, they hunted with their shadowy tendrils feeling out below.

None of them were surprised by the sight, and it made Soren think about the years Mihelik and Alcarond had spent together pondering the puzzles of the Demons of Dusk. He thought about their late nights brainstorming where they came from and why they had come. Soren thought about Firelight and wondered if it might be a key to the lock to the puzzle of how to rid the world of the beasts that preyed upon those that braved the night. The world had changed since the arrival of the Black Fog, and Soren hoped the Vellice dagger could be a weapon to use against them, the next time they met…

They all watched the fog meander like snails upon the plains, each deep in their own thoughts. To Soren, though, the Black Fog meant danger and certain death.

"Come with me," he said to Seph.

Seph followed him as he led her to the other side of the tower. Halfway across, he watched her hair transform from straight auburn to the frayed, midnight black he recognized. At the other side of the tower they stood side by side, gazing out east, back the way they'd come.

"What is it?" she asked. She turned her chin to her shoulder, shivering off the cold that blew in.

He sighed. "I'm worried about the road that leads ahead for us, for you…"

"I can take care of myself," she said. "I did that back home… I mean, back in Guillead. I'm tougher than you think. I'm tougher than how I look. I'll show you. You just haven't been able to see it yet."

"We're going to places where I can't know what we face," he said. "Don't be overly confident. If you were squared up against Glasse, you wouldn't be the victor."

"Kaile's going to train me," she said. "He knows a lot, and he's willing to teach me."

Soren sighed. "It takes time. It takes years to learn."

"I learned on my own," she said, trying to gain his confidence. She itched her cheek. "You're not proud, are you?" Her head slunk, and she dug her hands into her pockets.

"Seph. I'm extremely proud. I don't want you to think I'm not, because I've never been so proud of anything in my life. And that is the truth."

The whites of her eyes appeared from under her hood, looking up at him.

"I mean it. I've never met a single person who taught themselves the way you have. You're strong. I see that in you. But you need more training. More than that book could show you; you need a mentor. And I don't believe that to be Kaile. No ill intent meant for him, but you need to get back to Mihelik. He's old and beaten down, but he's sharp and still there. You couldn't ask for a better teacher."

"What did you two talk about last night?" she asked. There was a sincerity in her voice that showed she deeply wanted to know.

She doesn't want to be left in the dark about anything... I can understand and appreciate that... especially with the mission we're on.

"He asked me about the dagger. He and Alcarond were working on the mystery of the Demons of Dusk, before their fallout. Firelight is the first weapon that's been known to kill a Shade. He wanted to inspect it."

"Ah," she said. "So they don't know, then."

"There's another thing," he said. "But this stays between you and me."

She nodded eagerly, leaning to the side so their shoulders touched.

A stiff, biting wind blew in.

"There was something dark in the tomes that Mihelik burned. He hadn't gone mad. He was hiding something. There's another magic out there besides the Ellydian. Something from the old world."

"Something... other than the Ellydian...? What?"

"They don't know," he said. "But he was worried Alcarond was trying to use it."

"Does it have to do with the Black Fog?"

"They don't know."

"Well, that's a head-scratcher. I want to know the answer," she said.

"Me too."

They both stood watching light snow sparkle in the moonlight as it floated down to its final resting place below.

"What do you think of them?" Soren asked.

She breathed in and snorted. "I trust them."

"You do?"

"I trust Davin because I believe Mihelik," she said. "I'm not sure about Lady Drake. I haven't reached a conclusion about her. I just don't know what's going on in her head. Running a city, there's gotta be so many motives and plans swimming around in there."

"What about him?" Soren asked.

"Kaile…" she said, thinking, rubbing her chin. She turned her head to look back at him as he and Davin spoke on the other side of the wall. "I think his heart is in the right place."

"That it?"

"He's troubled," she said, turning back and looking down at the drop before them. "There's something in him. Something dark, but not evil. He's lost, or something. Imagine being taken from your family and home and thrown into the capital to the wolves like he was. Being told you're going to be powerful, but also being treated like vermin. I think it's taken a toll on him."

"He trusts you," Soren said.

Seph took a long moment to respond. "I think he just wants a friend."

"He jumped through that portal for something," Soren said. "I want to know what."

"It wasn't just to escape?" Seph asked, assuming as much.

"I suppose if there was a way to escape that life, that was the only real way to do it. All or nothing. He's put his entire hand in the pot, and we're it. He's joined the enemy. We all have now…"

"Your scars are back," she said, looking at his face.

He nodded.

"You know… you're more than those…" she said in a soft tone.

He nodded again.

"I'm glad I'm with you," she said.

He sighed.

"I don't want to die," she said. "Especially not now, now that I have a life and purpose for the first time since I can remember. But if we are going to the end, I'm having way more fun than I ever have. I mean, look at this view. Books just can't describe this kind of beauty."

"Makes you appreciate life," Soren said.

"I saw the way you looked at yourself in the mirror," Seph said. "I just want you to know. To me, you're more than the Scarred. You're my only family."

He put his arm around her and they squeezed each other.

"If things get hairy," he said. "I want you to find me. No matter how bad things get, or how dark it is... find me and I'll protect you."

"Thanks. I've wanted someone to say that for longer than you can imagine."

"I've been alone a long time, too," Soren said. "I've come to embrace it."

"Well, you're not allowed to be alone for a while. None of us are."

"Let's get out of here," he said. "You're getting cold."

∽

BACK ON THE DIMLY LIT, softly strewn, snow-laden roads of Belltop, Seph led the way to the loudest pub. It was a block down the road and the festivities were spilling out of the lively place. Music poured from it as well. Violens fiddling away were accompanied by a roomful of patrons belting out the lyrics to a song they all knew.

"C'mon," she said, waving for them to follow faster.

It reminded Soren of better times, traveling from city to city, camping on a barstool at the rowdiest pubs. Before Erhil.

The three of them followed Seph as she stayed close, but was on the outer ring of the spell.

"Stop," Davin said suddenly. All stopped and Seph looked irritated with her shoulders slumped. But Davin's serious tone took the group into an abrupt turn in the night's plans.

Davin was standing before a tall post with a large torch hanging from its curved top. He reached out and grabbed a posted piece of parchment, ripping it from the nails that held it firm. Water dripped from it as he held it out with two hands, stretching it out under the torchlight.

Between the writing at its top and bottom was an illustration. It was an illustration in ink of a man's face—a man's face with three long scars down the left side of his face. The title at the top read—wanted and dangerous, dead or alive. For the attempted assassination of the king.

Seph regained her posture as she went over and read beside them.

Davin read, "During the eradication of the dreadful outbreak that sadly took the city of Erhil, Soren Smythe, attempted to assassinate the divine King Amón, and killed dozens within the town. He is considered armed and extremely dangerous. If you see this man, report him immediately for a reward. He was last seen traveling with a thin, young woman with dark black hair and light skin. Another tall boy with red hair may be accompanying him. The boy and girl are not to be harmed, but reported immediately by order of the king."

The bottom said in bold letters, "armed and dangerous. One hundred-thousand torren reward."

Each of them looked at Soren, who folded his arms.

He didn't know what to say. It was official. He'd tried to murder the king, yes, but now they were framing him for killing the innocent people that died by the king's orders. And with such a bounty, he knew the real killers would come out of the woodwork.

"That's a lot of coin," Davin finally said.

"We should adjourn for the night," Soren said. "Leave at first light. Sorry, Seph."

"It's okay," she said.

Davin handed the parchment over to Soren, who held it out under the light. The illustration looked strikingly like him, with the scars exaggerated, of course, and he had a terrifying scowl on his face.

"They want you both alive," Soren said. "That answers that question, at least."

"They're going to torture us till they get what they want," Kaile said. "I've seen it before."

"What do you mean, you've seen it?" Seph asked.

"There's a room underground in the Tower of the Judicature. That's where they take Syncrons who refuse to bow and kneel. I can still hear the screams."

"Alcarond took you there?" Soren asked, perplexed. *Why would he take his prized pupil there?*

"Not Alcarond," Kaile said. "Zertaan. She said she was taking me to see something interesting. It was in my first few months of being in the capital. They'd found a Syncron from Zatan and took him all the way up north."

"What happened to them?" Seph asked.

"He died, but after a whole day of what they call the Re-Enlightenment."

Seph swallowed hard. "Yeah, I'm not in the mood to dance anymore…"

PART IV
WHAT DWELLS IN DARKNESS

Chapter Seventeen

※

The Borderlands

THE LINK BETWEEN REALMS. *Those that divide yet harbor their own majesty. In the lands between, those that are outcast from their homelands delve. It has become a breeding ground for the hopeless, wretched, and even vile.*

For those that seek refuge, seek the caves, seek the dark world beneath ours where light flourishes.

But travelers beware.

Those things that lurk in the dark are not always human.

And those that are without soul, are without remorse.

TRANSLATED *from the language of the Sundar. The Scriptures of the Ancients, Book V, Chapter XI.*

. . .

On the following morn, they sat upon their steeds at the break of the bitter dawn. A chill thinned the air, biting at their skin and eyelashes. It sent an icy shiver through their bodies as they breathed it in, and the hairs in their nostrils froze. The sun behind had not warmed the land yet, and the dirt road cracked as the heavy horses stomped on it. Plumes of vapor poured from their nostrils in the early morning light, and the vast beyond loomed before them. The borderlands weren't far, and there was no city for them to rest their weary heads the next night.

They'd have to seek the shelter of the forest or the mountains at night, and pray to the goddess she protect them from not only the cold, but the things that hunt in the night.

"What are we waiting for?" Soren asked, his horse spinning back as he pulled the reins to the side, angling it back at them behind him. "We should be off."

"Another moment," Davin said, patiently sitting on his horse, looking into the city.

Seph rubbed her hands feverishly, shivering.

Kaile sat stoically beside her on his horse, eyeing the horizon.

Beams of sunlight cut through the gaps in the city behind, glowing onto them, and Seph sighed in relief.

Belltop was just stirring to life as the sun slowly rose, and down the road, a rider turned a corner, heading toward them at a gallop.

Soren gripped Firelight, but Davin rode out to meet the man with a thick gray cloak. He had a sword in its sheath strapped to the horse, but it stayed there as he rode to them. Soren flicked the reins to join Davin.

The rider and Davin met, but Davin didn't say a word as the two eyed each other.

"Fine morning for a stroll," the gruff man said, vapor blowing from his lips, hidden by a bushy brown beard.

"The view is best down by the lake," Davin said, confusing Soren for only a moment. But as the rider reached behind him, grabbing a bag from the horse, Soren understood. It was code.

The rider rode up and handed the bag to Davin, who took it. The rider nodded and rode back off into the city. He disappeared as quickly as he'd come. He opened the bag, and from within, pulled two smaller bags from it, both thin, but roughly two feet long each, like branches wrapped in burlap.

"Come, girl," Davin said, holding it out for Seph to take.

She rode up and took it.

"Don't open it yet," he muttered. "Wait till we're away from the town."

"Is this what I think it is?" Kaile asked as Davin handed him the other.

"Aye," Davin said. "A gift from Lady Drake."

They said we'd be given weapons, Soren thought. *They waited until now to give them to us.*

Seph and Kaile both tucked them away in their saddlebags for later, but Seph had to bite her lip to wrangle her excitement.

They were two days to the borderlands, Soren knew. A day and a half if they rode hard. They'd need to ride southwest at a point, as Grayhaven—their ultimate destination lay on the coastline of the Sapphire Sea. That's where Edward Glasse would be, they hoped. But first, they needed to find Ravelle. Hopefully Davin could point them in the right direction, and Soren could let Firelight do the talking.

On the outskirts of Belltop, occasionally, makeshift shops lined the road that led west. If anything, they had fires for travelers to warm their frosty hands and sip warm mead at an affordable price. Soren didn't need mead, but he was in search of something else, and it didn't take long to find it.

Soren rode to the front of their line, as he'd been riding in the rear, and veered right to a merchant. The man behind the table had a wrinkled face worn by long years under the sun. His hands were callused, and his cotton shirt littered with frayed ends and broken seams.

Soren dropped down and looked at the wares—seeds, sprouts, and bags of dried fish for fertilizing.

"What're you doing?" Seph asked, still atop her steed.

"Do you have Bramblemud?" Soren asked.

The old merchant raised a weary eyebrow, eyeing Soren up and down. "What for?" he croaked.

"Fertilizer," Soren said. "Growing potatoes."

"Potatoes? What kind of potatoes?"

"The kind you eat," Soren said, turning and waving with an open hand and upturned palm for Davin, who rode over and put a small purse in Soren's hand. Davin didn't hesitate, and Soren took it, as Davin seemed to know what Soren was planning.

"How much?" Soren asked.

"Herum…" the old man groaned.

"How about five torrens for a pound?" Soren asked.

The old merchant folded his arms and thought hard, glaring down at the table.

"Listen," Soren said in a softer, kinder voice. "I'm one of the good guys. Just sell me some and I'll be on my way. I'm not going to use it to hurt anyone."

The wrinkled man stared deep into Soren's eyes, and whether it was Soren's sincere words or the man's need for the coin, he reached behind the table and began scooping something into a bag. He lifted it up, glaring down both directions of the long road, and exchanged the bag for the five coins Soren pulled from the purse.

Soren took the bag, nodded, got back up to the saddle, and they were back on their way.

Seph looked around for an answer, but Davin and Kaile

gave no signs of interest. "Is no one curious why we just stopped to buy dirt?"

Soren smirked, but continued riding. Davin did the same.

She turned to Kaile with a frustrated furrow of her brow.

"I'll tell you later," he whispered.

"You better. I hate being the only one not knowing."

Kaile's head suddenly glanced back behind them on the road. Seph noticed and looked, too.

"Is that?" Kaile asked. "Is that the same one from the other night?"

"I—I don't know," she said. "She's cute though."

Behind them, a slender black cat walked daintily through the snow.

"Did it follow us all this way?" Seph asked. She tugged the reins her horse stopped, causing all of them to stop.

The cat approached cautiously, with Seph's horse side-eyeing it. The cat came up and rubbed against the horse's ankles, purring.

"Well, hey little kitty," Seph said, leaning to the side. The cat looked up at Seph, and with a springy leap, climbed up the horse's side and was quickly on the horse's back haunches.

"Well, she's forward," Kaile said, as Seph petted the cat behind her.

"You make a new friend?" Davin asked with a laugh.

"Looks like it," Soren said.

"You coming with us?" Seph asked, as the cat purred under Seph's hand that glided over the sleek black fur.

Moments later, the cat was fast asleep in Seph's lap, as if it had always been with her.

Soren smirked at the sight, and Seph seemed lighter as the warm sunlight glowed on her back, casting a shining golden aura around her body.

Hours later, they stopped to rest. The sun hung high in the crisp blue sky. It was a vast open sky with clouds only dotting far to the west, hanging over mountaintops. There was no fire or shade. It was only the open plains and them along the beaten road of mixed snow and mud.

"Can we open them?" Kaile asked, already grabbing the sack Davin had handed them. All four of them looked around the area and didn't see anyone for miles.

Soren nodded.

Kaile drew his out first, while Seph still rummaged through her saddlebags. Kaile was as eager as Soren had seen him. Enthusiastic, wide-eyed, and quick moving. He pulled the staff from the bag, holding it up to inspect under the beaming sunlight.

The staff was two feet long, perhaps a bit longer, Soren thought. Smaller than most, but easier to conceal by far. It was made of a dark wood, almost black, sleek at its base and knobby and gnarled like an ancient tree at its tip. It housed inlaid green jewels with one white jewel at its tip. The way Kaile moved it through the air, it appeared light, no more than only a couple of pounds. Kaile grinned widely, showing the white of his teeth.

Seph's was the same length but gray wood with streams of sparkling silver. The base was also straight and wound up to a knobby top. Its top was inlaid with black stones with one golden one at its tip. Her mouth hung agape as she marveled at what Soren surely thought was her first staff.

Soren sat forward, folding his forearms over one another on the saddle's horn.

"They got names?" Soren asked.

"Not yet," Davin said.

"Where did it... I mean *they*, come from?" Kaile asked.

"Where do *you* think?" Soren asked, testing the boy's wits.

Kaile held it up with both hands before him. The sun's rays glowed off the jewels and the wood's finish.

"Organic, with polished emeralds and a moonstone," he

said. "Moonstone comes almost exclusively from Arkakus because of its volcanic nature. Emeralds aren't rare, but this type is. These are pure, with no visible imperfections. Perfect for casting and channeling. I'd assume those came through Lynthyn, as most precious stones like this would. The shaft, I'm unfamiliar with, but to find someone to assemble such a specific weapon, and so condensed—I'd guess somewhere far from the capital. To make such a staff without the king's knowledge would surely be a death sentence. I'd guess it's far to the south, far from Celestra. Perhaps on the coast?"

"You've been there," Davin said in a low, hinting tone.

"Me?"

"You both have, actually," Davin said, sitting atop his horse with his shoulders back as a bitter wind gusted through.

"Me too?" Seph asked.

They both looked at one another.

"Guillead?" they both asked at the same time.

Davin nodded. "I had them both with me when I came to Skylark. It seems Mihelik knew he'd need two."

"Mihelik knew what?" Soren asked in disbelief. "That old conjurer is full of mystery. How could he know that? He didn't even know Seph was still alive."

"He didn't?" Davin said. "Is that what he told you?"

"What's mine made of?" Seph asked. Kaile held out his hand, and she handed it to him as he handed his to her.

"Hmm... Brayburry wood with streams of elfvein. Flawless obsidian stones and dragoneye at its crest."

"Dragoneye?" she breathed in amazement. "The jewel of the goddess?"

"Yes," he said with squint eyes. "Unmistakable the way the light hits it. You can tell the difference of it from gold by the mild translucence. It grows deeper in color at its center. And it can't be melted like gold. It's hard, not soft."

"How did this stone find its way to this staff?" Soren asked, as much to himself as Davin.

"I just picked it up. I don't know the answer to your question," Davin responded. "You'll have to ask the old Syncron, next you meet."

There was a moment of thought as the wintry afternoon winds howled. It sounded as if the last breath of Cascadia was whispering to them, before they entered into the land of Londindam.

"Will you teach me how to use it?" Seph asked as Kaile handed it back to her, and she clasped her gloved fingers around the gray wood. She held it nervously, as it appeared heavy in her hand. It slid down her glove, so her fingers wrapped around it just below the knot at its top.

Kaile nodded. "I'll do my best."

"It seems like you know a lot," she said. "I want to know everything you can teach me."

Soren soured at the thought of the archmage's apprentice getting close to his only family, but he had no choice now, he knew. Soren knew about the workings of the Ellydian. He knew the way the notes channeled energy in waves from the world's core. He knew that specific frequencies carried unique abilities, and affected those that wielded it differently than others.

He knew how Cirella talked about it, and how she used her notes from her mouth and from, more easily, tuning forks. But Soren knew his knowledge paled in comparison to what the apprentice knew, even at his young age. And they were both Ayls. Soren didn't even know if Seph had gone through the Doren level or had skipped completely past, which took normally years of training to attain the upper level of Aeol.

"Let's start with what you *do* know," Kaile said. "Tell me about what you learned from Cirella's writings."

"You can talk on the road," Davin said. "We need to get moving again."

Davin rode first, as Kaile and Seph rode side by side, and Soren rode behind. He rode close, to listen in as well as he could.

The cat slumbered behind Seph on the horse still, a stowaway on their quest of sorts.

Chapter Eighteen

⁂

The fire roared as the smoke filtered through the trees above and into the sky of infinite sparkling stars. No new snow rested upon the remaining winter leaves, but the earth was hard as stone beneath them. They sat upon thick logs, warming their hands and drinking cold water from a spring along their journey that day.

They ate tough jerky and ate stale bread and soft apples. To Soren, that felt like a sense of home again. The air was fresh, and the smell of the wood smoke warmed him, and soothed him. It was far more freeing than the cell that had harbored them beneath Barringstone Castle.

Davin had released the spell from them, and Soren enjoyed their normal appearances again. She felt like Seph once again. She smiled warmly as the four of them talked. He thought she felt free as well. She'd shed her own prison bars, even though they kept her safe from the world as well.

They would be at the cave system the next day, if everything Davin had said was true and accurate. Soren hoped to speak with Ravelle and tell them about their need for the relic that hid one in the shadows, but he knew the truth—Ravelle had more than just the reputation for her skill in picking the guarded pockets of the rich. She had a taste for blood, too.

He didn't want to kill her. He didn't want to have to kill any innocent people. There was too much death already in these lands, he thought. But a deal was a deal, and he agreed to help Lady Drake, as long as she helped him to get what he wanted most in this world—his revenge.

"So," Seph said, chomping on a big bite of jerky. "You use C and E. Cirella said that A and E were the easiest to control, so that's what I've been using all this time. Why do you use C?"

Kaile coughed and cleared his throat. The fire lit in his eyes, shining with the spark of passion he held within. The Ellydian was his light, and he gushed with it.

"Cirella used A and E," he said. "A is the most stable of all the notes. It's steady and fluid in its power. C and E are similar to each other in that they are both more difficult to sustain magic through. A is the first we all learn, and the base for most Doren spells. The other notes are even more difficult to cast through, but possible. But if you really need to use a spell, you better make damn sure to use one that will work, and not break in the middle because the pitch is off."

"Okay," Seph nodded.

"I can use E. There's nothing wrong with it, but I've spent a long time working with C. It has a slight variance that gives some of my spells an umph that I get when using it compared to E."

"An umph?" Seph asked. "Like what?"

Kaile looked around at Soren and Davin, sighing. "I suppose there's no use in keeping the secrets, now. I probably won't live another year anyway, now that I've forfeited my life."

No one responded. Not one of them tried to give him solace, because they all knew the truth. Most likely, none of them would be alive in a year's time with the journey laid out before them. The life of a Silver Sparrow was unforgiving.

"So Dorens manipulate the world around them: move books from one table to another, and many things in between. Aeols like you and me can manipulate our own bodies, as you know. So, you, for example…" He pulled a tuning fork from his boot and struck it on a metal shoestring hole. It vibrated in the key of E. "You can make your body translucent, so you appear invisible." As they watched him raise his other hand, he twiddled his fingers. "Like this." As he waved his fingers, their tips faded into the air, letting the midnight air creep down to his wrist, and his hand was gone.

Kaile pressed the tuning fork against his pant leg and his hand reappeared instantly, the same as when Seph appeared once the Shades had sensed her—breaking her spell.

"But… if I use a C note, which I can blue away from the original note…" Kaile took another small tuning fork from his boot and struck it. It let out a high-pitched C note, and they all watched in amazement as the same twiddling fingers, instead of fading from view, turned to a stone gray, marbled and chiseled like rock. He slammed his fist down onto the log he sat upon, and it splintered under the weight.

Soren watched Seph as her jaw dropped and her eyes widened, marveling at the sight.

"You cast Claring Mist with E and it makes you invisible to the naked eye. If you cast the same spell with a tweak to it in C, then you cast Brittlex, turning flesh to stone."

"I want to learn that," she said, nodding as if in a trance.

Kaile smiled. "There are lots of examples of that. But it takes years of practice."

"I'm patient. I'll learn," she said.

From the shadows behind her, the black cat crawled from beside one of the horses into her lap. Seph stroked its neck and rumbling back as Kaile's hand receded back to flesh, and he put it back in his pocket. He put both tuning forks into their places in his boot slyly with a thief's hand.

"What *is* the Ellydian?" Davin asked, scratching his chin with sincerity in his voice. All wished to hear the answer from someone so close to the knowledge kept exclusively by the archmage, the closest to the clutches of the king.

"So you see it as magic, yes?" Kaile asked. "You know the world's most powerful Syncrons, and you've heard of their power. You know the king controls the knowledge most sacred to them, and he only doles it out to those who wield it under his command? For those lucky, or unlucky, enough to have it inside of them, it's tricky to control, and has spelled the end to many innocent lives. Either by accident, or by choice…"

"You mean the Black Sacrament?" Seph asked. "You either succeed and become a Lyre master, or die trying?"

"I think he means that, and if you don't pledge fealty to the king, then your life is forfeit," Soren added.

"Yes, both," Kaile said. "But if not wielded correctly, the spells can have devastating consequences, including to the caster." Kaile held out his right arm and pulled up his sleeve to his elbow. Angling his under forearm to the fire's light, he revealed scars that cut and gashed all the way up to his wrist. They were deep but healed into pasty whites and stark reds deep in the cuts. "This was from early on, when I tried a spell on my own. I'll never make that mistake again. I nearly bled to death."

Seph covered her mouth with the back of her hand.

"How'd you get the Ellydian?" Davin asked. "And do you know where it comes from? What it really is? I don't know much about it. I just hear the tales of the great Syncrons, and the dark Synths of old. We'd almost be better off without all them, if you ask me… but er, um… no offense."

"None taken," Kaile said. "The Ellydian is the source of all that fuels life in this world. It comes from deep down within the center of our world. And simply put, the only way to tap into that power is through sound, or music, or notes, or whatever you want to call it. You see… even the slightest reverberation, or pitch, changes the air. It can pass through almost anything, and when I let out an A note for example, that sound changes the air, passes through the ground beneath your feet, and forms a sort of string that connects to the source of the Ellydian deep within our world. With that connection through that note, you can bend the will of our reality, and form what you call spells, or magic."

"So when Mihelik formed that portal that saved you all from the king and his men in Erhil, that was him bending reality?" Davin asked.

"That kind of spell is something only he could use," Kaile said. "There's only a handful of Syncrons in all of history that could move things like that over vast distances, let alone multiple people, without killing them. As for who gets the ability to wield it, it's still a mystery. It can travel through families and blood like the Whistlewillows, or it can come seemingly out of nowhere, in the case of a poor kid like me."

"Have you thought of attempting the Black Sacrament?" Seph asked as the cat purred loudly in her lap, warm from the heat of the fire.

"That's a little too personal to answer," he said. "Ask me again later, if we survive this."

"I would," Seph said. "Once I'm trained. I want to be a Lyre master."

"You need to kneel to the king," Soren said. "There's no other way. You'd have to serve your entire life for that madman."

"Mihelik doesn't," she replied quickly.

"He did for most of his life," Soren said.

"Until he didn't," Seph replied again.

"You're right," Soren said. "But that's never how it worked before. He is the one, and now he's the most hunted man alive."

"Except for us," she said.

He nodded with a growl. "Except for us."

"You ready to tell us why you really came through the portal with us?" Seph asked. "We're in this together, you know. Mihelik may have known you were going to do it, but it still doesn't make any sense to me. Why leave one of the most prized positions in all the realm, abandon everything to join the 'bad' side?"

Soren deeply wanted an answer to that same question. And he wanted the truth. The real truth. No more vague notions, no more wishy-washy answers. He needed to know, if he was going to continue letting him get so close to Seph.

Kaile let out an exasperated exhale, slumping his shoulders and glaring into the fire. It cast a reddened glow upon his skin. His eyes burned gold from the reflection. There was a deep sadness within, something Soren knew all too well from many nights on the road; fatigued, cold, and lost.

"I did," Kaile said, clutching his knuckles to his cheeks. "I threw away everything. I had everything a wielder could dream of. But once I saw that fire burning, my entire view of life changed. I'd grown up thinking I was on the good side, and the Silver Sparrows were the embodiment of evil, and now here I am, on their side, and I feel like I see clearly now. The Chimaera is just an excuse for Amón to kill. I don't belong in that kingdom up there more than any of you. I took a chance. More than that, though, I abandoned everything to be here, right now, with you."

"Why us?" Seph asked. "Because you didn't have any other means to escape?"

"Yes and no," he said. "If I tried to escape the capital, then I would've been surely caught eventually, and put down in that dungeon to be 're-educated.' But..." He glimpsed Soren, and averted his gaze again quickly, almost bashfully. "I've always dreamed of meeting you."

"Soren?" Seph asked. "Why?"

"I heard of your feats back in Tourmielle. I heard tales of the way you defended the Syncrons. You were so brave and valiant in those stories. You killed giants and monsters in the Under Realm. I've never been that brave. I was just a kid in Ikarus, from a shite family with a good-fer-nothin' dad, a drunkard mom, and I can't even help my brother, who's still there with them."

Soren scowled into the fire. *Why would he idolize me? He has no idea who I really am. I'm a killer, and a vagabond who has lost everything now… Well, nearly everything…*

"You couldn't bring him with you?" Seph asked. "Why? If your family was that bad, wouldn't Alcarond let you bring him with?"

Kaile laughed darkly. "You don't know Alcarond."

"Explain him to me," Seph said. "Why would he separate two brothers, taking one forever away and leaving one like that?"

"A dangling carrot," Davin said, looking out into the woods veiled in darkness.

"If I do *this*, then they would bring Joseph to me. If I did *this*, then they'd let me write him a letter. If I do *this*, then they'll give him money secretly, so my parents wouldn't find out. I have no idea if any of it was true, or just constant lies."

"That's rough," Seph said. "Alcarond said those things, just to get you to grow your skills?"

"I feel… lost in my own thoughts sometimes," Kaile said, sliding his fingers into his hair and gripping it tightly in fists. He tugged slightly. "I obsess over things. I sometimes wonder if I am who I think I am. Am I the same kid they found and took from my village? Did he die when he set foot into Celestra for the first time? I want to think I'm me. I want to think I'm not totally corrupted by my mentors, but it gets so hard to tell what's real and what's not."

"This is real," Soren said, getting up, squatting beside Kaile and putting his hand on the boy's shoulder. "That warm fire is real. The moon up there is real. We are too. Erhil burned. You saw that with your own eyes. Believe in your instinct. What you see now isn't a dream or a nightmare, it just is."

Kaile nodded with a quivering lip, affirming the words to himself.

Soren clapped his shoulder one last time and went back to his spot by Seph.

"Was it real that you pierced the skin of the king?" Kaile asked. "I saw it, but everything I'd been told said he was as divine as Shirava. His skin is supposed to be woven in dragon-scale. His mind is righteous with the knowledge of the goddess herself, and no other. Even with a dagger from Vellice, how is that possible?"

"Because he's human, lad," Davin said. "It's a fairy tale you've been fed. He shits, pisses, and disappoints his lady, just like we all do. Ain't that right, Soren?"

Soren nodded, warming his hands by the fire as the winds howled above. "It's true. And now we are certain of it. That madman bleeds like the rest of us."

Chapter Nineteen

The hunt was on.
Overlooking the hills that were the borderlands —calm under the early morning sun, majestic in their power—the four of them glared down into the valley with a sort of apprehension that was hard for Soren to figure out. He loved the hunt. He enjoyed the mystery and the fulfillment of a long-sought after mission. And he always loved the reward.

But this was different. He wasn't alone, and others were relying on him.

Soren leaped down from his horse, took his gloves off, and unsheathed Firelight. He knelt on a stone, dried by the sunlight, and dug his dagger into the hard dirt beneath the fading snow.

None of them asked what he was doing.

A rare warm breeze filled the air, rustling dead blades of grass that dared peek their heads above the snow, above where their roots were kept alive from the winter chill. There was a faint smell of old fire in the breeze, which blew head on. Someone was in the hills, Soren knew. He didn't know if it was

Ravelle with the relic that Lady Drake wanted so badly, but there was someone, or something, out there.

Heavy cloud misted the lands in shadow, making Soren remember the relic, and its ability to hide the wearer in shadow. He wondered if the shade cast by the clouds would be enough to conceal its wearer. Could Ravelle be around them, hiding, waiting, watching…?

There were ways to tell if someone was hiding from magic, and chief of those was to trust his instincts; smell, sound, and touch, of course. She'd leave footprints, if anything. She wasn't completely gone from existence.

He cut into the frozen ground easily, not worried about dulling the infinitely sharp, otherworldly metal of the dagger. Firelight freed the dirt from the ground, and he scooped it in his hand. Within it he smelled the old earth, the iron in the minerals, the dying grass, and the faintest of animal scents that had crossed that path over the seasons. The dirt sifted back to the ground through his strong fingers, and he rose back to his feet.

"So this is it?" Soren asked. "They said she was in there?"

"Waiting it out," Davin said, resting his long, feminine arms on the horse's neck. "Waiting for the heat to blow over, expecting the lady to forget, or playing with her new toy."

"There's got to be dozens of caves down there," Kaile said. "I can count six from here."

"All caves aren't the same," Davin said in an uplifting tone. "She'd pick one to stay close to the surface. Don't want to be sleeping down in the depths with whatever roams in the darkness."

"Which is what?" Seph asked, warming her hands.

"The Shades go somewhere," Kaile said, with a nervous twitch in his eye. "The Black Fog and them disappear when the sun comes up. Alcarond thought they went underground, into the Under Realm."

"There's one way to find out," Soren said, shoving his boot into the stirrup and straddling the saddle. "If she's here, I'll find her."

"Let's do it before dark," Seph said.

"Agreed," Soren said. He rode his horse down into the valley, a mix of gray, aged snow and patchy, browning grass. The foothills were a dark slate stone, ridging up through the ground in brittle mounds before rising to immense mountains ahead—a deep shade of gray before their tall snowcaps of pure white.

They rode along the bottoms of the foothills, looking up at the rising peaks, and the caves that dotted high and low in the seemingly porous rock.

"What are we looking for?" Seph asked, gazing out, scanning the cliffside.

"Signs of life," Soren said. "Muddy, grass-beaten exits, footprints, even a long dead fire."

Entering the hills, they split up—Kaile rode with Seph, and the other two searched within earshot. There were far more entrances to the caves than Soren expected. There were crevasses a body could barely squeeze through. The sound of cold water dripping inside echoed throughout, signaling they indeed were vast below.

Soren considered entering the caves through one of the wide mouths in the rock, but since the hills and ridges went on so far, he decided to continue looking for signs of life, and not wandering into the darkness needlessly. There were also no signs of what else may lurk in the dark.

Midday turned, and the sun arced down her beautiful path. There were only a few stacked hands of sunlight left in the day, and Soren heard Seph's stomach rumbling from feet away. There were woods not far from where they searched, as they ran parallel with the ridge, so they'd be able to be within the thick woods within a half hour. So they continued their search.

The air grew chiller, and Seph was tucking into herself. Thick vapor plumed from their mouths as the shadows of the black slate mountains darkened. Davin and Kaile were further north, still visible but riding in and out of the hills.

"Soren," Seph said. Her voice quivered from cold and something else. "There…"

She pointed up to the top of a hill a hundred yards off. It was hard to see from that vantage point, and in the dying light, but there was something there. A dark object was outside of a narrow crevasse of a cave that looked something like a gothic door.

They both rode hard up the hill. Soren whistled loud for the others, who quickly were riding in that direction.

Soren rode up the hill first, with Seph right behind. He had Firelight ready to draw, but as he looked at the sight before him, he kept her in her sheathe.

Seph ascended the hill, covering her mouth, and muttering something behind it.

Soren got down from his horse as the other two rode hard halfway up the hill. He walked over to the body that lay before the mouth of the cave and knelt.

Davin and Kaile both summited the outcrop with heaving, frosty breath pluming. They watched Soren as he reached down toward the woman that lay on her back, on the blood-stained rock beneath her. Soren glided his fingers above her body. Her pale arms were strewn to the sides, splayed, frozen, and stricken with pain in her final moments. His fingers rose above her chest, the giant gash in her throat that was matted in thick, frozen dark blood, and finally to her chin. He pulled her head, twisted to the side, toward him. It was stiff, but she hadn't been dead long enough to completely freeze.

"That her?" Davin asked, irritation thick in his throat.

Soren angled her head toward his, and looking at her face,

he saw the freckles he recognized and the small scar over her left eyebrow.

"Aye, it's Ravelle," Soren said.

Davin got down from his horse, huffing madly. He spat curse words as he trudged over to her with powerful strides with his short legs. He stood over her and bent down to inspect her.

"You sure it's her?"

"I'm positive," Soren said. "That's Ravelle L'Aron."

Davin began patting her body as Soren stood back.

"Where is it?" Davin patted, irritated and fuming. "Where the blazes is it?"

"What is it, specifically?" Kaile asked politely.

Davin ignored his question.

"It's not here. Damn the goddess, it's not here." He drove his balled fists onto the rock.

"Davin," Soren said. "Look." He walked toward the cave's entrance and knelt, pointing to tracks in the snow and dirt, leading to and from the cave.

Davin stood and looked, suddenly seeing the tracks were everywhere. He was so distracted he hadn't noticed them before, but they showed the struggle, and the murder of the young thief. Whatever killed her, cutting her throat, went back into the cave.

Davin folded his arms, deep in thought.

"What are they?" Seph asked. Her question was to both of them, but Davin's refusal to look away from them, and his loud snorting, led Soren to answer.

"There are a couple of different prints," Soren said. "This one over here is large. And you see the five toes at the top? The ground is frozen, but it still made an imprint. It's big, and it's heavy. Can either of you guess?"

"Ogres?" Kaile asked.

"No," Soren replied. "Not that big."

"Trolls," Seph said.

Soren nodded. "Aye, two at least. Big, as I said."

"What are the rest of the prints?" Seph asked, shyly, perhaps not wanting to know the answer.

"Shades," Davin said grimly. He stroked his coarse, brown beard as he glared up at the sun as it slowly sank lower and lower with each passing second.

"Has she been dead that long?" Kaile asked. "Did we just miss it? We could have saved her."

"Been dead since the dawn," Soren said. "Trolls don't do sun, as we all know, and neither do Shades. By the cut, it was definitely the trolls. You can see heavy bruising on her arms and legs. One held her tight while the other nearly decapitated her with a jagged cut. But they didn't take her body, so that wasn't what they were after. Normally, a troll would take the time to consume, even cook their victims. But these ones didn't."

"Maybe they didn't have time," Kaile said. "With the Shades here? Maybe they had to retreat, leaving her here?"

"Perhaps," Soren said, rising to his feet and brushing off his knees. "More likely, though, is they got what they were after. Something for their horde, something for their collection. I'm guessing they could sense the magic in the relic she carried, and it was ultimately her downfall. Shame. She was beautiful and talented. She didn't deserve this."

"What about the Shades?" Seph asked.

"Hard to tell how old the tracks are, but the troll tracks cover the ones of the Shades. So the Shades could be long gone, or they could be waiting for us in there, watching us right now…"

"But the troll's tracks lead back in there," Davin said. "We've got to follow. We've got to get it back before it's lost forever."

"You want us to go in *there*?" Kaile asked. "That's madness."

"Lady Drake needs that relic!" Davin demanded. "It's crucial for the war ahead. We have no choice. We have to go in. Here…" He reached into his back pocket in his pants and pulled out a leather pouch. He unfolded the top flap hastily and held out the dark metal that was housed within. "Take what you need. You too, Seph."

Soren saw him hold out the pouch of varying arrays of tuning forks, small and medium-sized, labeled with the note it played imprinted into the leather pocket and on the fork itself. He walked up to them, and Kaile took two C's and two E's. Seph drew out two A's and one E. She struck it against the metal on the reins and a pure A reverberated from the small piece of metal, only four inches long.

"We're not going in there," Soren said. "It could be anywhere in that cave system. You'd have to be mad, suicidal!"

"We need that relic. There's no *no* about it!"

"You're going to have to tell me exactly what it is, if it's that damned important to her. You need to tell me everything about it you know," Soren demanded. "We're losing daylight and I'm already getting pissed."

"I can't tell you everything," Davin said. "Lady Drake has plans for it, but they can't be known. Secrecy is of utmost…"

"Don't give me that horseshit," Soren said, taking a great stride toward the half-height dwarf with his finger out. "What was all that about trust and whatnot back in Skylark? You want us to risk our lives in a dark cave when it's nearly dark already? You better start yappin', and soon, because those trolls already got a head start on us…"

Davin sighed. "Fine. I can tell you what you need to know, but no more than that."

"And no less," Soren growled.

Chapter Twenty

"It's a relic of the old world, before the tides washed away the past," Davin said. "It's not so much one relic, but two. The Twilight Veil is what it's known as. It's a small gauntlet, or more like a bracelet, and a ring. Separate—they're nothing but pretty and old, but together, they make you transform into nothing in the shadow. No sound can leave that shadow, no breath, no words, nothing. For as long as you stay within the shade, you are invisible."

"Twilight Veil?" Seph mouthed. "How are we going to find a ring and a bracelet in there?"

"Is it from the Sundar?" Soren asked. "Or the Polonians?"

"It was made by the Sundar, to the west, from the jewels that sift in the sands of the Dyadric Desert. Sapphires are inlaid in the bracelet, and the ring is crafted of gold with a single eldrite stone. Though I've never seen them with me own eyes, my people would love to have such a wonder in our city."

"What's Lady Drake's plans for it?" Soren asked. "What's the scheme?"

"That, Soren, I can't tell you."

"Why not?" Soren asked in a gruff tone.

"Because it's none of your concern," Davin said. "Even Mihelik decided to keep the plans for the relic secret. It's too important and is quite separate from this mission."

"It's separate from killing our enemies?" Soren asked. "Isn't this what it's all about? Freeing these lands and saving countless lives from those monsters?"

Davin didn't respond but looked down into the darkness of the cave in the quick fading sunlight.

"We need the relic," Seph said. "If it's that important, then we've got to get going. We can't wait for it to disappear in there, and we can't wait any longer. We've got what... a couple hours left? Let's get this over with." She hefted her staff in her hand, holding it out to her side. It held a golden glow as upon the vibrant stone of dragoneye at its crest. The sunlight shimmered white off the sharply cut obsidian stones below.

Soren watched her with awe. He still couldn't believe the woman she was becoming. So brave, inspiring even, but he still had to protect her.

"No," Soren said. "Kaile and I will go in. You two head for the trees. He and I will find the Twilight Veil."

Seph's nasty gaze snapped at him.

"That's not how we're running things," Davin said. "We all go in."

Soren sneered at the dwarf. "She's not going into that cave."

"Yes, I am," Seph said, pointing the staff directly at him, inches from his chest. "The longer you postpone this, the more dangerous it becomes. You're not going to win. It's three against one." She furrowed her brow and glowered at Kaile. "Right?"

He nodded, avoiding Soren's mean gaze.

"The lass is right," Davin said. "We all go. Don't fight it."

Soren sighed, exhaling through his nostrils as the vapor

plumed out. The air was growing more chill, and he finally dropped his chin to his chest.

"Let's get this over with. Seph, you stay behind me at all times."

She nodded eagerly.

Soren withdrew Firelight from its scabbard. It rang sharply as it kissed its way out. The layered lines of the Vellice dagger shimmered like golden glass.

Kaile stepped forward, hefting his staff of dark wood. The moonstone and emeralds darkened as they fell into the darkness of the cave.

"Seph," he said, waving for her to join him. The black cat strolled up behind her as she went to Kaile's side. The cat's long tail curled behind. "Have you ever used one of these before?"

She shook her head no, almost embarrassed.

"It's all right," he said. "Now, staffs like these are made to harness the power of the sound that flows up from the world's core. You use the fork to create the tune, and the staff pulls and concentrates that note's resonance within. So, strike the fork, draw it into the staff, and even without the note playing, the staff will hold the power until the note's resonance depletes. Try it. Use E."

Seph took the small E fork from her belt and struck it on the elfvein that flowed down the shaft. The pure note rang with a high pitch.

"I don't feel anything," she said.

"You will," said Kaile. "Now, we're going to use Lightbloom. Feel the resonance, and feel it surge into the staff in your hand. Let it flow from your palm and fingers into the wood."

"It's getting warm," Seph said. Her eyes were closed, and her focus was heavy. Soren watched intently.

"Good," Kaile said. "Now, while focusing on the note,

imagine the word Lumonose. Repeat it like a mantra. Let it fill your mind, drowning out everything else. Focus on it until there is nothing else that matters. It's just you, the sound, and the word."

Seph held the staff close to her chest with both hands. Her small frame appeared larger as she stood like a strong statue with her hair rustling in the freezing winds.

"I—I feel something," Seph said. "It's warm, and bright like the moon."

"Open your eyes," Kaile said softly.

She slowly opened her eyes to see the dragoneye, and the other stones glowing a majestic white light. They lit the cave's sides in a radiant glow. As she waved the staff around and further into the cave, a brilliant smile crossed her face.

Kaile's staff exploded into a brighter light. He'd struck his fork so quickly and caused the spell to beam, Soren had hardly the time to notice.

Kaile was indeed a powerful Aeol, and Soren both needed that, and feared it.

"Remember Seph," Soren said. "The Ellydian doesn't work on the Shades, if they're in there. Nothing works against them except this dagger, and your own fast legs."

"You don't think I remember that?" Seph asked. "I almost died when they killed my spell when I followed you. You think I'd let that happen again?"

"No," Soren said. "It's just a reminder. If there are Shades down there, then turn and run, as fast as you can. I'll do what I must."

"This isn't a suicide mission," Davin said. "Glasse is the real target. You're not allowed to be released from your contract yet."

"Let's get this over with," said Soren. "We're losing light."

Kaile led the way, and the others followed him in.

The cave was narrow and the scattered tracks below them fell into a narrow path, leading deeper into the cave.

"The troll tracks are on top," Davin said. "A good sign."

"What spell are you preparing?" Soren asked Kaile.

"Fire," he responded quickly.

"Aye," Davin said. "Trolls hate it."

It impressed Soren that Kaile knew to ready a fire spell, and naturally he wondered what other things the archmage had taught him over the years. Soren knew Kaile, as annoying as he could be to him, may be a powerful ally in the battles ahead.

They strode deeper and deeper into the cave, until a few minutes in, the cave opened to a vast cavern. The sound of dripping water echoed from the dank walls. Both Kaile and Seph had the forks still ringing in their hands. In this world, most beasts knew instinctively to fear the sound of a pure note in the wild. The ages had taught them to fear what came next.

Kaile muted his fork against his pant leg, and Seph did the same. They both waved their staffs, letting the light shine out into the darkness, but the cave was deep, and the shadows enveloped everything past the lights.

They walked cautiously into the open cave, the damp stone slippery under their boots.

"See anything?" Davin whispered with his ax in his hands. It was a single-sided one with a four-foot shaft of dwarven-crafted metal and intricate, carved design on its sides.

The cat making circle eights through Seph's legs meowed, and suddenly hissed. Soren's gaze snapped to it as it scampered back off to the entrance.

"Weapons up!" Soren shouted.

The two figures emerged from the shadows above, plummeting at immense speeds. Soren shoved Seph back as the shadowy beast landed right in front of him, swinging a huge mace in a massive arc over their heads. Soren ducked and rolled away to Seph's side.

The other landed nearly on top of Davin, but his stocky frame merely ducked away, running with quick strides back. Kaile had the sense to backpedal away, keeping his head low, but his staff securely in hand.

Beastly, the two trolls were immense, both nearly twice as tall as Kaile. They had sinewy arms with tight muscles down long arms and legs. Coarse, sharp hair was patchy down their long forearms that nearly touched the ground.

A predatory intelligence blossomed in their dark, cold, beady eyes. Their faces were creased with wrinkles. Long hair fell down both their backs from their colossal heads with pointed ears, both scarred at the tips. They let out menacing roars from behind yellow, jagged teeth.

The smell that came from them was putrid, causing Soren's nostrils to burn, and he kicked himself for not sensing them before.

The troll attacking Soren swung its heavy mace above again as Soren dashed to the side, and Seph clawed her way back up the cave's path.

As the two trolls attacked, they clearly had the upper hand. Soren and Davin were put immediately on the defensive, as the two Syncrons scrambled to get their wits about them. The glowing lights from their staffs strobed across the walls and floor of the cave as the two of them pulled back.

Soren finally got to his feet. Davin, too. Soren stood before the immense, hulking troll as it growled down at him. He had Firelight flashing in his grasp, holding it out before him. The troll's eyes seemed to be locked on the blade, and a slight hesitation gripped it. But it was only that—slight.

The two trolls attacked. This time the one with the mace swung it over its head and with flashing speed down at Soren, who evaded back as the huge mace, three feet in diameter, crashed into the stone. The ground under their feet quaked from the blow. Soren couldn't remember the last time he'd fought anything with that much raw strength.

Lunging at Davin, the other troll simultaneously attacked, but its attention seemed to be past the dwarf. With his thick forearm, he shoved Davin aside. Davin had time to attack, but his ax didn't cut deep enough into the thick skin, and Davin fell back onto the stone. The giant troll had Kaile in its sights. It pulled its weapon above its head, a four-sided club of stone, ready to smash.

"Kaile, fire, fire!" Soren yelled.

While backing away Kaile had tripped and was on his back still, scampering back with wide eyes as the troll was already nearly on top of him, ready to turn the boy to naught more than bloody paste. A sharp ring of C left somewhere at his hip, and he held his staff up high in front of him.

The white glow faded from his staff, and instead, an amber light shined. The troll held the club over its head, ready to crush Kaile. It stood with its legs spread, the several hundred-pound club nearly twenty feet above.

From his staff, the amber light spread. Fiery tendrils poured out from the staff's gemstone, swirling around quickly like a tide pool spinning outward. The flames gathered into a blazing mass, spinning around the staff of black wood.

The troll sent the club down, as Seph screamed from behind Soren. Soren was too busy distracting the second troll with the mace, and Davin was still gathering his senses back as Kaile was about to be killed.

"Infernous!" Kaile yelled, pointing the staff at the troll with his arm extended as far as he could reach.

The cave erupted in golden amber light and the staff erupted into a blazing inferno, casting its fiery breath upward. The flames crashed into the troll with an explosion that boomed and echoed throughout the cave. The fire blasted into the troll's face and chest, sizzling the fur, and the troll roared.

Its square club still plunged downward as the troll released it. The troll covered its face, wiping the flames away as Davin rushed to Kaile's side and yanked him away. The club crashed to the stone with a rumbling, thunderous thud next to Kaile's leg.

Davin continued pulling him to safety.

Soren suddenly noticed the troll before him was fully distracted by the commotion.

Now it's my turn…

He didn't hesitate.

Soren dug his heels into the rock, exploding forward with all his might at the towering giant of a troll.

The troll was slow to respond. They were known for their might, and toughness, but Soren knew a troll's greatest weakness was its slow mind.

Firelight flipped over Soren's knuckles, as he clutched it once the Vellice dagger's blade was at the backside of his hand. Soren ran under its two tree-trunk legs, cutting deep to the tendons at the backside of its right leg. The dagger, as sharp as it was, still only cut down to the bone, through sinewy, tough skin, but the troll howled in anger, swatting down at Soren with his free hand.

Soren escaped under the backside of the troll's legs as it stumbled backward, losing its sure footing as the blood ran down its leg. Soren slammed the back of his fist into the other leg, sending Firelight all the way in, feeling it pierce the bone.

The troll roared in rage, spinning to get a clear view at Soren, and smash him to bits. From under his legs, while the troll spun, Soren caught sight of another plume of fire erupting from Kaile's staff at the other troll. From underneath, Davin swung his ax wildly, heaving enormous blows at the troll's ankles and feet.

They were on the offensive, and thanks to the Ellydian, they had the upper hand. But Soren knew killing these two wouldn't be as easy as distracting them. It only took one grasp of their huge hands, or one swing of their immense weapons to spell disaster. They needed to find the relic and be done with it.

"Seph," Soren yelled while evading the troll's attacks, and sending a few of his own in. "Find it. Find the relic!"

She understood immediately. As she got to her feet, the sharp ringing of a tune hummed and light poured outward from her staff. Neither troll seemed to notice, as they then began stomping their feet to crush Soren and Davin, who battled underneath.

Seph ran around them and down into the cave. Her light still couldn't reach the top of the back of the vast cave, but she searched anyway. Hopefully, the troll's horde wasn't much further down, Soren hoped, and they could escape quickly.

We're running out of daylight…

Seph searched frantically, with the light of her staff darting around down the cave.

Soren didn't like her being separated, but he thought it was better than her being close to the trolls, and they needed to find that relic and be done with this!

Another shimmer caught Soren's eye, not from the light of the staff, but rather a reflection from it. As Soren fought the troll above, spinning in mad circles to get at Soren, he saw a flash of metal at the backside of the other. Sticking just barely out of a pocket of the frayed, stained linens at the troll's rear, was a glimmering silver.

"Davin!" Soren yelled. "Back pocket. The gauntlet!" Davin immediately looked above, scheming his way to get to the relic within.

But there was still the ring to find, and Soren assumed it was held by one of them. If they had one part of the relic, then they were sure to have both. As they fought, and Kaile blasted another plume of intense heat and flame at the troll, something seemed to make sense about the relic to Soren.

Above in the shadow, Soren couldn't smell the awful stench of the trolls, but down here, separated, the pungent odor was overwhelming, and it made Soren think about what Davin had said about the Twilight Veil—no noise could escape the wearer while concealed in the shadow.

Maybe that goes for stench too?

Soren took a chance and leaped. He jumped up and grabbed the tips of the linen clothing the troll wore. He had little time. The troll would surely grip him quickly and the battle would be quickly over. Hanging from one hand on the taught linen, he swung up and sliced with Firelight at the troll's back pocket. The slice was clean, and Soren let go, just in time for the monstrous fingers of the troll to whoosh over.

A shimmer of metal glittered down, falling to the rocks behind them. It clinked along the stone, bouncing quickly down the hill, leading further down into the cave.

"Get it! Seph, don't lose it!" Soren yelled.

She and her light spun to the small metal object bouncing haphazardly down into the darkness.

Soren moved away quickly from the towering troll, who also watched his sparkly possession escape off into the abyss.

Seph held her arms out wide as the clinking sound faded from Soren's ear, but grew as it approached her. The troll who Soren had cut the pocket of began to run down the hill toward Seph. Kaile let loose an inferno from his staff at the troll, crashing into its back, incinerating the coarse hair and linen there, sending the troll face first into the stone.

"Get it! Don't lose it!" Soren yelled.

The metal bounced one last time right in front of her, this time bounding high over her head. It spun end over end, flickering like candlelight in the wind.

Seph jumped. She stretched her body completely straight,

with the tips of her fingers extending as the metal flew high above.

Soren's throat caught, and his fingers spread. *She's not going to get it… it's too high!*

Suddenly, she rose another six inches, her fingers clasping into a fist, and she fell back to the stone. She heaved breaths as her boots touched the stone.

"I've got it!" she yelled. "I've got it!"

"I've got the other," Davin said from behind. Soren was so caught in what was happening below, that he was thrilled to see Davin with the gauntlet in his free hand.

"Run!" Davin said.

The troll between Seph and Soren got back to his feet, smoke still rolling up his back from the fire. He roared so loudly it echoed all the way down the cave, past Seph.

Seph ran with all her might up the slippery rocks. Soren knew he only needed to distract it long enough so that she could…

But then the trolls stopped. Their gazes both moved to the bottom of the cave. They'd gone from wicked fury at losing their prized possessions, to a palpable nervousness. Both of their weapons hung at their sides, and they seemed to have forgotten all about the battle and Soren and his friends.

Seph paused, looking back down into the gloom.

"Seph, run!" Soren yelled. "Run!"

Suddenly, the two trolls ran together. They were running to a side tunnel, not towards the exit, or further down. They were running from something.

"Seph, run!" Soren yelled again.

A clacking, chattering sound echoed up from the darkness.

"Oh no," Davin breathed.

Seph ran to Soren, and grabbed his hand.

The four were together again, and the trolls completely disappeared.

The chattering was growing, and the many footsteps were intensifying in the gloom below.

"We've got to make it to sunlight," Soren said. "It's our only chance."

"It's not what I think it is," Kaile asked with his mouth dry and a quiver in his voice. "Is it?"

"It is," Soren said. "Shades. Run!"

Chapter Twenty-One

They ran up the stone floor, slipping as fast as they were running. The dull glow of the sunset ahead cast a red aura at the mouth of the cave, and it grew brighter with each passing second.

Soren heaved breaths as he held Seph's hand. She was quick, perhaps quicker than he, but he held her tight, Firelight too.

The sounds behind of the ensuing demons rose; snapping of jaws, sharp claws scraping up the wet stone, and the growling of angry monsters hellbent on sending Soren to the afterlife. The Shades were gaining on them.

"Faster," Soren yelled. There was no reason to keep quiet now. *Pound your boots on the stone, scream if you must from exhaustion, but the sunlight is our only savior. I can't kill them all.*

The chasing demons were upon them, only yards back, but with one last push they turned a corner and faint, crimson sunlight wafted in the air. They ran into the safety of the sunlight, panting and wheezing. Kaile doubled over and clapped his hands to his knees, trying to catch his breath. They were outside the cave, next to Ravelle's body as the Shades came.

From the red glow of the setting sun, faint reflections from their eyes hung in the mouth of the cave. They stacked upon each other, little red dots of light on their black, obsidian-colored eyes. Dozens of them.

"Holy mother of all things holy," Davin said, trying to catch his breath, clutching his ax to his chest. "There's so many of them…"

"You said holy twice," Seph said, not panting nearly as bad as the others.

"Against those devils," Davin said. "Better twice than none at all. Those things are evil incarnate."

The Shades paused eerily, watching the four of them. The long, charcoal tails of the Shades slithered behind them as their heads hung motionlessly. Their eyes watched in a haunting, frightful manner. They were the unwaveringly dead eyes of a shark, ready to feed.

"Upon the horses," Soren said. "We're not out of this yet. To the trees! To the trees!"

He helped Seph up to her horse, and immediately clapped the horse's haunches, sending it off running in the direction of the woods, down the hill, and past the valley. Turning to glimpse the sunset, they only had moments left, as the red sun was sinking quickly into the mountains.

Soren mounted his steed, yelling at Kaile and Davin to hurry.

"Quick! Ride!" he yelled, and once the two were off down the hill after Seph, Soren finally drove his heels in. "Ride quick, boy, as fast as your legs can carry you!"

The party roared down the hill, down into the valley, and once the horse's hooves hit snow and dead grass, Soren gulped as the last sliver of sun died over the hill.

"Don't look back! Keep riding!" Soren yelled. He, however,

looked over his shoulder and his throat caught. An onslaught of creatures veiled in shadow poured from the cave's mouth, and not only the main entrance by Ravelle's body, but they slithered out of the other smaller caves, too. It was as if the mountain itself was purging a terrible poison from its body, and that poison was coming after them!

"Ride! Don't look back!"

Soren gripped Firelight tight, but he knew there was no chance of survival if he fell from his horse. He knew all too well the venom on the talons of the Shades. It tore into his leg last time, and he didn't ever want to have that feeling again.

So ride. Ride hard!

A wave of Shades as quick as wolves ran down the mountain, eventually pouring out into the valley. Their gazes were fixed, set upon murder, as they filled the valley. Soren had never seen anything like it, and even when Seph rode safely into the tree line, he pressed her to ride in deeper.

Kaile and Davin made it to the outskirts of the wood—their horses frantic and spooked. And as the first of the Shades, snarling and flashing their black fangs, came so close to the back of Soren's horse, he spun with Firelight at the ready.

His horse dove into the woods as Soren felt the thin, young trees scratch his legs. They snapped under the power of his horse. He whipped the reins though, pushing the steed further in, but as he glanced back again, he saw the Shades halted at the outer rim of the woods. He pulled back the reins, which the horse fought at first, but eventually calmed, and Soren stared at the Demons of Dusk.

There must be a hundred of them.

They stalked the perimeter like lions waiting out their prey. But Soren knew better. They couldn't wait forever, for when the sun rose, they'd retreat back to their holes. But Soren watched out of sheer curiosity—the way they moved, the way their legs bent, the motion of their long, black tails, and their eyes—those obsidian eyes that didn't blink.

"C'mon," Seph called to him from deep in the wood. "Let's go."

Soren spat in the direction of the Shades, and rode far into the woods, deeper to safety.

∽

SOREN TWIRLED the ring end over end, inspecting it in the fire's light. He'd never think another thing of such a plain band ring. Sure it was made of solid gold with three tiny blue stones on its underside, but to think this was a magical relic from the old world—he wouldn't have even guessed. The bracelet, however—that was different.

Kaile held the bracelet, holding it up close to his gaze, letting the amber light of the fire gleam off its intricate craftsmanship. It was gold too, but adorned with elaborate floral patterns that filled the entire three-inch band. The same blue gemstones dotted it like fireflies on an autumn night, and thin strands of that same blue flowed throughout the curling designs. It truly was magnificent, and Seph watched it in amazement, sitting beside Kaile.

"No wonder the trolls wanted it," she said. "It's beautiful. I don't think I've ever seen anything so enchanting in all my life."

"Aye," Davin said. "Waste of a life, though. She was a thief but didn't deserve to go like that. Didn't have a chance either against such monsters."

"You knew her?" Seph asked Soren.

"Yes. Off and on," Soren said, scratching his brow as he put the ring in his fist and looked down at the fire as it popped and hissed.

"I'm sorry," Seph said.

"It happens," Soren said, trying to keep the spite out of his words, but partially failing. Seph reached over and put her hand on his forearm, squeezing.

After a momentary lapse in conversation, Kaile broke the silence. "Seph, I saw what you did back there. That was quite impressive."

Soren knew of what he spoke, but Davin raised an eyebrow.

"Yes, that was quick thinking," Soren said.

"I wasn't going to be able to reach the ring," she said. "So I tried to use the resonance left in my staff to use a spell I knew from Cirella's book. It lifted me just enough to get it."

"Yes." Kaile nodded. "And to use a spell without the sound itself, only relying on the staff in that short of time, with no practice, was really, quite impressive. I'm actually astounded."

"I knew it was the only way to get it before we lost it."

"And good thing ya did, then," Davin said. "No way we would've found it with all those demons down there."

Soren was proud too, yet he didn't show it as much as he should have, he thought. Because there was another thing on his mind, another piece of the puzzle which hadn't been solved yet over the decades. What about the forest could keep such unrelenting demons at bay? What about the cities kept them out when they unquenchably thirsted for blood? He'd seen a Black Fog tempt the outskirts of a forest, but that was it. There was something keeping them out, and Soren wanted to know what. Perhaps that would be something he'd ask Mihelik, when next they met.

The cat purred as it lay in Seph's lap, sleeping sound.

"That thing doesn't seem to be going anywhere," Soren said. "Except right by your side."

Seph grinned as she stroked its back.

"Have you named her yet?" he asked.

"I was thinking about Bella."

"Bella, huh?" Soren asked. "Sounds good. Welcome to the family, Bella."

Seph smiled wide up at him, and then went to petting the black cat.

Moments later, after giving the Twilight Veil back to Davin, who tucked them deep into his pack, Soren noticed Kaile staring intently into the fire. His eyes were glossy and fixed upon the flames, almost as if by enchantment.

"Everything all right?" Soren asked him, snapping Kaile's gaze away from the flames.

"Er, um. Yes. Well… no," he said. "I keep thinking about the Demons of Dusk. You know, I've never actually seen them up close like that before. I… I don't know what to think. I've spent so many days and nights researching them with my master… er, Alcarond, rather… But to see them like that, up close. They're terrifying. There's no way we could stop a force like that. The way they looked at us. They looked like they'd been raised in the depths of the Nine Hells."

"They probably were, lad," Davin said.

"I don't think so," Kaile said. "Alcarond used to allude to something else. Something he delved over constantly. Something dark that created them. But I don't think he knew what it was. But it was there, in his mind, always."

Soren remembered his last conversation with Mihelik about the very same thing.

This is not the time to discuss that matter. If ever. So far, my trust for Kaile is growing, but that kind of knowledge I'll keep. At least for now. There is one other thing I've meant to tell him, though, and this seems to be the right time.

Soren shifted in his seat upon the log under him. "There's something I've been meaning to discuss, and this seems like an appropriate time."

All three of them waited with eager looks on their faces. Kaile especially, his skin pale and his eyes strained and reddened. His thirst for some kind of answers to the problems their world faced was palpable.

"Mihelik told me something before we left Skylark, something about the Shades and the Black Fog. Kaile, do you remember the riders you mentioned in Guillead? While I listened to your conversation with Alcarond, you mentioned your friends that disappeared while traveling back to you."

"Benjamin and Thorn," Kaile said. "Never saw them again, and no one ever heard from them. I assumed the Shades, or the fog, got them."

"I believe I saw them meet their end."

Kaile swallowed hard, rubbing his brow.

"The Black Fog got them as they crossed the plains at night. They were trying to get word to you of the Silver Sparrows in Erhil. There was nothing left of them. I'm sorry."

"Why are you telling me this now?" Kaile asked.

Davin leaned back with his arms folded. "So you can have closure, and answers."

"Not quite," Soren said. "Yes, that too. But Mihelik told me something no one knows about the Black Fog…"

"What?" Seph dug her fingers into her thighs, leaning in.

"Whatever the Fog consumes, people at least, turn to the Shades. They were once humans, and so your friends Benjamin and Thorn turned into them."

There was a thick silence that hung in the air, almost so thick if anyone were to speak, it may not reach each other's ears.

Kaile's head sunk and he gripped his hair in his hands, clenching tight.

Davin's head hung also, shaking back and forth. Seph stared at Soren as if waiting for something else to leave his lips. Something to help explain why such insidious monsters existed.

"These things…" Davin said, almost as if speaking to himself. "They're making more of themselves?"

"Yes," Soren said. "It appears that way."

"And there's no way of killing them," said Davin, frustration heavy in his voice. "Except for that blade you carry."

"Also, yes."

"So they're just gonna continue multiplying until there's no one left?" Davin huffed. "We're all just waiting to be eaten by those bastards? And there's no way to stop them?"

Soren didn't respond. Davin already knew the answer.

"Well… fuck," Davin said.

"I'll second that," Kaile said.

"Me too," Seph added. "I'll third it…"

PART V
THE SPY IN GRAYHAVEN

Chapter Twenty-Two

❧

L*ondindam*

OF THE SIX KINGDOMS, *Londindam reminds of most of the turbulent past that haunts. A beautiful kingdom in all its mighty glory, its vast lands embrace some of the wildest beasts and spectacular monuments.*

It is but also famous for its veiled shadow. A darkness dwells there. It lives in the earth, it breathes with the wind, and it watches from its mountaintops. Yet, that shadow creates a form of braveness, righteously coveted within Aladran. Mighty sailors brave its famous fog. Courageous soldiers defend ancient cities with but forks if they must. The Ellydian sprouts there too occasionally, and we must hope it finds those worthy of it, and not fall into devious minds with itchy fingers.

TRANSLATED *from the language of the Sundar. The Scriptures of the Ancients, Book III, Chapter XII.*

. . .

Above them, paint-brushed clouds swirled in the sky above, circling like a vortex to a distant world. It was so eerie and mesmerizing that they all stood by their horses on the outskirts of the woods staring up at it as if it was a sign from Shirava herself.

Soren himself had never seen a dragon, but he imagined this would be the type of sky in which they flew. Cast in tendrils of smoke, illuminated with the fiery light of a rising sun, the clouds twirled around one another in an infinite circle.

Perhaps it was a dragon, but pushed that thought from his mind. *Dragons don't come down to Aladran. They're all so aged they may be stuck in their caves, sunken in their treasure. It's been centuries since one was last seen here. If there are any left, they're still in Eldra, on the far side of the sea.*

"Let's press on," Soren said, mounting his steed. He briefly thought of his own horse, Ursa, and wondered where she was, if she survived the king's burning of Erhil.

The four of them rode through the valley with the early morning frost crunching under the horses' hooves, and into the dead grass below. This was where the Shades had been waiting throughout the night, and the ground was littered with their tracks. Even Soren felt the weight of their presence in his stomach still. He looked back to the rising sun and thanked Shirava for the sun's protection.

They talked little as the horses trotted. The horses were eerily calm, seemingly as spooked by the twirling, storming sky as Soren and the others.

Two hours later, as the sun rose from behind, the winds warmed, and the mountains drowned out to the rolling, open plains—a stone pillar stuck from the earth like a monument of old. A tattered banner hung from its top, limping along the stone's surface, waiting for a gust of wind to lift it to full glory. Soren didn't have to get close to know what the black, white, and blue of the cloth referred to.

They had arrived in Londindam.

Normally, this meant little to Soren. As a wanderer, he'd traveled nearly everywhere in the last decade, even roaming Arkakus and its black stone. But this time was different. This time, he had a purpose.

"We're here," Davin said as they watched the banner lay against the gray monument that rose ten feet out of the icy ground.

"This is the furthest I've ever been," Seph said.

"That's only going to get further from here on out," Kaile said.

Soren watched carefully for prying eyes on the plains. Davin had erected the concealment spell on them, but Soren was vigilant, nonetheless.

"C'mon. Let's go," Davin said. "It's four days of full riding to Grayhaven. Let's be on our way."

Soren knew four days was pushing it hard on horseback, but as long as the weather held, and these strong horses remained so—it was doable.

"So four days to get there, and how many there?" Kaile asked. "How will we get back after? We are going to Skylark after, correct?"

Davin cleared his throat. "Lady Drake has thought all that through. Don't worry your little head over it. All in good time, lad."

"What if I don't like that answer?" Soren asked. "What if we demand specifics? I don't like a job without an exit strategy."

"Well then, we've got four days to talk about it all, don't we?" Davin said. "We shouldn't expect any trouble as long as we stick to the main roads. Don't attract attention and let my necklace do the work. Enjoy the scenery. And stop *bugging* me."

Chapter Twenty-Three

❦

Four days later.

THE WARM SUN rose from behind. It was a welcome one. The night in the forest was bitterly cold. It was the kind of cold that seeped into one's bones, freezing the very core. Exhaustion was thick in them from shivering. Soren was up most of the night, but that was almost always the case, anyway.

The four of them left the safety of the forest, Kaile yawning and stretching his long arms high over his head. Seph had a desperate look of a deep craving for sleep in her weary eyes. Davin just came off more grumpy than normal.

Cold sea winds blew in from the south to their left, blowing in from the Sapphire Sea with a vengeance. Gulls flew overhead by the thousands, weaving in and out of the thick, gray sky in a dizzying madness. There was truly nothing welcoming about these lands, Soren thought. But he knew in Grayhaven, they would at least have beds. Fully in their disguises, not a soul gave them a third look on the day's long road, and would allow them the comfort of a couple nights' rest while they surveilled their target.

They packed their bags and made their way back onto the main road that led to the capital of Londindam. It had been a long road, and Kaile and Seph had become worn down. Davin seemed used to the damp, wet, cold winter travel, but to a boy of Lynthyn, used to warm hearths and all he could drink? Soren thought he was the most miserable he may have ever been. Seph, on the other hand, craved to see the rest of the world, and well, here it was—in all its frozen glory.

Over the past few days, they'd spent time doing the things they needed to prepare for the assassination the best they could. Soren constructed three digger bombs from the fertilizer he purchased outside of Belltop. Kaile taught as much as he could about using staffs and more about the basics of the Ellydian she didn't know from her book. Davin filled them in, mostly, on what the plan would be, but that much of the remainder of their plan was to be discussed with one of the lady's spies within the city.

Soren had used the Twilight Veil, testing it in the shadows. And indeed, it was a great weapon, he thought. Any powerful being in existence would surely want this weapon on their side, and not on their enemy's. It made sense, after, why Davin was so urgent in going into the cave to retrieve the relic.

Two hours later, through the thick fog that rolled in from the Sapphire, the highest, lofty peaks of the keep of Grayhaven came into view. Where Skylark was a golden city, seemingly placed there by the goddess herself, crested upon the peaks of the Cliffs of Blackstone with a waterfall pouring from its mouth, Grayhaven resembled anything but.

As they rode closer, and the city came into view, Soren saw Seph's fatigued gaze look upon it with dread. He could tell she didn't want to go into it. Kaile, too, seemed withdrawn at the sight of such a place.

Reaching immense heights, the keep at its center resembled a mountain in its own respect, monumental and stoic, rising to three lofty towers. The city sprawled outward toward the coastline with massive walls to keep intruders out, and perhaps keep trapped taxpayers within. The dark mists hung along the towers, weaving in and out of the other thousands of scattered buildings like a scratchy, wool blanket.

Another howling wind blew in from the sea, knocking Soren's hood back.

"Well, there she is," Davin said. "All in all, not the worst trip, eh?"

Kaile and Seph didn't answer. Either they were too tired, or couldn't be further in disagreement.

"You've traveled across the sea," Soren said. "That may be the only trip that may be considered worse to these two."

"Aye," Davin said. "Nary worth it. It's a coin toss if the ship'll make it or not. I'll only do it again one more time in my years. And that's reserved for the trip home."

Home. What a concept. Of the four of us, he's the only one who has a place he can go back to and call it home.

Soren watched Seph slump onto the horse, shivering under her coat.

Why is she here? What went wrong that she has to endure this sort of life now? This was never what I pictured for her.

"What day is it?" Kaile asked, rubbing his face to wake up. "Anyone know?"

"The seventeenth of Decimbre." Soren didn't hesitate. He knew the answer immediately.

"It's been eleven days since the king destroyed Erhil?" Kaile gawked. "It feels like it's been months."

"We'll be back in Skylark for year's end." Davin bit at the dryness on his lips.

Seph turned her head slowly to look at him with a sincere wish for his words to be true.

"Let's get down there and get you warm." Soren flicked the reins. "Everyone remember each other's names?"

They each gave their own mumbled signs that they understood.

"Good," Soren said. "We are the enemy here, remember that. You're going to be Synths to these people, not Syncrons. Keep those staffs hidden always. Lord Garriss is a spiteful man. He doesn't love King Amón, but is wise enough to appease him at the minimum."

"Are we sure Glasse is here?" Seph blew into her cupped hands to warm them.

"We'll know soon," Davin said. "Einrick is our contact here. We're to meet him at the Hunter's Moon tavern. But yes, Glasse was heading back in this direction after the genocide at Erhil. Glasse's estate is further north. He owns Riverward Castle between the Lyones mountain range and the Ambler River. But he'd be on his way to fill in Lord Garriss personally about them 'saving' the lands from the Chimaera in Erhil."

"Evil knows no bounds," Kaile said.

"Quite true, lad," Davin said. "Takes root deep, and even if you cut it, it still grows back. Gotta get those deep roots out, and get your hands dirty doin' it."

Soren looked over his shoulder at the apparent young, tall woman who just said those words. "That was nice. You just make that up?"

Davin laughed. "Ha! No. It's a mishmash of things I've heard over the years. But I'll gladly take credit for it!"

"You fooled me into thinking you're not only stubborn and rude," Soren said. "But wise, too."

Kaile snickered. Seph was still too tired for anything else.

Davin laughed. "You know, Soren, in a different life, I may

actually have enjoyed your company, when you're not moping about and constantly pecking at my ears for everything."

"You're not so bad yourself," Soren said. "Until I saw you fight those trolls, I thought you were going to be a wailing baby that I needed to swaddle when the swords came out."

"Me?" Davin gasped. "A coward? You obviously have not met enough dwarves in your time."

"Apparently not." Soren smirked. "You have the pleasure of not only being the first I've really gotten to know, but also the smelliest."

Seph finally broke out of her stone-cold gaze and laughed.

Davin lifted his arm to sniff his pit. "I've been on the road. We've all been on the road! I'm not usually like this."

"Sure," Soren said. "Maybe in another life you wouldn't smell like horseshit."

Kaile laughed from behind his covered mouth to keep the enraged dwarf from sending his anger his way.

"We dwarves are a clean and tidy people," he muttered. "This is not the time to be judging. It's fuckin winter and I'm wearing fucking bearskin! Of course I'm gonna smell. And it ain't like you're smelling like rosy soap either!"

Soren erupted into laughter. He couldn't tell if his insomnia had thrown him into spiraling delirium, but it warmed his core, so that was enough.

They rode up the hill to Grayhaven, with a little more warmth, and the sun shining on their backs.

Droves of people poured in and out of the gate of the castle as they approached. With the snow all but melted away, and with a clear, blue sky, it seemed an invitation for those who lived within the city walls.

There were over a dozen soldiers stationed at the main gate, leaning up on the stone walls, striding back and forth, or scanning the people who lingered around. The high walls of the city were indeed huge. Soren knew he could scale it, but they were definitely over twenty feet, and where other city walls were made of stone and mortar—these were mostly smooth. *Wise design*, he thought.

Davin didn't need to say it, because they all knew to stay tightly together. Soren remembered the one night in the inn in Belltop where Seph's extended fingers turned to her natural shade, once the reach of the pendant's spell had been exhausted.

The soldiers had seen the four of them coming up the hill from far away, and as the four approached the gate, they were met by a pair of soldiers in their path.

One of them motioned with his two fingers for them to dismount, which they did.

"Good day," Davin said, pulling his hood down, revealing the tall, slender woman's face. She only glanced in the soldier's direction. He didn't want too much attention from the soldier. Soren watched intently, even moving to be between the soldiers and Seph.

"Names," the soldier said, walking up and inspecting Davin's horse. The other soldier stood behind with his hand on the hilt of his sword. Most of the remaining soldiers watched from the perimeter of the gate as well. Most citizens paid them little attention.

"Bonnie Rifken," Davin said. "This here's Alfred Duncan. She's Pricilla Lightfoot, and that glum mate there is Victor LeSabre, but we call him Uncle Vic."

"Where you headin' from? And what's your business in Grayhaven?"

"Traveling through." Davin waved his hand out to the side, motioning to the other side of the gate. His voice was chipper and playful. "We've ridden down from Redbridge. Picking up supplies and continuing on our way. We'll only be a few nights."

"Where you goin' after that?" The soldier had a mean,

hard, worn look on his face. His deep wrinkles tightened, and a whistle came through his missing front tooth as he spoke.

"Was planning on chartering a boat for fishin' in the spring," Davin said. "Shouldn't be too far off now with weather shaping up the way it is."

The soldier looked up at the sky, squinting. He snorted and spat at the ground. He looked at the other soldier behind, who shrugged his shoulders. The soldier with the missing tooth stepped aside.

"Thank ya kindly," Davin shot her gaze to the ground as she pulled her horse forward.

As they passed through, Soren glimpsed the second soldier from under the side of his hood. The soldier noticed, and his eyes narrowed at Soren. He walked over with forceful strides. Soren resisted the urge to move his hand to Firelight. That would only erupt the situation into an uncontrollable one, and a bloody mess.

The soldier gripped Soren's hood tightly and jerked it back, rustling Soren's dirty hair. Leaning in, the soldier glared at Soren, inspecting the features of his face, especially where Soren's scars should be. His gaze traced all the way down both sides of his face, with a twitch spasming in the soldier's eye as he glared at Soren. The soldier grunted, shoving Soren away. Soren remained calm and his heartbeat was steady, but he could tell the other three were nervous. Kaile wasn't even breathing. He'd been holding his breath subconsciously.

They walked into the city of Grayhaven, and heard the coughs echo down the long, drab roads immediately.

Chapter Twenty-Four

Walking into the market in Grayhaven caused a sense of gloom to wash over the four of them. Soren had been here before and was used to the state of melancholy from the dingy old city. Seph reached out and grabbed Soren by the hand, squeezing it tightly. Davin walked at the front into the early morning market, looking up at the huge wooden sign, with deep black letters branded into it, "Beware the Chimaera, if sick isolate immediately by order of Lord Garriss."

Kaile too looked up at the sign as a burly man reeking of brandy bumped his shoulder, coughing hard as he did so. Whether on purpose or by accident, Soren hadn't seen, but Kaile showed an annoyed, perturbed look on his face.

"Stay close," Davin didn't need to say, but did anyway. "We're not here to dawdle. We're here for a purpose. Remember, this isn't going to be a welcoming place to strangers in the time of the plague."

"The soldiers didn't seem to mind too much," Kaile said, wiping his shoulder.

"The lord still wants money, and taxes from wealthy travelers." Davin turned back to them. "Even if it means people perish."

"Even in the summer, the place feels like this," Soren said, a sternness in his words. "Eyes watching down every alley, itchy fingers ready to slide into pockets, cutthroats eager to cut for a few coins. The city needs to be cleaned, in every sense of the word."

"The plague may do it if it has its way," Davin said gravely.

"Where are we headed?" Kaile asked.

They were in the middle of the market, a horseshoe-shaped area with half the shops and stalls empty, with those braving the cold getting all the attention. Those who sold warm food had the longest lines, one with over a hundred people waiting with most of their faces covered. Others waited, with small fires burning in between the stalls.

The faces of the street children were what Soren hated most about Grayhaven. Every city had its forgotten sons and daughters, but Grayhaven's abundance of children with dirt-covered faces and hungry eyes caused his stomach to burn.

What's the point of collecting all these taxes if you let your future generation suffer so?

"To the seaside district," Davin said. "By the docks."

"Lead the way." Soren pulled his horse beside him, with Seph's hand still clenching his.

From the main gate, they walked southwest. The city was a spiderweb of huge streets, all shooting out from around the central keep. They cast out from the keep like the sun's rays. Each time passing a major intersection, a clear view of the massive, sky-reaching three towers was visible. Even in the fog, their tips could be seen. Thousands of smaller streets connected them like the veins that scattered from the major arteries.

Soren liked to imagine the vision of the architects and kings who built such a place, before the floods and bastards that let the place fall to hell. It must have been a modern marvel at the time of its construction. Surely in its first hundred years it was a marvel of the world, a symbol of hope and the ingenuity of the human spirit. Now… it was anything but…

They walked down the sloping streets toward the sea. The cold sea air bit at their nostrils and the smell of fish was nearly overwhelming the closer they got. Gulls swarmed by the thousands overhead and along the coastline in the deep fog.

It was over a half hour before they reached the tavern, which Davin had to ask for directions twice. But once they made it, they tied the horses up to the hitching post and Davin tipped the young girl to tend to the horses and get them to the stable. Before they entered the Hunter's Moon tavern, clearly stated by the swinging wooden sign, Soren scanned the crowds. The problem was—everyone looked suspicious and didn't hide their gazes back at him.

Davin went in first, and Soren, last.

The smoke from inside the inn was thicker than the fog outside. It was a robust mix of flavored tobaccos, musty, stale beer, and the roaring hearths on both sides of the room. During the day, and with the Chimaera ever present, the inn was only half as full as Soren would have expected, which was a pleasant surprise.

Davin led them to an empty table in the room's corner, beside the hearth at the right. Kaile was nearly collapsed into a chair when Soren cleared his throat at him.

"I'll be sitting there," Soren said as Kaile nodded and stood back up, moving to the next. Soren sat in the chair with his back to the wall and a clear view of the rest of the inn.

An elderly woman came over and wiped the table clear with a dark rag, setting a candelabra at the round table's center. "Drinks? Food?"

"What do you have today?" Seph asked, licking her dry lips.

"Cooks prepared fish pie," the old woman said, forcing a wide smile at Seph. "He cooks sort of on the spicy side, so fair warning. But it's warming! Bread's just making its way out of the oven. Piping hot with honey."

Seph nodded eagerly.

"For everyone?"

Soren nodded. "Yes."

"Drinks?"

"Water and coffee," Soren said. "For all."

The woman nodded, but her smile faded as Soren spoke.

"My legs are burning," Kaile griped.

"Mine too," Seph said in a high voice, letting her chin fall to the table. "I'm exhausted and in life-or-death peril for a bath."

"This is what life is like, outside a city," Soren said. "Isn't this what you wanted?"

"Don't be an ass," she quipped back, not lifting her head. "Just because I didn't want to spend the rest of my life in that shithole, Guillead, doesn't mean I want to be walking in the freezing rain from city to city. There's an in-between."

"Not for me," Soren said. The black cat was beneath him, making circle eights between his legs, with her tail wrapping around his boots. "This is my life. Welcome to it."

She frowned, dropping her forehead gently to the table with a sigh. "I just want to eat and go to sleep."

"Soon enough, lass," Davin said. "You'll feel better with some warm food in your stomach."

"Where's this man we're supposed to meet?" Kaile asked. "Einrick. You know what he looks like?"

"Shh," Davin hushed him. "Don't be throwin' around names. You never know who's listenin'."

Kaile swallowed, leaning back with his arms folded.

"And the answer is no," Davin said. "He knows what I look like, though, and he's sure to know that there's four of us. So we wait."

There were others in the tavern. A broad-shouldered, aged man behind the bar, the old woman moving from table to table like a moth from flame to flame. There were perhaps twenty others—some playing cards, a couple snoring with their heads on tables or the bar top, and others laughing with women of the night at the other hearth.

"After we eat, we'll get some rooms and wash up," Davin said. "Then we'll come back down and try again. I'm sure the place fills as night. Weird thing how alcohol makes ya feel like you're impervious to things like disease."

"Weird thing. That's for sure." Seph looked wearily around the tavern, especially at those attempting to muffle their coughs behind napkins.

The food came, and they lapped it up as if they hadn't eaten in weeks. Even Soren, after the meal, and the soup's contents warming his entire body from ears to toes, relaxed. His eyelids drooped, feeling weighted, and he let out a mighty yawn.

Davin asked the elderly woman for information on rooms, who helped book two upstairs. Davin gave her payment, adding a couple of bottles of wine to their order, and the four made their way up. The woman showed them the rooms, but Davin insisted they needed two side by side, which these were not.

She took them further down the hall, after telling them they weren't as nice, but Davin waved it away. All they needed was for the spell to continue working through the wall.

"Bathhouse is downstairs at the back," she said, before bowing and leaving them.

"Well, let's get to it," Soren said.

They dropped their things, locked the doors and went to bathe.

Immediately upon entering the bathhouse, warm steam escaped the room, falling onto their faces like the most welcoming clean, warm sheets. They walked in, disappearing into the steam. An hour later they left the bathhouse, feeling absolutely refreshed and like new. They had to walk past the bar area in the tavern, returning the sense of where they were to them. This was an unwelcoming, miserable place. The weary, mean glares of the wet patrons told them as much. They went to their rooms, tucking in for a long midday nap.

Soren and Seph closed their door behind them, leaving Davin and Kaile to share the other room. Soren closed the heavy curtains, casting a dark shadow into the room. A thin sliver of grayish light peaked through, cutting the room in half. Soren on one side, Seph on the other.

They both tucked in, and Soren let out a loud yawn. He placed Firelight on the table beside him, and Seph had her staff and a tuning fork on hers. He rustled in his sheets, lavishing in the feeling of the clean, soft sheets on his bare arms and chest.

"Soren," Seph spoke while on her side, facing the wall.

"Yes?"

She yawned too, in a much higher pitch. "Being here, in this place. I don't get a good feeling about it."

"Neither do I," he replied. "But we won't be here much longer."

"You don't think so?"

"This is what I do," he said, staring up at the ceiling, watching the specks of dust pass through the beam of gray light. "The only thing that makes him different is the Ellydian, and we've got Kaile, and you. I'll deal with the rest."

She didn't respond, tucking the covers tighter around her.

"What's wrong?" Soren asked, turning his head to look at her.

She flipped over to look back at him.

"What if something goes wrong? What if he's expecting us? What if it's a trap?"

"I don't think it's a trap," Soren said. "Guys like him think they're invincible, because they do everything to appease the king. They think they are near gods themselves."

"Well, you injured him, and the king," she said.

"Yes, I did." *And it felt damn good.*

"I can't help shake this feeling that something is going to go wrong," she said, looking straight into his eyes. She didn't look like his Persephone from the spell, but she was in there. He could feel it.

"Trust your gut," he said. "And don't let anyone tell you otherwise."

She feigned a smile and then turned onto her back. "You ever think about death? What is it like? What it is?"

He didn't reply, but he knew the answer. *All the time.*

"I used to think it was going to be like they told us in the orphanage. I thought we all go, the good ones at least, to the Halls of Everice. That's where I'd see my family again." The cat rose from its rest, stretched its legs, and tail out, meowed and lay on her chest.

"Your mother and father would be very proud of you, Seph. I hope you know that."

"Cirella would be proud of you, too," Seph said. The name jarred Soren. To hear her name aloud shuddered him to the core. She was his baby, the one he wanted to take care of, the one he wanted to grow old with. And now he sometimes had trouble remembering her face. His lip quivered, but he bit it.

"You all right, Uncle Soren?"

"Yes. Get some rest, child. Don't think about things like this before sleep. Think of the good things."

"Think of the good things, huh?" The cat purred loudly as it nestled in upon her chest. "I can count those on one hand, probably."

"Which are?"

"Well… you, Kaile, and Davin."

"That counts as one," he said playfully.

"This cat."

"Who still needs a name, mind you?"

"To be out of Mormand and Guillead finally."

"Two more," Soren said.

"My magic, and my music," she said.

"Those are sort of connected," Soren said, again in a playful tone. "One more then. Give us a good one."

Seph thought long and hard, and as the words left her lips, Soren let out a great grin, as he hoped those might be the ones she came up with.

"A shot at revenge. Real… fucking… revenge…"

He'd never been so proud for her to be at his side on this journey. "That a girl…"

Chapter Twenty-Five

They didn't have to wait long.

Soren and the others had only been sitting ten minutes in the bustling bar before a round of drinks was sent their way without them knowing. He even tried to send them back, thinking they were sent to the wrong table. But a point by the busy server to the far end of the room, and a nod from a bearded man over there, said otherwise.

Twilight was just sinking in through the windows to the tavern, and the fires were stoked. Voices bounced off the walls and filled the room with a rumbling, constant chatter. Soren was surprised they'd even found a table, and it just so happened to be the one they sat at hours earlier, in their *rougher* condition.

Davin was the first to drink from the round that came their way. He even had a sort of satisfaction on his face—or rather —her face. Soren pushed the drink away as the bearded man with thinning blond and gray hair squeezed his way through the crowd. Seph pushed her drink gently away too, and then Kaile followed suit.

Davin pulled a chair from a side table, from someone

who'd left the seat only moments earlier. He put it between him and Kaile, who scooted over to make room.

"May I join?" the bearded man said, setting his mug down on the table, and already taking his coat off.

"Please." Davin waved a hand for the man toward the chair.

Seph sat back with her arms folded, leaning back, with her shirt slightly hovering over her mouth. Coughs filled the room, but this was where they were told to meet, and supposedly this man would give them the information they needed. So Soren would put up with it for as long as needed, but no more than that. A bottle or two in the room would be far more welcome than any risk before they would be able to make their move.

Something suddenly caught Soren's eye in the room's far corner as the bearded man sat. In the room filled with unfamiliar, mostly jovial faces, he thought he saw a familiar one. It was just a flash, an inkling, but in an instant it was gone.

I'm losing my mind. I need to get more sleep. I've been here before. Of course, I might recognize someone from back then. Focus on what's important.

Ever since they'd washed and readied up, Seph had slept like a softly snoring angel, and Soren lay with his eyes closed on the soft bed, with the constant trudging of awful thoughts and memories through his head.

"Remind me of your names," the bearded man groaned as he sat. His shirt was thin and showed his lean arms and sunken chest. Before he removed his long coat, Soren thought he was a much larger man, mostly because of the bushy beard and his tall stature.

Davin went around, naming everyone in the circle. "Bonnie, Pricilla, Vic, Alfred, and…"

"Einrick," the man said, taking a deep drink of the ale and then wiping the foam from his mustache.

Soren felt a sense of relief at the man's name, but still kept his guard up, and drank his own drink.

Davin finished his quickly, shrugged and took Soren's from before him. Appearing fine, Seph and Kaile both took theirs and sipped.

"We should find somewhere more private," Soren said in a gruff voice.

"This is fine," Einrick said. "No one cares here. I've been in this tavern for a full week now. Trust me when I say they're all far more concerned with getting through the next week and bombarding their livers, than in any fresh faces coming in for a break from the weather."

Soren clenched his jaw, but the conversation quickly moved on. The tavern was so loud and brimming with noise, Soren could barely hear Einrick at the other end of the table, feet away.

"Just don't be using names too loud," Einrick said, finally leaning in and putting his elbows on the table. Each of them did the same. Soren raised his arm and waved for another drink. Before they talked, the woman came over and Soren ordered a bottle of red wine, a pitcher of ale for refills, and a glass of whiskey for himself.

While they waited, Einrick seemed most interested in Seph, eyeing her, not directly, but his gaze kept trailing back to her. Soren couldn't tell if it was because she was a young woman, or if the stranger knew more about her than he should.

Soren had to remind himself that Einrick was a spy, and that trading in information was not only a sought-after trade, but a dangerous one—for everyone involved.

As he spoke, Einrick's breath stunk heavily of harsh alcohol from deep in his gut. "You got here in good time. I trust you found no obstacles on your path?"

No one answered, or didn't seem to know how to the stranger.

"The lady wants to know. Did you find the piece she requested from the thief?"

"Ravelle was dead." Soren had an irritated tinge in his voice. "Trolls got to her first."

"Dead, eh?" Einrick asked with an upturned eyebrow, using his fingernail to fish out something stuck in his yellow teeth. "The lady might be happy to hear that. The bitch snuck into her house and stole it."

Soren's fist tightened under the table at the way he spoke about Ravelle.

"No matter, so trolls, then. Did ya get it? Do ya have it?"

Davin said, "Aye, we got it. With no shortage of luck, and the fortune of having these two along with us."

"I see," Einrick said, taking a deep gulp, leaning back in his chair, looking around, and then putting his elbows back on the table, hunched. "You're to use that relic, Soren."

"Don't use his name." Seph's lips drew taught together.

"Sure, fine," Einrick said. "Like I said, no one can hear us in this mess, and no one gives two shits about who ya are."

"A reward is a reward," Davin said. "And most of these people think the king was just in burning that town full of people. No one would think any different."

"You're wrong in that," Einrick held a dirt-smudged finger toward him. "There's a stirring. Whispers in the night. Even those who once believed burning those towns was right, are starting to be turned on their heads. It's gettin' to be too much. They're getting more frightened of that bastard than of the plague. I hear it. I've seen it. And you can bet your ass of one thing—the king ain't gonna like it when he figures it out."

"Good," Seph sneered through clenched teeth.

"Any word on where everyone from the burning is?" Davin asked.

A glimmer of candlelight reflected in Einrick's eyes.

There's the spy. Hiding behind this scrawny, drunken fool.

"Well, the man you want is here," Einrick said in a low voice. "Arrived the day before yesterday."

"Anyone with him?" Soren asked quickly.

"The lord Garland Messemire is here with him."

"Garland?" Soren spat. "What's that needled prick doing here?"

"I don't know," Einrick said, gulping another sloppy drink.

"Before we get on with them," Kaile suddenly interrupted. "What about the others from the attack? Do you know where they are? Where they went off to?"

"Aye, most of the dogs followed their master back to the capital."

"Most?" Kaile prodded. "Who?"

Einrick raised an eyebrow at the boy, glaring at Kaile with a renewed sense of curiosity. "You're him, aren't ya? The apprentice?" Kaile didn't respond but didn't shy his gaze away either. "Don't blame ya for wanting to know. You may be the third most wanted man in all of Aladran now, because of what you did."

"Third?" Soren asked, but suddenly realized whom the other was. "The old archmage, yes…"

Einrick put his drink down and pulled them in close with a wave of his curved index finger. They all drew in close on the table, and Einrick's breath fumed with a putrid stench. "They're on their way back to Lynthyn—the king, the archpriest, that awful Knight Wolf, his bitch sorceress, Sophia the Synth, the drakoons and all their army."

Seph could tell Kaile didn't want to specifically say his name, to show his true question, so she did it for him. "What about Alcarond? You didn't say his name."

"I don't know where the archmage is," Einrick said. "And if the lady doesn't know, then he may as well be out on the open sea, traveling to Eldra for all we know."

Kaile pulled at his collar, as if it were tightening on its own, and he began to sweat.

"Can't say I blame ya, being afraid of that one," Einrick said. "They're all rotten scoundrels, but that man wields enough power to uproot a mountain I've heard."

"I don't think that's the case," Soren said. "But he could damn well uproot a tree. A very big tree."

"Let's just hope he's not here," Davin said. "Now, what about the ones here? What can you tell us?"

"They're difficult to get close to, so I don't know much about what they're doing here. I know they met with Lord Garriss yesterday. Mutterings were that they informed the lord about Erhil, and word from the king that the fight against the Silver Sparrows was intensifying."

"Glasse and Garland both met with the lord?" Soren asked. "What's Garland got to do with any of this? Why didn't that rat scurry back to his nest in Faulker?"

"Maybe you put the fear of the goddess in him?" Einrick asked. "Ever think about that? You see the look in your friend's eyes when I mention the loose archmage out there? Well, the reverse can be true about you. They all know you're going to war against them for what they've done, and they know Mihelik got you. They know about her, here, and they might not say it out loud, but they might be afraid of *you*..."

Seph, Kaile, and Davin all looked at Soren with a newfound sort of respect, or perhaps a sense of gratitude—that he was at their side, and he may lead them to an impossible victory.

"Where is Glasse now?" Soren asked, pushing aside the compliment.

"He's locked up in Grandview Tower," Einrick said, finishing the rest of his drink. Davin refilled his mug to the top. "Ain't no getting him up there. Even with the relic. Too dangerous, even for you."

"Don't be too sure about that," Soren said, with a hint of a curl at the side of his mouth.

"Well," Davin cleared his throat. "I hope you have something you've been working on, then."

Einrick leaned in. "I believe I know where he'll be, tomorrow."

"How sure are you?" Soren asked.

"Mostly."

"Mostly?" Soren pressed.

"Yes, mostly."

"Where?" Soren asked.

"Usually this is the part where I tell ya how much it'll cost ya," Einrick said with a twinkle in his eyes and a crooked smile.

"But this ain't that kind of conversation," Davin growled back. "I'm sure the lady is taking care of ya in that realm. Isn't she?"

"Aye, she is," Einrick smiled widely. "Edward Glasse has a sort of fascination with a young man here."

"Fascination?" Seph asked, scratching her cheek.

"He gets his needs met," Einrick said. "But he goes to the young man for some reason, and doesn't send for him. He went once already, but word has it he goes every other day while in the city. It's just as twilight hits, and right as the booze takes hold."

"Sounds solid to me," Davin said. "If your sources are right."

"My information is rock solid," he said with a droplet of spit flinging from his dry lips. "People are much more predictable than we like to think, especially when eager cocks are involved."

"Where?" Soren asked, ignoring the man's crass words in front of Seph.

"Down in the Broadmoor," he said. "He enters through the front door, still heavily guarded. His arm's in a sling, so he's got double what he normally does. That going to be a problem?"

"No," Soren said, with his fist balled on the table. "Not at all."

"Forty-nine Broadmoor. Stone building with a cluttered outside and green curtains on the inside. It's got a copper door latch."

"Forty-nine Broadmoor, at twilight," Soren said in a low growl. "He'll be coming from the capital?"

"Aye," Einrick said. "From the north."

"Anything else?" Davin asked. "Anything else we need to know?"

"Use the relic, Soren," he said. "And then once your mission is done, you'll take it back to the lady."

"How?" Soren asked. "What is the plan for getting out of the city?"

"There are two," Einrick said, scratching his chest and glancing around the bustling room before he leaned in.

"By sea, outside of the Salt Maid's Pub. There will be a ship waiting. It's covered and has two good men aboard. It's not big, but that's the point. The other… is under."

Seph swallowed hard. Soren noticed. He didn't have a problem with getting dirty in the dark if that meant he'd escape to safety, but Seph didn't seem to care for the second option. Kaile also shifted uneasily in her seat.

"Are we going into the Under Realm?" she asked, biting her nail.

"Not really," Einrick said. "Most is just below the surface in man-made tunnels."

"How will we know where to go?" Soren asked.

"I have an acquaintance who will help us find the way. You find your way underground and I'll find ya. There's an exit to the east. I'd highly suggest changing your appearance again once you're out in the sunlight. If and when he's dead, there's not gonna be much of a mystery about who did it. And the wrath upon the Sparrows will be tenfold." He waved his hands, breaking their hushed conversation at the table's center. "But that's neither here nor there. It's not for me to decide to talk you in or out of anything. You do what needs to be done, and I'll arrange the rest. Thanks for the drinks."

He poured a fresh top-off for himself, turned to walk away with a nod, but then spun back and grabbed the still half-full pitcher of ale to take off with him.

"Charming," Kaile said under his breath.

"Doesn't have to be charming, lad," Davin said in a stern voice. "He just has to be *not* wrong."

Chapter Twenty-Six

There was no reason to wait.
They made their way down to the Broadmoor immediately after their meeting with Einrick. Soren wasn't entirely sure how the others felt about the upcoming attack upon the Synth and his entourage, but he was sure as shit ready to kill. He'd get revenge for Glasse's part of the burning of Erhil, and he was only the first step in his ultimate revenge—to killing the king himself.

With the darkness of night fully enveloping the city, and the smoldering of torches scattered throughout, Soren felt right at home. The four of them stood beside a hanging torch on the corner, just houses down from forty-nine Broadmoor. The torch's flames rustled in the cool winter winds. A man lay next to them, crumpled over like a sack of flour. He snored soundly, and Seph bit her lip nervously.

They each scanned the area, looking down all four directions. Up north, the road led straight to the capital's three towers, including where Glasse stayed, Grandview Tower.

"This is good," Soren said. "This is real good."

"Why do you say that?" Davin asked. "We're completely

out in the open. You may be bloodthirsty enough to want to attack a whole platoon of soldiers in the middle of the road, but I could think of many preferred locations to attack a Synth."

"It's better than at the top of a tower," Seph added, nudging the man at her feet to make sure he was still alive.

"I'm going to go up there," Soren said, motioning to the rooftops above. They were mostly single story with a few two stories. The building that housed the man Glasse visited was one of the latter.

"We should all stick together…" Davin said, but Soren was already on the roof behind them. "Wow, he's fast."

Soren glided from rooftop to rooftop, scanning every doorway, window, every hole in a side wall. He wanted to know exactly where every in and out of the vicinity was. The shadows drew his attention the most, though.

Where were they darkest? Where did the light least shine? What paths did the shadows create? Where could Soren become invisible? That was the path to true power. The shadow was his ally. He'd trained there, thrived there. With the Twilight Veil, he truly would become invisible, and would become the most feared killer in all of Aladran—once again.

Already wearing the immaculate bracelet of the relic, he marveled at its construction. The way the floral patterns wove around the three-inch wide metal band was masterfully done. The blue desert gemstones sparkled in the dim, distant torchlight. He took the ring from his pocket, honestly to him, looking like no more than a normal gold ring, except for the same three blue gems on its underside. He slid it onto his ring finger.

He'd tried it on once while out in the wilderness, on the way to the city, but here, in the deep, dark depths of the nightly shadows, the world snapped to a clear, hunter-like focus. The edges of the surrounding walls tightened. The air grew crisper, and he could feel the sounds around him. Beneath him, in the building under his boots, he could feel a man snoring, with a dog beside him doing the same. The still-unnamed feline companion of Seph was on the far side of the roof, following him and licking her paw.

Gazing down the road, distant objects became alive. A woman walking across the road with a child, with no torchlight around, was as clear as if they were walking under the midday sun. He scratched his temple, though. It wasn't as if they were illuminated under a fake sun. No, it was as if he could see them in the shadows.

If only Landran, my master, could see me now. With the Twilight Veil and Firelight. I may have a chance at retribution with these two. With my new allies, and these new weapons, I may have an actual shot at revenge! If only he was alive to see it…

He jumped from roof to roof, gliding in and out of the shadows. Each time when in a new one, the clear focus of the Twilight Veil erupted in his mind and eyes. Making a complete circle of the area, crossing each of the four intersecting roads, he made his way back to the others. He leaped down from a rooftop to land, without muffling his landing, beside them.

Soren was no more than three feet beside Kaile, who stood glaring out at their surroundings. They were deep in a conversation about positions, corners to be aware of, and their exit strategy after the battle. Soren was impressed with Davin's acumen, devising his plan. It seemed sound, and Soren appreciated certain things he pointed out to the inexperienced Seph and Kaile.

Little did Seph know Soren would put her as far away from danger as possible. She'd only have to fight should the absolute need arise. He'd rather give her the relic to use in a distant shadow than put her life at risk.

But…

He also was getting to know her more and more. And he had to remind himself—*this isn't just my revenge. It's hers too.*

As they walked, Soren fell from shadow to shadow. Clicking Firelight upon the stone walls, stomping his boot into puddles, and even whistling. But nothing... they didn't hear a thing.

Again, Soren was astounded by the craftsmanship that existed in their world. The Sundar creating such an incredible artifact, and the masters of Vellice designing the infinitely sharp dagger. He'd always assumed, and been told, the Ellydian was the modern marvel of the world. But he was beginning to see the magnificence and splendor possible.

Soren stepped out of the shadows. Kaile's breath caught as he fell back in surprise, but Soren was delighted to hear the ring of a C note at his side. Normally, that would send Soren into a mad rush to survive. But this time, it pleased him to know the boy would be ready. He'd need to from now on. Einrick's words about him being one of the most hunted men in all of Aladran weren't an exaggeration.

"Good," Soren said, pointing down to the small fork ringing at Kaile's side. "Very good. What spell would you have ready?"

"Goddess, Soren," Seph said, catching her breath. "You scared the nine hells outta us. Easy with that thing!"

"Just making sure it works," Soren said with a grin.

"Of course it works," Davin said gruffly. "Now, can we get back to it?"

Soren nodded.

"He'll be coming down from the north," Davin said as a stiff wind rushed down the road, causing Soren to hold his hood to his head. "Kaile will attack from the rooftop over there." He pointed to the roof across the road from the house where Glasse would enter. "A bright plume of magic to not only distract, but terrify. I go in, no disguise, with my ax, chopping them down from over there. Glasse is the tricky one, obviously. As soon as he hears the attack, he is immediately our biggest threat. So, Seph will be over there." He pointed to the roof right next to the house. "And she'll cast another spell to draw his attention. It'll give us the moment we need, while he's confused at the two sources of magic, that you rush in and get him. Cut him down as quickly and ruthlessly as you can. Once the head of the snake is gone, the rest is throwing the writhing body into the refuse pile. Sound good?"

It did sound good. Similar to what Soren thought as well. Create the distraction, attack from multiple angles, overwhelm and kill Glasse as quickly as possible.

"Seph will be over there." Soren pointed to a roof six houses down, on the opposite side, as Davin said. "She'll be our backup plan, in case something goes awry. Kaile will be sufficient a distraction. Something bright and loud would do. Some sort of fire spell, or lightning, even if you are able. That will give me all I need. I'm going to be close, very close, when the time comes."

"Soren," Seph growled. "Don't push me out of this. I'm here to fight, too."

"I know," Soren said. "You're still in this. We're all part of the team. But don't let your emotions get in the way of the mission. You are integral. If shit goes south, you're going to be the one to help us get out of here. This isn't a one-way mission. We are all going to get out of here once he's dead, and we are going to make it back to Skylark. We need to be smart, methodical, and fucking precise to make this as efficient as possible. And then we get the hell out of here."

"Agreed," Davin said quickly, folding his arms, seemingly waiting for Seph's rebuttal.

Her face twisted in anger. She scrunched her nose and furrowed her brow.

"I think they're right," Kaile said. "You're also the least

experienced, so it's wise to keep you back. In case we need your help, if something creeps up."

Seph's face flushed with rage. Her hands even began to shake. She balled her fists and took an enormous, shaky breath.

"Fine. But you're not going to all do this to me every time. You may look like a woman, Davin, but you're all a bunch of dumb men who don't know what you need until it's gone. I'm tougher than you all think, and I'll prove it to you someday."

"I know," Soren said in a softer tone. "It takes time. You're going to be a great Syncron someday. We just need you to live long enough to get there."

"We good here?" Davin asked. "Any final thoughts while we're here?"

They began to walk back toward the Hunter's Moon.

"Edward Glasse." Kaile waved for them to stop. "I've heard of him over the years in the capital. He's no mere Dor. Every one of us should be quite clear on that. He may not be an Aeol like us, but just because he can't use his Ellydian inward, on his own body, doesn't mean he's not a notoriously powerful Synth."

"Go on," Soren said.

"I've known of the powerful, well *Syncron* to me in the past because I thought he was on the good side, wizard in Londindam for years. He specialized in spells that manipulated the air around him. He'd do favors for King Amón in exchange for the knowledge of such spells. And just to be very clear, he knows many spells. Many destructive spells. So just because he focused on air, don't think he's going to be an easy fight. He could suck the wind from your lungs or expand it in a second. He may not be able to turn invisible like you Seph, or turn his body to fire, but if he can cast a note, then we are all in terrible danger."

"Aye," Davin agreed. "Well said, lad. Couldn't have said it better myself."

"I'll be there, right in close." Soren held his hand out, twirling the Twilight Veil ring in his fingers. "Once you cause the distraction, I'll send Firelight through his heart. He deserves as much for the people of Erhil. I felt his attack that night. He attacked Bael, Alicen, and I in the tavern there. I felt the force of his magic, and no, I won't forget his power. He and Garland attacked us that night before the burning, making way for that devil William Wolf to come and kill Bael." Soren's teeth gritted and his stomach twisted.

Seph laid her hand on his shoulder. "We'll get him too. We'll get all of them. This one first, though. Glasse, then the others. We'll make them all pay."

Soren's mouth tightened, and he dropped his chin to his chest.

"For Bael."

Chapter Twenty-Seven

❦

In the upstairs room of the Hunter's Moon, the four of them sat around the room. The thick curtains were down, and Davin's spell of disguise was gone. Seph sat up on her bed, Kaile beside her, Davin in the chair in the room's corner, and Soren sat on the floor with his back to the wall, an open bottle of wine between his legs. The floorboards nearly shook from the commotion below, but warm air seeped up between the floorboards, which they were all grateful for.

The room flickered in the light of the four candles on the round table by Davin. Each of them was deep in thought, and the cat purred in deep sleep beside Seph. She stared with glassy eyes at the thick, burgundy curtain as she stroked the cat's back.

Kaile scratched his thigh and then clapped both hands to his forehead, rubbing it hard.

Soren noticed but went back to glaring at the open bottle. He knew how Kaile felt. He'd been there many times.

The night before a fight was always the hardest at first. He knew Kaile wouldn't sleep more than a couple of hours, if he was lucky. There were always so many scenarios running through your mind.

What if this happens? I'll need to react this way. What if I get hurt? What if she gets killed? It's enough to make a man go insane.

They'd be outnumbered, but not overpowered. Soren had seen what Kaile could cast when he needed to, and that should be enough, at least for what he needed from him. Glasse was only human, after all. Cut an artery and he'd bleed out and die.

Deep down, Soren, though, was extremely relieved that he knew the Knight Wolf was far, far away. As much as Soren feared the potential for magic in a fight, he was as helpless as a naked baby in a sea storm when it came to the spell the Wolf and his Synth bitch, Zertaan, had over him. Not to mention, the more Soren discovered about the amazing craftsmanship and power of the Vellice blade he carried, he was also reminded the Knight Wolf carried the Ember Edge, a sword from Vellice, and possibly the most legendary sword in existence. The only other Vellice blade Soren knew of absolutely, was the king's sword, Storm Dragon.

Davin sat with his head back, staring up at the ceiling, a pipe hanging out of his hand on the table, smoldering. Soren was glad to see his true form again, the grumpy dwarf, who he still butted heads with. His other form was prettier to look at, but in the coming fight, the stout, broad-shouldered fighter would be more than welcome.

He'll have to fight viciously through the ranks of soldiers until Glasse is dead. He's going to be outnumbered twenty to one until I'm free to help. Soren smirked. He loved those odds.

Most times, anymore, Soren tried his best not to kill, unless absolutely necessary, or the job required it. But here, in the dank, rotten, corrupt city of Grayhaven, where children roamed the frozen streets by the thousands—a little slaughter might cause the rotten lord to wake up. Soren assumed it wouldn't, but a thorn in that bastard's side would be a pleasure to sting in deep.

Soren took another deep drink.

"Don't get drunk tonight," Seph said, not tearing her gaze away from the curtains.

Soren gulped it down. "Excuse me?"

"You heard me," she said. "You need to be on your game tomorrow. Not delirious and angry like normal."

Soren sat forward. "Excuse me?"

"You need to sleep. We all do," she said.

He sat back, laughed, and took another drink. "You don't know what you're talking about."

"I know more than you think I do."

"Oh, yeah?" He glared up at the ceiling, as Davin and Kaile watched them.

"Yeah." She snapped her gaze at him.

"What do you know?"

"I know I care about you, and I don't want to die tomorrow," she said.

Soren sighed, pushing past his rough guard at the sight of her tears. "No one's going to die tomorrow. I promise. You just stay where I told you and we'll all stick to the plan, and we'll be fine."

"How do you know that?" Seph asked. "You can't. You act like you have all the answers all the time. But what if something happens? What if Glasse gets a spell off at you, or Davin, or Kaile?"

Davin and Kaile kept silent, deep in thought. Kaile hunched over his elbows on his thighs, scratching his hair.

"Listen, Persephone, I've done this many times. I can see it all playing out in my head already. I've seen it. I've been here. But you, for your first time, it's natural to be nervous... scared. But this is just a stopover in the longer journey. In two days, we'll be out of this goddess-forsaken city and back where we belong… far away."

She wiped her tears away with her sleeves—exhausted, but it always impressed Soren how Seph had the ability to push past pain and hurt. It's as if the pain was embedded so deeply inside of her it was muscle memory to push past it. She took a sip of hot tea from the table beside her.

Kaile cleared his throat. "What are you going to do if Garland is there?"

Soren glared down into his drink, letting it spin back and forth between his hands, watching it swish around the glass. It seemed like ages ago he brought Garland out of Faulker to bring him to justice in Erhil. That seemed to be the moment that began his entire cycle of pain all over again. Garland was more than a bastard, arrogant, creep of a lord—he embodied something worse to Soren. He reminded him of the rotten allegiance to a king that would burn an entire town of helpless mothers, babies, and frail elderly.

"I saw his face when the king burned Erhil," Kaile stroked his chin. "Garland, as much of a scoundrel as he is—he was horrified—like I was."

"What's that got to do with anything?" Davin asked in a gruff tone. "Not everyone who sends an innocent person to the gallows is the man heaving the final ax."

"True," Kaile said. "But there's still good in people. He may not have known what they were going to do to Erhil once they got there."

"Why are you standing up for him?" Seph asked in a curious tone. "Lord Messemire was brought back to Erhil by Soren for having a forceful relationship with a thirteen-year-old girl."

"I'm not defending him," Kaile said. "At least for that. But you can't blame every lord and lady for what King Amón did."

Soren scowled, remembering the Knight Wolf sending a

bolt through his friend, while Soren was helpless to stop it. "He helped kill my friend. He and Glasse attacked us while the Wolf came in and killed Bael."

"Garland may deserve to die," Kaile said with his hands up. "I don't know, but did he pull the trigger to kill your friend? He may be rotten to the core, a sexual deviant, and up to his eyeballs in greed, but does that warrant death?"

"Yes," Davin said immediately.

"Listen," Kaile said, leaning again on his thighs, motioning with his waving hands before him. "I know a lot of people in Celestra. They're not all bad. In fact, some of the people I love most in this world live there. They're genuine, good, loving people. I need to know that we're not out to destroy everything, just because of a few evil people. There's a whole world out there of people who don't know what's really going on. We can't just destroy for revenge, just to destroy in the sake of revenge. We need to understand the balance of good and evil —or else we may become what we are out to destroy."

Soren was taken aback by the impassioned speech by the boy. He didn't expect such an eloquent reminder of the balance and fragile existence of the difference between good and evil. Soren knew history was written by the victors, so that would play a big part in such actions, but still.

"Syncrons and Synths, for example," Kaile said. "No one alive considers themself a Synth. No one believes they are evil. Everyone has their own *right*, and the more passionate, perhaps the more blind."

"Glasse is evil," Seph said, somewhat taking Kaile off guard, with his mouth left agape, as she interrupted him.

"Agreed," Davin said, puffing on his pipe.

"This is war," she added. "We are on one side, and they are on the other. Glasse wouldn't hesitate to kill any of us, or Lady Drake, or especially Mihelik. You'd do well to remember there is gray in this world, and then there are your enemies. And in this game we're playing—it's kill or be killed. And like I said, I don't want to die tomorrow, so take it easy on the fucking wine, Uncle! Okay?"

Soren put the bottle aside, raising his arms, giving up at her insistence. "Better?"

She didn't reply, and Kaile seemed complacent enough to have voiced his opinions. Soren wasn't exactly sure what he was arguing for. It seemed he was trying to have Soren spare Garland's life—should he be there tomorrow. The thought was brief in his mind, but to be honest with himself—he wasn't entirely sure what he'd do if he saw him.

Garland and Glasse led the attack on Erhil, attacking them in the tavern that led to the Wolf killing Bael in cold blood. But that was also the Wolf—as ruthless and bloodthirsty as any other predator that stalked the lands—as deadly as the Shades and as terrifying as the Black Fog.

Sure, Garland had abused that young girl in Erhil, and Soren was charged to bring him back for justice. But he was released. He paid the girl's family, and they let him go. The law said he had nothing left to pay for, so Soren was left with the decision—kill a man who had a part to play in his friend's murder—which he assumed he would, or, spare his life.

He was much more concerned with killing Glasse, that much was certain.

Hours later, after Davin and Kaile had said their farewells to return to their room, Soren slept soundly, dreaming of nothing—an absolutely beautiful, soothing, blankness.

Then something bit him. It sunk its claws in deep. The pain in his foot caused him to sit up instantly. His abdomen muscles tensed as he grabbed his dagger and held it up high, ready to kill whatever had attacked him in his sleep.

At his feet, the black cat stood on its hind legs, claws extended, pawing at his feet, which lay bare, sticking out from under the covers.

The urge in him was to put the dagger down and pick the cat up by the scruff of the neck and set it outside the door. But the cat ran like a maniac to the door and back, clawing at something Soren couldn't see. He instead threw the blanket over his feet and cursed the cat for interrupting such a welcome sleep.

He sighed, put the dagger away, and looked over to see Seph, wide awake, lying back in bed, staring up at the ceiling. The spell of disguise was enacted, so it didn't look like her, but it felt like her.

"What's wrong?" he asked.

"Can't sleep. Too much to think about."

He rolled onto his side. "Want to talk about it?"

"Go back to sleep," she whispered. "I don't see you sleep like that much, if ever."

"Hmph," he said, rolling onto his back. Fatigue was heavily in him, and his limbs felt weighted against the soft mattress, but the stinging of the new holes in his feet kept him alert—in case another attack was forthcoming.

"What're you thinking about, this time of night?" he asked.

"Oh," she moaned. "Everything."

He nodded. "I know the feeling."

They both lay there for what felt like ten minutes of silence. Staring up into the dimly lit room.

"There's something I've been meaning to ask you, Seph."

"What?"

"In Guillead," he said. "When I heard you play that organ in that abandoned monastery. You were amazing. How do you play like that after all this time?"

"You thought I was good?"

"I thought you played wonderfully," he said, putting his hands on his chest and exhaling deeply at the thought of the notes, and the melodies. The wind blowing down from the bellows through the pipes, filling the room with a thunderous mélange of depth, feeling, and excitement. "I couldn't believe it was the same girl playing that I taught to play all of those years ago."

"That organ isn't much different than the one you taught me on in Tourmielle."

"You remember that?" Soren asked. "You were seven. I'm surprised."

"I don't remember everything about back then, but I still have bits and pieces. I remember a few times when I got through a piece with you, and saw the smile on your face. That meant a lot to me, I remember."

Soren grinned. "So, you just remember how to play from the things I taught you back then?"

"No. I practice."

"On that organ, in that monastery?"

"No, by myself, at night, during the day. I wrote the keys on a tapestry and practiced on that."

His brow furrowed. "You practiced… on a drawing?"

"Well, you didn't leave me with an organ."

"I—" he began, but then he stopped. He didn't know what to say. He was so overly impressed by the thought of his past pupil practicing on a drawing, with no pitch, no weight of the keys, no pedals, and no sound at all.

"Not bad, huh?" she asked, turning over onto her side. "I think, you know, being alone for all those years, I kind of had fantasies that everyone was still alive out there. My parents, you. And that someday I'd make them happy by how I turned out in such a shitty place. That one time I thought I saw you up on that rooftop gave me enough will to keep practicing."

"Well, you did well," Soren said. "I'm proud of you."

She grinned and turned back onto her back.

Saying those words out loud had an unexpected reaction in him. He was proud of her—for so many things, in so many ways. She was truly her parents' daughter. Her father's flair for curiosity and intuitiveness and creativity was alive in her, and her mother's stubbornness and charm, too. The words made him feel older, responsible for her life, and indeed proud they were together. He was getting to know the woman she was becoming. It made him remember how miserable and worthless he'd felt all those nights alone with Ursa. He didn't feel that way as much anymore. She made him feel like he had a purpose, like his mission was great again.

He turned to say something to her, but instead heard her yawn.

"Thanks, Uncle," she said. "Goodnight."

"Goodnight, child," he simply said instead. "Dream of brighter days ahead."

PART VI
THE SYNTH OF LONDINDAM

Chapter Twenty-Eight

❦

D*eceit.*

W*ROUGHT from the firmest of bindings. Ironclad and unbreakable—the rust is slow, rotting from the inside, until the stress builds too much for the welds.*

Trust snaps.
It breaks.
Unrepairable and irreversible.
The chain may be repaired, but the rust lingers. Always there, coloring the metal with a tarnished discoloration. Never fully fixed, never fully healed.
There are many forms of deceit, but in this world—be cautious with whom you trust your secrets. For those that break the bond of trust, are often the most rewarded.

. . .

Translated from the language of the Sundar. The Scriptures of the Ancients, Book II, Chapter X.

It was the day of the attack.

Everything was lined up.

Soren had waves of adrenaline bursting in his veins—pushing him past the shit for sleep he got. His mind was racing with the thirst for murder. He'd have his revenge against all the ones who wronged him. But it all started with one man, and today was the day Soren would end his miserable life.

The plan was sound, he knew. Now they just needed to execute, and he had faith in the others that they'd live up to their roles. Davin—brave and strong, as tough of a fighter as anyone Soren had fought alongside in ages. Kaile—talented, courageous when the time came, and had the god damned Ellydian, which was the one thing Soren couldn't get, no matter what. And Seph—the dearest thing to his heart. She was his only family, and would fight one of those silver bears in Myngorn Forest with her bare hands if it came to that.

Now… they just needed to wait for the sun to arc all the way across the sky, and fade into night.

The table they sat at was shaking. Kaile had his lanky elbows on the table as his coffee steamed into his face. His bobbing knees under the table transferred that same energy to the table, sloshing their drinks.

Davin glared at the far end of the bar. He, in his female form, pulled heavy drags from his pipe as he glared at the far corner of the tavern. Soren imagined his pale violet eyes and graying brown beard under there somewhere—the rougher, grittier—him.

Seph sat hunched onto her thighs, scooted away from the table. Her hair fell over her eyes, and she sat motionless as her tea steamed and swished on the table.

Soren glared at the shaking table, one leg tapping on the hardwood floor. He deliriously stared, stroking the stubble on his chin. A fog rolled thick in his mind. Normally, before an attack, he was focused, yet calm. He normally had no one else to worry about. If he died, he died. It had been a path of turmoil and self-loathing since all those years ago in Tourmielle. One thing was clear through the fog, though—a crystal clear vision of Cirella's face.

The blues of her eyes were the color of an afternoon sky over a snow-capped mountain, or the top layer of clear seawater on a warm day. Her flowing golden hair framed her tan face angelically. Cirella laughed in his vision. It was a moment from long ago, on one of their first dates. He'd made a joke about the matron forgetting their order at a tavern, bringing Cirella a full roast of lamb instead of the vegetables she ordered—perhaps thinking Cirella was too thin. He remembered the smile on her face, the whites of her perfect teeth, and the glow on her face.

Soren was in a trance, but he didn't want to let it go. He wanted nothing more than to be back with her, and he felt tears wet his eyes. Cirella's laugh faded with a wry, sexy smile and a wink. She leaned forward and grabbed his hands, stroking his finger. He didn't want it to go away. But just like the best moments of the last bits of dreams before you wake, her image began to fade. He focused hard with all his strength to keep her there. He wanted to keep that image forever.

There were too many nights alone where he couldn't summon that memory. He couldn't remember her hair that way, or her smile was too brief—too distant, too faded.

He was jolted back to reality, like waking from a dream with a damned cat's razor claws sunk into your damned feet!

The elderly woman was standing beside him, holding the table with her firm grasp. "I'd ask if you need a top-off, young man, but it seems you may have had enough."

"Huh?" Kaile muttered, leaning back from the table in his daze.

"You're shaking the whole damn place," Davin said, leaning on the back legs of his chair, blowing out a fresh plume of smoke at him.

The elderly woman gave an upturned eyebrow at the pretty woman, in her—not so womanly manner. But she smiled, shaking her head with a laugh. "You sure are an interesting lot. You traveling through? Where ya from, and where you headin'?"

Kaile opened his mouth to speak.

"Nowhere," Soren said, moving his fingers from his chin to scratch his nose, and then down to cross his arms.

The woman gave a humph and topped off his coffee before making her way back to the bar.

"Didn't have to be rude," Seph said. "She's just being polite."

"How do you know that?" Davin asked her, interrupting exactly what Soren was going to say.

"She seems nice," Seph replied, sitting back up with her hands scratching her thighs.

"Seems nice," Davin said, hitting the front legs of his chair back to the floor. He tapped the pipe into the ashtray. "Tomorrow, who do you think the soldiers are going to be rounding up? When we're long gone? You think they're just going to forget? That lord up there in that tower is gonna want answers, and where do you think he's gonna start lookin'?"

Soren watched as Davin hunched over the smoldering ashtray. If Davin got much more intense with Seph, then Soren would intervene. But he knew he was right. The city was going to be in a wild disarray the next day. The lord was going to want answers, and even more than that King Amón himself was going to want some.

"We're not here to be nice," Davin said. "Even to nice old

women. Who I might add, are probably the biggest gossips in this whole fuckin' wretched city."

"You're right," Seph said. "I'm sorry. I'm just really tired."

"Welcome to the fight," Davin said. "The only rest we're going to get after this, is when we get back to where we came. Until then, we will turn once again from the hunters… to the hunted."

∼

THE WINTER SEA air bit Soren's nostrils and wetted his eyes as the winds blew in from the sea. The four of them stood beside one another on the arching bridge that paralleled the southern beach below. Warmth from the sun heated the air just enough to make it feel fresh, and hint at a spring that felt far, far away.

Fishermen were pulling their nets in for the day, and the fronts of the taverns were filling with patrons, soaking up the last rays of sun. With fresh drinks in their hands, they were celebrating a day's hard work, and replenishing their spirits for another day.

Soren, Seph, Kaile, and Davin—however—still had their work ahead of them. And in only an hour's time, they'd have blood on their hands.

Soren's mind was washy like the waves below. Fatigue hit hard. Much harder than he'd allow himself to feel before a fight. He was prepared to not sleep, but this was a fight against a Synth, and one who helped kill his friend. Soren would allow himself a bit longer in his fogginess, but he trusted his instinct would kick in. And there was more at stake this time than just gold.

They stood there, watching the sea's waves as it may be their last time. Silent, deep in thought, and ready to get it on with. The wait had been the hardest part, especially for the younger two. They'd been nervous messes ever since they woke up. Even pressed, they hardly ate any food, and were scattered in their thoughts.

"What're you thinking about?" Soren asked, cutting the silence sharply.

Seph jolted, as a wagon was pulled under the high bridge by a set of gray horses. "Oh, nothing." She steadied her breath. "Just thinking about things. Things back in Guillead. I wonder if anything is different without me there, or if it's just going on like before. I wonder if they even noticed I was gone."

"I'm sure they did," Soren said.

"I'm pretty sure they counted their blessings and my bed was taken halfway through the night when I didn't return."

Soren laughed. "It's possible. What about you? What's going on in the wizard mind of yours?"

Kaile had a dark look on his face. He glowered out at the waves. His brow was tense, and an eyebrow shivered ever so slightly. His lips were pressed together tightly, and he scratched his cheek angrily.

Seph stood straight with a worried look.

"Everything all right?" she asked softly.

A tear dropped from Kaile's eye, which he wiped away quickly. Soren saw again the scars on the underside of his arm from the spell that had gone awry in the past. "Sorry. I just..."

"It's all right, boy," Davin said. "You can feel whatever ya need to."

"I—" Kaile gripped the bridge with his arms out wide and his head sunk. "I was just thinking about back home."

"Lynthyn?" Seph asked. "Or..."

"No. My home."

"Oh," she said. "What're you thinking about, back there? Your brother?"

Kaile nodded. He squeezed the handrails of the bridge, with the veins in the back of his hands bulging. "Yeah."

She put her hand on his back between the shoulder blades.

"Want to talk about it? Might help," she said. "We're like family here, now. You can tell us."

A tear dropped from the tip of his nose as he glared down. He wiped away the stream that led to the droplet.

"I just worry about him. I worry about him all the time. And I'm so far away. I can't do anything to help him. I'm supposed to be this powerful Syncron, but what use is that power if I can't do anything to help the one who needs me most?"

Soren felt for the boy. He knew that feeling all too well.

"What're you worried about?" Seph asked. "Isn't he there with your family? Your mother and father?"

Kaile leaned his head over slowly to look at Seph. Even in his disguise, Soren could see Kaile under there, in pain.

"That's what I'm worried about," Kaile said in a low tone. "You don't know them. You don't know what they're capable of."

"I'm sorry." She rubbed his back. "I didn't know."

"That's part of Alcarond's game with me. He uses that to keep me training. Always training. Always trying to get better. Do this spell better. Learn this other spell quicker than any other pupil did. He says I need to become something special if I want to save all the other kids, like my brother, out there."

"That's fucked up," Seph said. "He's using you, and telling you if you do what he wants, then he'll help you save… everyone?"

Kaile's head shot back down, spitting. "I know that's a lie. More propaganda from the capital, but it's the only way I can think to help Joseph. If I get strong enough, and get enough money, then maybe I can buy him from our parents. But now… that's all long gone now. My life is ruined, and he's stuck there… with them."

"What's wrong with them?" Davin asked. The female voice helped in that instance, Soren thought. "They hit? Yell?"

"Yes," Kaile said. "But it's more than that. They're mean. Mean like sin. The hatred in my father's eyes is like looking directly into the nine hells. Burn with brimstone, they do. My mother, so blinded that Shivara will bless her soul in the afterlife, that whatever misery she creates in this world is just an in between to the Halls of Everice. That woman knows no bounds in her scorn and wrath, and I left him all alone there with them."

"After all this is over, then we'll go get him," Soren said.

Seph and Davin gave astonished looks at him as he said that.

"Family is the only thing that really matters in this world." Soren's words held a palpable weight as Kaile looked up at him with wide, wet eyes.

"It's more than that," Kaile said. "They won't let me take him. He's theirs, they say. I was theirs, until they sold me to the king. They won't let me just take him."

"Listen to me, Kaile," Soren said, walking over to him, behind Seph. Kaile stood up and turned to face Soren. They both stood there, squared-shouldered and eye to eye. "You can do whatever the fuck you want in this world. You're a god damned Syncron Aeol. And we're not going to let those miserable bastards ruin the rest of your brother's life. Someday, we're going to go get him, and we'll take him wherever the wind calls home. If that's what needs to be done, then I'll help you do that much."

Kaile bit his quivering lip. "Thank you."

"Now," Soren said. "Ready to help me kill this murdering bastard?"

"Hell yes," Kaile responded.

Chapter Twenty-Nine

The shadows stung his skin. They enveloped him like death, and in a sense—he had become it. In the darkness, he found his home. He felt the way he felt best—dangerous. Soren was a predator. As deadly as the Black Fog itself, perhaps more so even. For he could excel where the Demons of Dusk lacked. He had a hateful intelligence. He could move with the night and the day. There wasn't a destination Soren couldn't track his prey to. And as he stood along the rooftops in the Grandview—stalking, waiting, hungry for blood—this time, his prey was coming to him.

Davin was down in the cold winter streets. He was tucked into a dark crevasse at the backside of where Glasse would arrive with his guards. Soren couldn't see him, but knew the dwarf was patiently waiting, also thirsty for blood. When the attack came, Soren knew he'd come out fighting as if the world was ending, for if they lost—it was the end.

Kaile was just across the road, opposite the front entrance to where the man Glasse was going to pleasure, or receive pleasure from, lived. He was upon a single-story roof, to cast his spells down upon the soldiers when the time came. High enough up, Davin could slaughter whoever tried to climb up to him, but low enough he could leap down if the need arose.

Soren could see Seph. Her silhouette messed with the dark rooftop a half-block down. Her dark hair trickled out from under her hood in the whistling winter winds. She was their trick up their sleeve, should they need it. A Syncron joining an attack like this—especially from the rebellion of the Silver Sparrows—would draw the attention of every corner of Aladran. But two Syncrons? This was going to start all-out war.

They were far enough that the spell of disguise didn't work.

Fuck it. It'll be better to scare the shit outta them anyway, letting them know who had come to end their miserable lives!

Soren blended into the shadows in a way he never had. The bracelet and ring of the Twilight Veil were on his wrist and hand, and the Vellice dagger was already in his hand. He thought about getting another weapon, a second dagger, but put all his confidence in Firelight instead. Under the moonlight, the silver blade glowed a fiery red. That red couldn't escape the shadows, but Soren could sure as hell see it, and he sneered at the thought of Glasse's blood replacing that red glow.

The sun had set moments ago, and with a clear view of the road that led north to the central towers, Soren should see them coming—any time now. Einrick's intel needed to be right, though. He said every other night at twilight he came down, and this would be that night. They were moments away from knowing if that was true or not.

And bless the goddess, Soren didn't have to wait long to find out.

Up at the top of the hill, they emerged.

A full escort worthy of a lord.

Torches in their hands, in arms with metal gauntlets and plate armor all the way up their shoulders and necks and down to their boots. Twelve of them, at least. All wrapped around their prize. From this distance, Soren couldn't wholly make out every detail, but then he caught a golden flicker off the spectacles of the man at the center of the entourage. He clasped Firelight so tight the leather squealed.

"Glasse," he growled.

It had been almost two weeks since the burning of Erhil, and the murder of his friends. That sent a hatred into Soren's stomach at the sight of the Synth, who had been beckoned by the king to aid in the burning. All those innocent lives were gone in the name of an outbreak of the Chimaera but was secretly a warning to the world. There was to be no opposition to the king. If you were a wielder of the Ellydian—you bowed fealty, or you died. There was no in-between.

As the Synth made his way down the hill, Soren saw there were other figures within the circle of soldiers, though he couldn't make them out in the dim light, and under their cloaks. But there was something oddly familiar about them: the way they walked, their body shapes under the concealing cloaks.

Soren thought one may be Garland. Soren had no fear of that man. His fingers were more accustomed to counting coins than holding a sword. But Kaile's speech lingered in his mind. Did Garland deserve to die? Soren didn't know, but anyone keeping Soren's prey from him was fair game. At this point in the war, revenge was all that mattered.

Many were going to die in this war, and better on their side than his.

Soren moved deeper into the shadows, never taking his eyes off his target. Glasse was moving closer with each step, and the twelve soldiers around were vigilant. Soren could tell they were well trained and aware that this was their moment to be alert, and die fighting, should the need arise. The two figures with Glasse still had their hoods up, and Soren still couldn't see who they were.

What if they're Synths? That would be disastrous. Too late now, though. This attack is happening, and if Kaile needs to distract three, then he's going to have to carry that weight. I'll kill all three in seconds. I just need the chance.

They were nearly there. The soldiers were about to round the corner toward the house in the Broadmoor. Once Glasse took the corner, that was the sign.

All hell was about to break loose.

Soren stayed at the tip of the shadow on the rooftop, overlooking the corner. One soldier even looked up directly at him, his eyes quickly glancing back away.

Glasse walked casually, yet with a quickened pace. His tan, bald head steamed slightly in the winter winds. His heart rate was elevated, and he sweat. His arm was in a sling—Soren's doing, but the other arm wielded a long staff of oaky brown, with striking plates of metal along the shaft. A red stone perched at its peak.

This is it. Wait for the signal.

Glasse took the corner, as the two in hoods did too.

Soren saw the faintest flash of light by Seph, upon the rooftops halfway down the road. The flicker became a solid dot of flame, as she cast it down onto the street. Soren waited. On the edge of the building, he waited for his moment. Firelight was hungry.

Edward Glasse paused, spoke something muffled to the other, and just in front of the house with the copper door handle, they both took down their hoods.

Garland, certainly. Soren knew that pale, plump face anywhere. But the other figure slacked his jaw. His mind raced and whirled. He couldn't believe what he saw as the woman pulled down her hood to reveal her sandy blond hair. Her back was to him, but she turned enough for Soren to see a sliver of her face. It was just enough.

Alicen.

His arms felt infinitely heavy and in a flash he thought of all the reasons she could be there with Glasse, and with Garland.

You're alive! How is that possible?

Glasse spoke with them and took a step onto the front stoop of the home. The soldiers spread out into a semi-circle, glaring out with their weapons sheathed, not speaking, and their stances wide.

Something is wrong. Something is very wrong. She shouldn't be here. She shouldn't be in Grayhaven. She was with me that night in the tavern when Bael died. She was with us when we first met the Silver Sparrows… she was…

He didn't want to say the word. All the trust he had in his instinct shattered in that instant, but then again, sex was a heavy swayer of judgement.

"…Alicen… was… *a spy?*"

We need to stop this attack. I need to talk to her. We can't…

But it was too late.

The digger bomb on the road below Seph exploded into a gigantic explosion. The ground shook, the air coursed with a shockwave shooting out from the fiery explosion, and every soul in the Grandview was surely alert.

The attack was on. There was no turning back now, and Soren's hatred doubled on Glasse. He couldn't think about Alicen. But he needed to protect her. He needed to know. He needed to know how she could betray the thousands of souls that died that day. He had to speak with her, so he'd now have to make sure she lived.

Glasse, Garland, and Alicen huddled up together with a pair of soldiers, as the other ten tightened their circle. They all drew their weapons as the road burned down the street. Seph lit another digger bomb from a vantage point only Soren could see.

Then Kaile emerged from the shadows. He gripped his

short staff in his hand, holding it up before him as the tune rang deeply from its core. His arms were spread, and his hood flew back from his head, letting his reddish hair show. His cloak whipped behind him in the winter winds. He looked as dangerous, yet as valiant as any Syncron Soren had ever seen.

As the C note filled the air, and Seph cast down another digger bomb onto the road, Kaile's arms and sleeves were cast in a brilliant orange glow. His free hand was illuminated in a fiery light, bright enough to mimic the sun, small enough to fit in the palm of his hand.

In a flash of movement, he cast the small ball of light down into the ring of shoulders. As it tumbled down, so did Soren. His boots left the ledge perched above, and he fell.

Glasse struck a tuning fork onto his staff quickly, as any well-trained wielder of the Ellydian would. An A note rang out from it, the simplest note to cast too, and a good one for quick, defensive spells.

The ball of light fell to the road at the soldier's feet and exploded on impact. From the small ball of brilliant white, an intense fire roared out from it. It blew the soldiers back, many catching on fire and falling onto their backs, cursing and screaming.

Glasse moved to cast a spell of violet light up at Kaile, who was preparing another ball of what he'd called, Orb of the Sun. As Glasse moved to attack, and Garland and Alicen ran to the door behind them, the other digger bomb exploded down the road, causing more chaos and confusion.

Soren's boots hit the ground, back into the shadows. As he made his plan to get to Glasse, he saw the two soldiers guarding him weren't dazed or stunned. Those two were veterans, and would be need to be taken down.

Glasse's spell paused in his hand as another, more immediate danger entered the fray—in the form of a half-height, ax wielding, maniacal dwarf. He came from nowhere and cut a soldier's leg clean off with a solid swipe through the knee. The soldier, partly on fire, collapsed, screaming and clutching at his leg. Davin raised his ax over his head and cleaved the man's head in half. Blood gushed up, hitting Davin in the face.

Kaile threw down another ball of light, and Glasse's spell erupted from his hands in a pillar of violet light, colliding with the ball in a blinding explosion halfway between them that shuddered the air, and sent electric, searing waves all around.

Soren made his move.

There was forty feet between them.

Soren slid through the shadows, silent as death.

As the battle raged and grew to a mad fever, Soren's gaze was heavy on Glasse, possibly the most powerful being of Londindam. But out of the corner of his eyes, Soren couldn't stop the feelings of betrayal as Alicen pulled back, staggering in terror at the attack.

Soren was halfway to Glasse. Alicen and Garland were at the door to the room. Garland and she pounded on the door, screaming for help. Soren was nearly upon Glasse, but he'd have to leave the shade to cross the road.

So he did.

He felt the torchlight break the spell the Twilight Veil had upon him, as many of the soldiers instantly snapped their gazes to him—especially the two guarding Glasse.

"Kill him!" Glasse spat as he hurled another pillar of violet magic up at Kaile, who continued to bombard the area with Orb of the Sun spells.

The two huge soldiers moved between them, both with sharp swords and heavy armor. Their eyes narrowed, and both saw the scars on Soren's face. That didn't deter them, though. They held their stances, and Soren rushed in to meet them.

One soldier's sword swooshed over Soren as he ducked low to evade. The other's came crashing down immediately after, far quicker than a big man like that should be able to move.

The first had another blow incoming with a wide arc as quickly as Soren dodged the second.

That's when he knew—the soldiers were imbued with some form of enchantment. Soren would have to end this quickly.

All the battle was happening so quickly. The remaining soldiers were still in a mad daze, trying to deal with the berserking dwarf and the onslaught of magic reigning down like a maelstrom of the goddess. Glasse was well aware of Soren, as he glowered at him when the moment arose. Glasse remembered him, and his arm in a sling was a stark reminder of that.

"Soren!" Alicen yelled, covering her mouth with her hands.

Soren clenched his teeth and stuck Firelight into a soldier's thigh up to the crossguard. It slid in between two plates of armor like hot piss melting through fresh snow. The enormous soldier with the enraged, dark eyes behind his helmet didn't even flinch. He raised his knee and drove it into the side of Soren's face, the heavy metal cracking into his jaw.

Soren was dazed momentarily, but leaped back to put distance between the two lumbering soldiers, one with fresh red blood pouring down his shining silver armor.

"Soren! I didn't know!" Alicen yelled in the chaos behind Glasse. "I didn't know what they were going to do!" Tears streamed down her cheeks, and Garland continued pounding on the door.

"Open this goddamned door immediately!" he yelled.

Soren didn't have time to deal with the two seasoned, enhanced soldiers. Glasse was the target. Not them.

Instead of heading straight, he darted to his right, into the building, and leaped up, grabbing onto two beams that supported the roof. He lifted himself up, disappearing once again into the shadows. The two soldiers were immediately baffled, hollering at one another to search for Soren.

Glasse noticed too, and his jaw slacked. He spun quickly

and launched his spell up at the section of roof Soren had disappeared into. It exploded into the building, and shot clear through, knocking the roof back onto the snowy street with a tremendous boom.

Soren had already moved from the spot, and saw dozens emerging into the road to see the battle.

Need to kill him and get out of here!

Alicen and Garland were nearly directly underneath, as another digger bomb exploded down the road. They both jumped and screamed—Garland muttering to himself, "I don't want to die, I don't want to die."

The plan was working, and Glasse, with sweat pouring down his brow, had to spin to deal with the incoming spells of the archmage's apprentice. Davin continued tearing through the ranks of soldiers, who didn't seem to share the same enchantment as the two hulking ones searching for Soren in the shadows.

Alicen looked up above her into the empty shadows.

"Soren, I didn't know! I didn't know what they were going to do! I swear! I swear it!" Her eyes were glassy, reddened and showed the deep panic and sorrow in her. "Please. Help me. I didn't know they were going to kill them. I didn't know."

Whether or not you knew about it, this is partly on you. What did you think was going to happen? You told them about the Silver Sparrows in Erhil!

Glasse was right there, right past Alicen and Garland. All Soren had to do was leave the shadows one last time, and feed Firelight what it desired most. But something else emerged into the battle Soren didn't expect.

From the hole in the building, small fingers clasped the shattered wood from the inside. Soren watched as the two sandy-haired children began climbing out from the inside. Alicen ran to them. She yelled with her hands up, trying to force them to stay in, as they cried for their mother. Two young girls, both not older than ten, cried, panicking for their mother.

Garland ran over too, but began climbing over into the building, disregarding the mother and her two young girls.

Shake it off, Soren, deal with Glasse. He's what matters.

But Soren couldn't shake it off. The amount of hatred he had for Alicen then took him over.

He pulled the ring from his finger.

"He trusted you," Soren said, hanging from a beam above. "I trusted you."

She looked up in panic, her frantic gaze snapping at his enraged one.

"I know, I know," she cried. "But I didn't know what they were like until after. They lied to me. I'm so sorry."

"Bael died because of you! They all died because of what you did!"

The two hulking soldiers were moving toward Soren, and Alicen pulled the two young girls, possibly her daughters, over the broken structure to her. Garland fully disappeared inside.

"Soren," Davin yelled. "What are you doing? Get him! Get him!"

"You betrayed everyone," Soren said, as Alicen clutched her crying girls in her arms as she knelt.

"I know. I know," she cried. "They said I'd have a better life for us. And I'd be helping save everyone from them."

Soren felt the anger in his stomach, boiling up into his throat.

"You're either a terrible liar, or a complete fool! You should die for what you did to that town! Think of all the children that burned alive! Think about them!"

"Soren," Davin yelled while in the thick of battle. "He's getting away!"

Soren was so filled with rage, he didn't even look as Glasse was making his way further into the road, into his platoon of soldiers.

"I can't stop thinking of them!" Alicen yelled. "They haunt me every second of every day. And I deserve to die. I know it! But I don't want my daughters to grow up without a mom. Please, Soren, remember me for who I was. I cared for you, and you cared for me."

He did. And he still did.

Soren sensed an immediate danger—more so than the encroaching soldiers—he spun, and with Firelight, knocked away a rock the size of a fist. It hurtled to the side of his arm, and he was left staring into Davin's mad eyes.

"Glasse!" the dwarf shouted. "Get him!"

Chapter Thirty

"You and me..." Soren growled to Alicen, as he fell from the beams above to the front stoop beside her and her sobbing children. Firelight glowed in red waves as it reflected the torchlight. "We are not done. Not even close."

With the two huge soldiers nearly upon him, they both stabbed with their swords as he evaded, running after Glasse.

Glasse was halfway down the road then, with the remaining soldiers following. Davin, swift with his short legs, followed. Blood dripped down his ax as he ran. Two soldiers lay dead behind.

"After him!" Davin yelled. He then motioned up to Kaile, running along the rooftop beside the Synth below. "Stop him!"

Kaile cast another Orb of the Sun before Glasse, erupting in the road before him. Soren was swifter than anyone else in the battle. Weaving through the soldiers, making his way to Glasse, Firelight gripped tight.

Kaile cast another spell, with the C note ringing out from his staff, filling the air. He leaped from the building's edge, and where a normal man would have plummeted hard to the ground, he flowed down as if walking down stairs, but his legs hung stiff. His cloak tails flowed behind, making him look like a demigod to Soren. It was even enough to make Soren stagger.

With his staff erupted into flames, still floating down from the rooftop, Kaile suddenly shot out a pillar of flames at Glasse. It sizzled the air, and Soren felt the heat on his face.

Glasse, with his staff in one hand, flung it to his side, knocking Kaile's spell to the ground, erupting the road in head-height flames.

"You son of a bastard," Glasse snarled, blocked by the wall of flames. The soldiers around stopped and turned to face Soren, Davin, and Kaile. Kaile's boots touched the ground and the three of them stood surrounding Glasse and his eight soldiers. The two lumbering ones weren't far behind Soren.

"Edward Glasse," Soren spat. "For your part in the murder of all those in Erhil..." He glowered hard at the Synth with his brow furrowed, fists balled. "You're going to die, right here, right now!"

"Ha!" Glasse laughed. He twisted to the side, letting his deep, ocean-blue robes kiss the ground. He indeed held a powerful presence, and his ego and confidence gushed. "Still crying about your friend the Knight Wolf cut down? I would be too. Since you didn't do a damned thing to stop him." His words cut deep, though Soren tried hard not to let them.

"It was more than Bael that died that day," Kaile said in a stern, harsh voice. "How can you live with yourself knowing all those innocent people that died there? How can you even go on?"

"King Amón is a spiteful, cruel man," the Synth said with the corners of his mouth smirking up. "Far better to be with him, and have to deal with his... *dark wishes*... than to be standing where you are. You think you're going to live much longer after this? If I don't cut your life cords here and now? It will be all-out war upon you. The king doesn't allow defeat.

What you're doing is far worse than idiotic—it's a death wish for so many in Aladran. Did you ever stop to think about that?"

"Glasse," Kaile said, extending his arm toward him. The soldiers around Glasse looked to one another, to figure out what Kaile was doing—if he was about to cast a spell or not. "Come. Join us. Help us fight our good battle."

"Kaile, no!" Soren shouted. "He's one of them. Don't be foolish."

Davin turned and ran at the two oncoming soldiers, clashing into battle. Soren knew he needed to join him, but the fight was now on both sides of them.

"Ha, you think I'd join you? Defy the king? I may be old, but I'm no madman. You've made your bed, traitor! Alcarond will come for you, and soon."

A nervousness washed over Kaile as if he'd been stricken to the bone with icy water on his skin. He recoiled, pulling back to Soren's side.

"Yes," Glasse said, with wicked fire burning high behind him. His blue robes glowed from the fire's light. A dark, grim look overcame him as his face shadowed and his golden spectacles glistened. "You haven't the slightest idea what you face. Opposing our king is certain death." An insane smile grew on his face as his eyes slightly misaligned. "But there are things even worse than our mad king in this world."

The soldiers before him muttered, and turned to watch the Synth as his voice grew raspier and deeper.

"King Amón wishes to purge this world in the cleansing heat of pure fire," Glasse said, his face deepening in color, and his wicked teeth showing. "But I don't want that. I don't want the world to burn. I want the world to know fear… I want it to feel it in its veins. I want it to pour from every orifice in every person of every kingdom. I want the world to seethe in misery until it all crumbles and falls into chaos. Then, and only then… will it be ready for what *awakens*."

"Awakens?" Soren asked, with his fingers spread in his free hand. "What awakens?"

"You don't know?" Glasse asked as Davin slammed his ax into a soldier's side, causing the man to curse out in fury. "You've seen it. Face to face. You and your friend both, Bael, was that his name?"

"What are you talking about?" Kaile asked, scratching his sleeve, as the soldiers, also unsure of what Glasse spoke, pulled away from him.

"Oh no," Soren muttered as Davin heaved his ax into the soldier's head behind, killing him as he fell to the ground. The soldiers around Glasse stepped away from in between Glasse, Kaile, and Soren.

"What?" Kaile asked. "Soren? What's he talking about?"

Glasse laughed as his face twisted in darkness. He took a tuning fork from his hand and struck the metal on his staff. It rung not one of the major notes, but a B minor.

"I may not be an Aeol like you," Glasse hissed. "But even a Doren as powerful as I am, I will still beat you." He took his staff up and slammed its bottom tip into the ground. The B minor seized the air, roaring out of the city like a lightning strike. Soren felt it in his chest and it weakened his legs.

"A B minor?" Kaile said, shaking his head. "What's he using that for?"

Soren grunted, and his eyes narrowed. "Get ready…"

"Get ready for what?" Kaile asked.

"You think you know the true power that exists in this world? You think the Ellydian is the one gift of the goddess? There's more to this world than just that. So… so much more…" Glasse said as the fire raged behind him, and his face became shadow behind his golden spectacles.

Kaile sent the note from his staff ringing clear and hard, standing in a defensive position, as Davin and the soldier behind both stopped fighting to watch the Synth grow as dark as obsidian.

"Welcome," Glasse hissed, "to the new world."

Suddenly, a crash erupted to the western edge of the city.

"Soren," Kaile muttered. "What's he doing? What's going on?"

Soren looked down at Firelight, watching the red glow off of its edge.

His heart pounded, and he swallowed hard.

"Suddenly," Soren said. "I think this dagger here is the only thing that can save us."

Screams filled the air in the western part of the city, as buildings crashed to the ground. Something was coming. Something big. Something dangerous.

"What is it?" Kaile asked. "What's going on?"

"It's him," Soren said. "Can't you see? He's the one that tried to kill Bael and I out in the forest with a cursed coin. Glasse is the one who started all this. He's the one who brought them here… he's the one… who brought the Black Fog."

Kaile spun to face the crashing creature flying through the city. "The Black Fog? Here?"

"Your magic won't work against it!" Soren yelled. "Kill him! Kill him now!"

Kaile turned back and cast his fire at Glasse, who deflected it with a raging, violet fire of his own.

Soren turned to the west, toward the cause of the thing destroying the city.

The soldiers turned and fled, and Davin came to Soren's side.

"No one has ever survived the fog," Davin said as Kaile and Glasse fought behind them.

"I did," Soren growled.

"This is different, lad," Davin said. "It's in the city."

"I don't fear death," Soren said. "And I don't fear the Black Fog…"

"Speak for yourself," Davin said. "That's the one thing I fear most in this world, and you'd be a fool not to."

"I killed Shades," Soren said. "I can kill this too."

Davin clapped his thick fingers around Soren's wrist. "Fight bravely and fight hard. You are our only hope, Soren."

"Help Kaile," Soren said, as the oncoming destruction was nearly upon them, only six blocks away.

Davin turned and ran to help Kaile as Glasse walked backward through the flames and deeper into the city behind.

Soren's feet spread, and he held Firelight up to his side, cocked just over his shoulder. "Come on, you fucker. Let's see how invincible you really are!"

Chapter Thirty-One

The night sky darkened. The fires roared, crimson and violet intertwining in an unworldly inferno. Glasse stood before Kaile, the Dor of Londindam, against the Ayl of Lynthyn.

"It's too late to stop what's coming," Glasse said, his words thick with disgust.

Davin hefted his ax, only twelve feet from the Synth, surrounded by the roaring inferno. "Distract him and I'll cut him in half."

"Will do," Kaile said through clenched teeth. The ringing of his C note flooded the air, mixing in an awkward, twisted sound with the very rare B Minor from the Synth's staff.

They heaved fresh spells at one another, with both fires erupting into a violent, crashing explosion that sent Kaile and Davin back to the ground. Glasse still stood, having erected a glowing violet sphere around himself that soaked up the last bit of fire from the explosion.

Glasse, his eyes fierce, his face as dark as shadow, and his golden spectacles cracked, threw them to the ground and strode over to Kaile, who lay in a daze—moaning and struggling to find his staff, laying on the cobblestones feet away.

Davin got back to his feet quickly, heaving his ax over his head, but with a movement of Glasse's hand toward him, Davin went flying back. He fell back again to the ground and tumbled shoulder over broad shoulder until he lay on his stomach with his nose pressed flat against the gray snow. He tried to get up, but fell back quickly. He turned his head to the side to watch Glasse stride over to Kaile.

Glasse stood over Kaile, sneering with yellowed teeth. He heaved raspy breaths as Kaile reached out hard for his staff, still inches away. The sounds of the oncoming Black Fog still roared through the city, nearly upon them, and Glasse shoved the point of his staff between Kaile's eyes.

"Alcarond chose you to be his apprentice? You? A fisherman from the house of a drunk whore and a miserable, mean father? What he saw in you, I never knew. But he'll respect me when he sees I bested you. He'll respect me when I'm one of the most powerful Syncrons in the world!"

"You're no Syncron," a voice called from the side. Both Glasse and Kaile looked over to see a small woman walking through the flames. Her black hair whipped wildly behind her thin neck and pale face. Her lime green eyes sparkled with hate as she glowered at Glasse. "You're the devil in disguise."

Glasse kicked Kaile in the jaw hard with the tip of his boot, as Seph gritted her teeth and the flames roared behind.

"You don't know the devil," Glasse said. "You've seen nothing of my power yet."

Kaile groaned as he rolled to his side, moaning, cobweb deep in his mind.

"And what power is that?" she asked, striking her staff with a tuning fork swiftly. A beautiful E note rang out from it. "Some form of dark magic. Something from the old world?"

Glasse stepped over Kaile, knocking the boy's short staff

away with a flick of his long staff's tip. "So here you are, alive after all these years, eh? The last Whistlewillow, here to reclaim a name that's lost all resonance in this world? You can't redeem your parents', or your uncle's, failures. It's a lost cause, girl. You've should've stayed in that forgotten hole you hid under. There's nothing but pain out here for you, girl."

Seph bit her lip and choked down her anger and spit. "I *am* the last Whistlewillow, and I'm here to get my revenge. Your king killed my parents, and to get to him, I'm going to wipe that miserable fucking smirk off your face and bury you in the fucking ground."

"I'd love to see you try," he hissed, holding his staff up at her, and she pulled hers in front of her.

"Bring everything you've got… old man…"

∾

Soren stood hardened, unwavering, fearless.

The Black Fog burst through a stone structure at the far western end of the road. As the black monster appeared, not a single soul was seen. Everyone that drew breath fled, tucked away and silent, or running as fast as their legs could carry them.

The fog slowed as it entered the wide road. The tip of eyeless, black head was pointed like a beacon toward Glasse, behind Soren. But the huge black mass slowly turned, cocking its head as if sniffing something it hungered for.

It walked with its dozens of spidery, black-as-coal legs over the rubble, making its way fully into the middle of the road. It was over a hundred yards from Soren, but it turned to squarely face him.

Its body was enormous, over fifteen feet high and stretched over eighty feet long. It was by every definition a monster, and the largest Fog Soren had ever seen. Its smoky black body moved slowly, inching toward Soren like a centipede. Wisps of black tendrils flowed out behind it as it moved as silently as the night.

Soren took two steps forward.

"Come on you monster!" he yelled at the top of his lungs. "What are you waiting for? C'mon!"

The Black Fog steamed forward, hurtling down the road toward Soren. It moved faster than any horse, with its legs scraping the stone road, crawling forward like mythical legs a great sea monster might bear.

"C'mon! Let's see what you've got!"

Soren took another two strides forward, then shifted his weight to his back leg, and stood in a side stance. He held Firelight in his right hand, twisting it slowly with its tip pointed directly at the oncoming beast.

The Black Fog was halfway to him when Soren twisted the dagger further, causing its red glow to shimmer. He shifted it upward, letting the starlight and firelight catch the rippling metal of the Vellice dagger with a majestic, ethereal glow. The fog halted instantly, silently, and eerily. The smoke of its gigantic body wafted around it, steaming up from beneath the creature.

And then something happened Soren did not expect.

The fog at the front of the monster fell back. It pulled back like something had blown fresh air at the front of the fog, and as the smoke pulled back… eyes emerged.

They were eight, as lifeless as death, yet as wise as ancient trees.

Looking at the tiny eight eyes in two vertical rows of four, Soren saw the black, onyx orbs weren't looking at him—but the dagger.

Soren waved the blade in front of him, doing a slow swoosh of the dagger through the air, and the eyes never flinched away from it.

"You know," Soren said low to himself. "You know what this is, and you're afraid. Good. Now you know fear and know that you're not the top predator in these lands anymore. I am... This is my home."

Soren walked forward as the winter winds blew past him. His hood flew back and his cloak tails and hair whipped behind him. He didn't need the Twilight Veil. He didn't want to hide from the monster before him. He wanted it to see him. He wanted it to see he wasn't afraid. And he wanted the Black Fog to see what its true enemy was.

"I'm here, you bastard!" Soren yelled with both hands out wide and Firelight glimmering crimson. "You want this dagger? Then come and get it!"

∾

SEPH SQUARED OFF AGAINST GLASSE, who was darkened with seething hatred. Her frail frame paled to his as her skinny arms had her cloak sleeves hanging at her elbows. The winter winds gusted hard, smelling of fire and powerful magic. Glasse hunched over in his dark blue robes, which whipped behind him. The snow at their feet had all but melted from the magical flames surrounding them—and the battle had begun.

Glasse, killing the B Minor from his staff and striking a D instead, let a spell of roaring red fire erupt from his staff—firing at Seph.

Seph, still using E, sent a shockwave of pure, biting cold from hers, flying at his spell as they collided in a violent explosion that sent a steaming mist shooting out and rising into the air. It hissed as they hit, but was loud, like a thunder boom from the heavens.

Glasse's expression soured, and he shook his staff angrily in his veiny hand. Kaile still lay struggling to get up, and Davin, too. But both were stirring from the fresh magical fighting.

"You bitch! You're no Whistlewillow. You're a miserable, loser vagabond, just like your worthless uncle."

"I'm whatever I need to be, to beat you, you monster. You can summon the Black Fog. How many have those things killed? You're part of that. You're part of that evil."

"Evil is just another term for those that don't understand," he hissed. "Evil and heroism are all taken in the eye of the beholder. You don't see, yet. You can't. There's a beauty coming. Something this world has not seen in far too many ages."

"You'll die before I let that happen," she said, swaying her short staff before her. She let fly the icy spell at him. It froze the air itself as it hurtled toward him.

His flames caught the spell, and again they collided in a hissing mess of steam. Seph glowered in anger, clenching her teeth and twisting her hand on her staff.

"Seph," Kaile moaned from the ground, still feeling out helplessly for his staff. She could barely hear his words, but they were just loud enough for her to hear his next ones. "You're an Ayl. Use the Aeolian." It was a whisper, but just enough.

The E ringing out sharply from her staff sparked alive, ringing a clear tone all around the battle. A golden wave surged out from the dragoneye stone at its crest. It poured out in all directions, soaking into her arms, clothing and face as it hit.

Glasse's face twisted, heaving a huge plume of unimaginably hot fire. The fire burst on in a huge swath from his staff, completely enveloping Seph in its wrath. A shimmer of blue light flickered behind the flames around her body. The barrage of violent flames covered her, but began to grow outward from her, like a chick emerging from its shell. Blue light broke through the flames like the egg cracking, letting the chick breathe its first breaths, feel its first air… come alive.

The blue light beamed out brightly in sheets like heavenly

ribbons stretched tight. And suddenly, the blue light broke out in a wide sphere, pushing back the flames that poured out from Glasse's staff. His face twisted further in rage. His dark eyes glared in hate; the corners of his mouth turned down—disgusted.

The sphere widened, and Seph emerged, with both arms out wide over her head, and a blue angelic light beaming from her skin. The dragoneye stone glowed a pure, intense, starlight white. With a great push of her magic, the magical flames of the Synth burst backward, extinguishing in the cold air. His spell faded, and he had a nervous twitch in his eye.

"Skin of a Fae," he grumbled, hating the words as they left his lips.

"Do you hate it?" she said, soaking the blue rays back into her skin. "I've heard there are powerful Ayls here in Grayhaven. How does it feel to be a lowly Dor from some shitty castle up north? Does it bother you what they say about you in the late hours of the night, laughing over wine? Do you think they laugh about you? How weak you are? How stupid you are? I bet you do. I bet it tortures you—knowing you're not as good as them. You'll never be as good as them."

"Fool!" he yelled instantly, bursting a pale white spell from his staff at her. As if knocking the wind from her lungs, the blue light was cast out of her, leaving the form of her body in blue light falling out of her, behind, like a frail ghost.

It was such a jarring spell. She fell onto her back, struggling to keep hold of her staff. She knocked both elbows hard onto the ground and slammed the back of her head on the road.

"Seph!" Kaile moaned, watching with blurry eyes as Glasse walked over to her, putting his boot onto her wrist which held her staff, straddling her, and bending over to stare into her eyes.

"Skin of the Fae." His words were filled with resentment. He spat on her, hitting her on the cheek as she turned her head

THE LAST WHISTLEWILLOW

to the side. It oozed down as she turned back to look at him, fighting to break her hand and staff free from the weight of his boot on her arm. "Funny thing about young Syncrons like yourself... they forget all the other spells. You think you're impervious when you cast a spell of protection like that. I've grown too powerful for spells like that to have any sway."

A glimmer of light flickered on that dragoneye stone at the crest of her staff. It was only small enough to reflect off the road like moonlight hitting a shimmering snowflake as it twirled down from the Halls of Everice.

"One thing I've learned about old creeps like you," she said with a wink. "You're easily distracted by your desire. Even if that desire is killing me."

He raised his eyebrow and tried to fight it off quickly, but it was too late, as the claws and teeth sunk and cut into his hand.

"Damn! What the?" He shook his hand, still wrapping his veiny fingers around his staff—as the black cat bit and clawed at it. His other hand hung in a sling, but he used it trying to grab the cat's tail. Its claws scraped through the skin on the back of his hand, and she bit into his fingers as he cursed. His boot still remained on Seph's wrist, but as the dwarf's ax came in swinging hard from behind, Glasse spun, swinging his staff so hard it threw the cat off. He unleashed a spell of blasting fire at the incoming dwarf.

Davin fell back in a heap of flames that enveloped his body.

"Davin!" Kaile shouted, crawling to his friend, rolling on the ground in flames, screaming in pain.

"I'm done with this!" Glasse cursed, spinning back to Seph, angling the tip of his staff down at her, only to find hers up pointed up at him. Their tips clacked as they touched.

"Then let's get this over with," Seph growled.

On his dark face, the color of deep charcoal, a maniacal grin crossed his face, and then an intense, hateful scowl emerged. Looming over Seph, it looked as if the devil had found flesh, hosted a body, and was holding a huge staff at her.

Wisps of black magic trailed out of his knuckles and rolled down the staff, to its tip, and toward her. "Daughter of the famous Calvin and Violetta Whistlewillow. Pff. You could've been great. You could've been one of the greatest to ever live. You could've even become one of the great Lyrian Syncrons given enough time—but you had to come here. You had to make the choice to spite me, in my home! You came to my home! Well, girl, that will be the last mistake you ever made, and I'll be the one who wipes your miserable, stained family legacy from time."

The black magic flourished. It hung on the staff like mist on early morning water, but spun like a slow, eerie whirlpool.

"It's all about power to you," Seph said, lifting the back of her head from the ground. Hints of golden magic emanated from between her palm and the staff. "Nothing else matters as long as you have that."

"Yes," Glasse hissed. "Power is everything. Power is all there is."

"You're wrong," she muttered as the magical flames of both staffs intensified and glowed. The deep, abyssal black swirled around his staff, causing Seph's hair and robes to whip on the ground. Her golden light poured out from her palms, creeping up the front of her shirt, illuminating her skin with an angelic glow.

Kaile reached Davin, helping extinguish the flames with his own robes, as the putrid smell of seared skin filled the air. "Kill him!" Kaile shouted in the torrent of magic.

"I hate to lose good Syncrons," Glasse said through clenched teeth. "I really do. But I must deny there's no better feeling than seeing the last bit of light in their eyes before they fade."

Seph didn't reply, but clenched her teeth, squinted, and

focused on the raw power of her staff, as a bright beacon of golden light surged out from the dragoneye stone.

"Goodbye, daughter of the Whistlewillows," Glasse said as the B Minor poured out of his long staff, growing to a deafening tone that made Kaile and Davin cover their ears. "May the afterlife treat you better than this miserable world did…"

With a great roar, the black smoke of his staff turned to scorching flames as they consumed his staff and went crashing down onto Seph. The searing fiery flames overwhelmed her, covering her body and pouring out all around her on the street.

"Seph!" Kaile shouted, barely audible in the ringing B Minor.

The black flames pulsed from his staff in waves, pummeling her tiny body in his dark spell. The heat was so intense it emanated all around, melting all the remaining snow for one hundred feet in all directions.

"Seph!" Kaile yelled again with his hand up toward her, his staff still strewn away, and with a forearm over his face to shield himself from the heat.

Glasse poured the black heat on without mercy, teeth gritting and mad eyes wide, lavishing in the sight.

There was a subtle laugh from within the flames. Glasse cocked an eyebrow. At the tips of the black flames, a golden, sparkling hue emerged. From within the ball of black flames that covered her body, an orb of golden glowed. It was like a divine egg that covered her body.

Glasse was enraged. He cursed as he shot down even more flames onto her body, causing the air to heat further, and Kaile had to hide his face and skin as he draped his body over Davin, who lay motionless on the ground.

"The thing about obsessing about power," Seph's voice said from within the golden orb, "is that no matter how strong you are, there's always someone more powerful, and it can really bite you in the ass."

The golden light of the dragoneye stone exploded in gushing light. It tore through the air, and the pure sound of the beautiful E note of her staff overwhelmed his. The orb that protected her body burst outward, erupting with a thunderous boom from high in the heavens. With its explosion, it pushed his own dark spell back, sending his own black, scorching flames at him. They crashed into him, instantly catching his blue robes alight, causing him to shield his face as the undersides of his arms burned the skin away.

He cried out in pain, moving back as the black flames consumed his body. It had all been so chaotically fast, and incredibly violent, that it took Glasse a moment to think, to kill his own spell. The black flames receded to within his staff, but the damage was done, as smoke rose from his skin, and he staggered backward.

"You bitch, you spiteful, nasty little bitch!" He stumbled backward, trying to recollect himself, and his staff hummed in B Minor again. But as he got his feet under him, and his robes still burned in patches, he opened his eyes as the heat had abated. But it was only just in time to see Seph standing before him, her lime eyes staring into his. She was flying at him with such quick speed, he tried to react, but the shimmer of something in her hand caught his gaze.

Seph moved with such speed, and Glasse was so completely caught off guard, that he couldn't concoct a spell fast enough, or even get his slung arm up in time. Seph lunged, and stuck the tuning fork so deep into his eye she heard the pop, and drove it all the way in, to its handle.

Chapter Thirty-Two

The world faded away.

There was only supreme focus.

For if Soren lost this fight—then there would never be another one.

Seph would fall just after, the only thing Soren cared about in this wretched world.

But there was a catch. *Why was there always a catch?*

Looking up into the eight soulless eyes of the Black Fog, as it raised up onto its back spidery, centipede-like legs, Soren knew it wanted more than to just kill him.

He knew the Black Fog didn't just want to kill and consume him—because if Soren lost this fight, and almost surely would, then he'd become one of the cursed—one of the Shades.

The Black Fog towered over Soren, casting a long dark shadow across the road and onto him. Its underside had the same tendrils of black that splayed out from behind as it normally hunted on the plains. It looked like a portal to another world, and in a sense, absolutely was.

Its arms spread wide at its sides as it glared down at Soren, silent as the night, as destructive as a tornado.

"C'mon!" Soren yelled, flashing the red glow of Firelight before him. "If you want me, then here I am!"

The fog cocked its head, its obsidian eyes never blinking. Its head then lowered, arching its back, looking down at him like a hunched worm. It was only twenty yards from him then. He'd seen them move on the plains, and Soren had every ounce of his strength ready. Every muscle was ready to explode with movement when the time came. For any wrong movement he made, would be his last.

"What're you waiting for, you worm?" Soren asked. "I'm the one who killed your babies! Remember? I killed your Shades! I made them bleed. I cut them down. They're dead. They're gone because of me. And I'm going to do the same to you, you monster!"

The Black Fog did something unexpected then. Its body fell to the ground, never taking its eyes away from glaring at Soren. But it began to hiss. It was a low-pitched hiss, almost like a low groan, as its sharp legs clattered against the stone ground. Soren felt the ground beneath him shake. Its hiss intensified, and it hummed from deep within its body.

"She's angry," Soren muttered to himself. "Good…"

This is it, Soren. It's all come down to this. All your training over the years with Landran. He was preparing you for this. Don't let him down. Don't let Seph down.

Make it dirty.

Make it count.

You're only going to get one shot at this.

"Come on, you bitch," he growled. "I want to watch you bleed…"

In a flash, the fight erupted.

The Black Fog shot at Soren with immense power and speed. It flew at him far faster than Ursa could ever run. Its legs hurtled its immense body toward Soren, who only had one option for such a massive incoming force.

His boots dug into the stone and he leaped hard to the side. He tucked his chin to his chest and rolled, landing on his feet as the fog barreled beside him. Its legs were only feet from him, as he stood there with his weight low and his feet spread.

Its head turned to see Soren, still standing. Soren thought that was perhaps the first time it had ever missed its prey, and Soren waved the Vellice dagger at it tauntingly. Its hiss intensified as its legs dug into the road, breaking into it with its sharp, claw-like tips.

As the fog readied another attack, angling toward Soren, he did the opposite of what any sane man would do. Instead of running… he ran at the fog.

Its legs were only feet away, and bent like they were, were half his height. He flipped Firelight over in his hand, letting the blade stick out the bottom side of his fist as he swiped at the legs.

The legs of the monster, as thick as a muscular man's arms, to Soren's astonishment—and anger—evaded his swipes. The legs lifted over his whooshing swipes with a quickness he'd never expected from such a huge monstrosity.

The fog lurched to the side, its head careening toward Soren. Its legs pulled in tight to its body at that side, pulling back into its foggy skin. Soren rushed with quick steps down toward its tail. The long body of the Black Fog nearly folded over to chase him.

Soren knew the only reason this fight was still ongoing was because of the dagger. He needed to keep it between him and the monster at all costs. As he raced, he kept its point pointed behind him. He had nowhere to run, nowhere to hide, and no idea how to combat such a force. His only hope was the dagger.

Firelight is the key.

He reached the tip of its body where its black tendrils spread out like sharp octopus legs. Soren thought he may be the first person ever to approach the backside of a fog, and with the adrenaline pumping hard in his legs, arms, and chest, and his heart beating like a drum, he turned off his mind—and let the animal come out.

Instinct roared within him, and his body and heart took over.

He felt the whooshing shadow beside him and felt the fog's legs clicking on the ground from within its huge body. The fog towered over him completely, almost like fighting a full-grown dragon in tales of old. Every sound, and every nuance of the situation became a song all around him. The clicking sounds were beats, the hissing was the rhythm, and the shadow was the overtone. But every song ends, and as the monstrous head of the fog was just behind Soren, the shadow pulled back from its head, and a round mouth of thousands of slick teeth emerged. It was pink as daises with splotches of black rot embedded in its gums, from which the needle-like teeth curled inwards, ready to pull whatever came within its maw in deep.

The mouth was as round as Soren was tall, and its eight eyes glared down soullessly as it prepared to feed. Soren glanced back, with Firelight still propped out at the back of his fist.

And as he saw the mouth, with the great hiss pouring out nightmarishly from deep within, Soren had a single thought burst into his mind—it does have a hard body inside. It's not all smoke. And what is hard… can be cut.

Soren took a chance, as he was mere strides from the tendrils at its back, with its mouth ready to devour. He knew not what the tendrils were or would do to him, but he leaped on top of them—dozens of snake-like tentacles slithering far behind the beast. His boots fell deep into them, knee deep, and he was stuck. He spun to see the head of the fog pause, as Soren held Firelight out, glowing and shining red from the light of the stars above, and the fires that burned around.

He felt them slither along his shins and calves. Some began to curl around his ankles. The fog's head hung only six feet away, frozen in place as the waves of curled teeth stretched within its mouth.

"Let's see how this feels, big girl…"

Soren pulled his arm up, angling his elbow out and aiming his knuckles at the tendrils. As the enormous Black Fog's hiss turned to a bellowing, deafening roar from deep inside, Soren drove his fist, and Firelight cut into the arm-width tendrils.

The Vellice dagger cut through easily, slicing two in half instantly, and left a third hanging together by only an inch. Black blood poured from the cuts and spurts of it shot onto Soren's legs, as he knew he needed to escape quickly, as the fog writhed.

Its roar was something like what might come from the depths of the Under Realm itself. It was guttural, filled with rage and pain, and low like an erupting volcano.

Its head lifted in pain, angling up to the sky, as Soren lifted his legs high to crawl over the squirming, powerful tendrils. But he didn't get far.

The tendrils, far stronger than he expected, wrapped around his legs, and began reaching up for his torso like thick, heavy, powerful vines, like constricting snakes. He slashed at them wildly, fighting to break free, and as the Black Fog roared, its legs moved quickly, carrying its body forward.

The speed jolted Soren's upper back as it plowed down the road, back from where it came, then bursting up on top of a two-floor building, causing Soren to fall onto his back on the tendrils, still wrapping around his legs.

Once atop the building, its gigantic body began to coil, and as the fires burned below, and Soren found himself quickly staring into the eight eyes of the beast once again, this time glaring down on him from above, Soren finally got back to his feet.

The tendrils continued to wind up his legs, but the eight eyes wouldn't move their glares from the red glow of Firelight—dripping in its thick, oily blood.

He waved the blade in front of it as a warning, but Soren knew he was in trouble. He was stuck, pinned to its back, and the monster was still mostly unharmed except for a couple of tendrils gone. Its eyes were still brimming with hate, and its mouth salivated as it was aimed directly at him.

Soren looked behind him, to a full two-story drop, and then before him to the black body that curved up to the evil head, ready to devour.

He knew there was only one real option left. Soren knew he needed to defeat this beast, or it would be left to kill everyone. Never before had a Black Fog entered a city, and here it was, in the middle of Grayhaven—a pure form of absolute destruction, chaos, and death.

Soren had to fight, there was no escape.

So, he tore into the tendrils once again, with the dagger crafted from one of the masters of Vellice cutting in deep, without hesitation, and with all the power he could muster. But this time, he wasn't trying to cut out, this time—he was cutting in deeper. The monster roared as the tendrils whipped all around him, and their sharp corners slicing into his skin. One cut across his forearm, another nicked his chin, another crashed so hard into his thigh he worried his femur may snap. But he just kept cutting, moving further into the beast, even pulling himself forward with his muscular fingers, pulling him in with the tendrils, as they grew thicker and strong.

He was soon completely enveloped in them, so far into the backside of the monster that the smoky body of the beast wafted around him like dark mist. Soren had nowhere to go but forward, so he sliced and pulled, trudging through like an infinitely black jungle full of vines that pulled him, and snakes that bit him. His heart pounded in his chest, and the full rage he was in held any pain he may be feeling at bay as he cut, harder and deeper.

Finally, just as he was gasping from the lack of air and the smoke of its body, Soren found something he didn't expect.

Light.

It wasn't much, but it was there where it shouldn't be.

A thin sliver of pure white light was before him, seeping through a gash he'd created from the dagger. The tendrils whipped over it, hiding it past them as they curled and slithered.

He shoved his arm forward, almost completely wrapped in the strong tendrils that squeezed. He cut the gash again, and as the dagger's tip slid into it and across it, a spectacular light emerged. It glowed in waves as the gash widened. Past the black smoke of the fog's body, it appeared as though a pool of silvery-blue liquid flowed within.

Soren's clenched jaw relaxed at the sight, and his jaw hung open at such a wondrous, unexpected sight. But the moment was brief, as he remembered the gravity of the fight, and remembered Seph was somewhere out there, outside the slithering tendrils and suffocating darkness around him.

He gritted his teeth, and with all the strength in his arm, drove the dagger directly into the glowing liquid. He drove it in so deep, that his hand and wrist disappeared into the silvery blue. The Black Fog erupted in a roar that shook the world around him. The tendrils tensed in pain, cutting deeper into his arms, neck, face, and legs.

With his hand still in the liquid, he twisted his arm and cut deeper into it, feeling the thick liquid ooze around his skin. The roar of the beast was deafening, sending a piercing ring in her ears. Something strange was happening with his hand—it didn't feel as if it were a part of his body anymore. While it was inside the beast, and as he felt the Black Fog moving again down the building, he worried his hand was gone from him forever. It felt distant, cold, and separate.

The fog found the ground, and Soren fell hard onto his shoulder, hitting the side of his face and ear onto the hard stone. The light pulled away. The silvery liquid dimmed, and he felt his hand and dagger slide out of the gash. The tendrils eased on his body, slithering away.

An overwhelming sense of worry flooded Soren as the tendrils left him. He felt he needed to kill the monster, not let it go. It would kill others. It would turn them to Shades. He couldn't let it escape. There was too much to lose to let that monster go back out into the plains.

But it was too late. The speed of the gigantic monster slid away without a sound, back the way it came. Soren watched the back slide away, with broken bits of tendrils falling from it with black, oily blood leaking in long streaks behind.

As the Black Fog disappeared back out into the city, heading out back into the plains whence it came from, Soren felt a regret that he had lost the battle. And then the pain poured into him. It seeped into every cut in his body. A searing hot pain like red hot nails being prodded into his veins. He roared in pain before falling into a dark place he didn't want to go. The pain was so overwhelming, it overtook him. His whole body felt as if it was burning from the inside out, and the only place left for his mind to go from the unbearable pain—was death, he thought.

Chapter Thirty-Three

Glasse fell to the ground, dry from the scattered flames that had brushed all snow and ice far away. He lay awkwardly on his side, with his pale, skinny arms held up before him. His blue robes were half gone, left to scorched black edges that left his scrawny chest and bony back bared. The darkness of his face had retreated as blood rolled down from where the handle of the tuning fork protruded from his eye. The blood gushed down and pooled on his collarbone and the bottom of his neck.

He didn't scream, but his teeth gritted and his hands shook with anger as he pointed his staff up at Seph, still humming with the B Minor.

Seph, looming over him, appearing far larger and more menacing than she possibly ever had in her life, reached forward and grasped the tip of his staff. As the smoke still poured off his hands and forearms, skin still torn away from the heat that melted it, she yanked.

The old man didn't have the strength left in his fingers to match her rage. She tore the long staff from his hand and threw it back over her shoulder. It arced behind her and clattered on the ground, as the Synth's fury quickly faded. His head slunk, and he sighed deeply. Somehow the old wizard was managing to deal with the surely overwhelming pain all over his body.

"It's over, old man," Seph said. "Your time is done."

Kaile helped Davin get to his feet, still twenty feet away. Davin was covered in burns and groaned, muttering curses as he staggered toward Seph and Glasse.

Seph stood tall as she held her staff firmly aimed between Glasse's eyes.

"And who's to take up my role?" Glasse asked. "You? An orphan?"

"I will fight for what I believe in," Seph pressed the staff to his brow. "That should be enough."

"Perhaps you're right," Glasse said with a hint of defeat in his voice. "But isn't that what we all do? In time, you'll question your own mind, also, as we all do. Grow powerful enough, and you will carry regret for even those decisions you believed were most certainly just. Sometimes to kill a god, you must become the devil."

"Is that what you tell yourself at night?" Kaile asked, helping Davin over. "To sleep in your satin sheets, justifying bringing those monsters here? How many lives have been destroyed because of you?"

"Many," Glasse said. "Lower your staff." He moaned. "I'm powerless against you now."

"Don't," Davin said. "He could use his voice or use a fork. Don't trust him Seph."

She didn't budge.

"You're defeated and broken," she said. "And you deserve to die."

He looked up at her as his lip quivered. He was angry, bitterly angry from defeat. Seph's black hair whipped past as a stark, cold winter gusted past. His eyebrows lowered, and he gave a nasty scowl.

"I'm not done." His voice was bitter and seething.

"Give up," Kaile said. "This is over. Look, your beast is gone. Soren beat your Black Fog."

Glasse looked over his shoulder to watch just as the tendrils of the huge fog were disappearing back into the city, and people screamed in the distance.

"Uncle!" Seph said, covering her mouth with her free hand. She lowered her staff to run to him.

"Hold," Davin said in a grim voice to her. "We'll go to him once this monster draws no more breath. If he gets away, how many more will suffer, Persephone? You need to end this. Kill him, now!"

"I—" she said, sending shivers from her hand to the shaking staff between her and the Synth. "I—I can't…"

"What? Why in the Nine Hells, not? Kill him!"

"I—I've never… I've haven't…"

"Seph…" Kaile muttered. "You can do it. You have to!"

Her green eyes were wide, but her head shook subtly from side to side. "I can't…"

Suddenly the Synth's hand flashed before him, knocking her staff wide to the side, yet still securely in her fingers. With the same movement, while Seph was trying to collect herself from his blow, Glasse struck a tuning fork at his side on the ground. It hummed in a low A note.

"An A?" Kaile asked himself without thinking.

"Kill him, lass!" Davin yelled.

Seph cast a plume of blazing orange fire at him, but the spell washed over a circular, invisible orb around him. With the tuning fork still protruding from his eye, and a fresh one ringing in his hand—he stood.

Seph continued to pour the flames onto him from her staff,

but they flew over and past him into the building behind. Kaile ran to his staff, while Davin staggered before falling to a knee.

Kaile grabbed his staff from the ground and instantly struck a C note. Flames erupted from the tip of his staff and surged at Glasse, who stood with his arms loosely held at his sides. The fires both blew past harmlessly.

"Stop," Kaile finally said, and Seph's flames returned to her staff, as did his.

"I suppose it's all come to this," Glasse said, seemingly more speaking to himself than them. Sweat beaded on his brow as he used his burnt, torn sleeve to wipe them from his thick eyebrows. "Sooner or later, it all comes down to this moment."

"Huh?" Seph raised her eyebrow, and the fingers on her free hand spread. She turned to Kaile. "What's he talking about?"

"He's using an A note," Kaile said in a grim tone that was as bleak as wet, dark ink.

"What's that mean?" Seph asked.

Glasse lifted his chin and looked to the heavens. His arms spread out wide as he looked straight up at the star-filled sky. "The time has finally come. The true test. I am worthy. Goddess Shirava, protect me with your light. I am worthy, and I will become…"

"Kaile…" Seph yelled, "what's he doing?"

"Don't ya see, lass?" Davin said in a hollow voice. "He's attempting…"

Seph gasped. "…The Black Sacrament…"

Glasse began to hum. It was also an A note that rang from his throat and closed mouth. He closed his eyes, as if not feeling the pain from the fork cut into his destroyed eye. He raised his arms as he glared up at the night sky.

"Can we stop him?" Seph asked, running to Kaile's side, while Davin fell to both knees.

"No," Kaile grumbled. "Once the sacrament has begun… it's between him and the goddess."

She swallowed hard, lowering her staff to her side.

In the dark sky above, clouds floated in from the far corners of the sky. They pulled together like pulling the center of a bedsheet up, pulling in all the surrounding pillows with it. But as they watched it happen in the complete winter sky above them, they felt as if the goddess herself was present, squeezing the dark clouds together above Glasse in what would be his ultimate test.

"What happens if he passes the test?" Seph asked. "Can we beat him?"

"I—I don't know," Kaile said, shaking his head, frustrated with himself. "He'd be only the third Lyre in all Aladran."

"So Ayls can't kill Lyres?" she asked.

Kaile furrowed his brow and scowled at Glasse as the dark clouds twirled in an apocalyptic funnel above him. "There's a first time for everything."

"We've got to stop him," Davin said. "If he succeeds, then even after all this, not you or even Soren can kill him."

"Should we run?" Seph asked. "Get Soren and get out of here?"

Kaile stood tall and squared his shoulders. His demeanor darkened, and an aura cascaded down over him that made him feel vastly powerful, far stronger than an apprentice. He was more.

Seph noticed and took slow steps back from him. His reddish hair blew in the strong, gusting winds that swirled around them.

"You go," he said in a stern voice. "Save yourselves. But I have to stay. I have to bear witness."

"No," Seph said. "You'll die if he succeeds. I can't let you die. I can't lose you like this."

His gaze slowly turned to meet hers. He was as stoic as a

man three times his age, and he exuded more power than he ever had, yet no magic left his fingers or staff. "If I die, then I will die fighting." He faced Glasse again as the dark clouds above funneled down to the ground, flowing onto him as the A note rose to a thunderous volume. It was as if the storm itself rang with the same low note. "I have to be here for this. But you go! Run! There isn't much time!"

"Goddess Shirava!" Glasse yelled from within the cone-like funnel, where it appeared the sky itself was rushing into him. "Hear my words, and grant me the strength to become. I am strong. I am deserving. I am… a Lyrian!"

Seph couldn't take her eyes away from the monstrous storm that swirled around the Synth Glasse. His hands were completely enveloped in the swirling black clouds. His arms were still scarred in fresh burns, his eye was still bleeding down his face and chest, and it felt as if the world itself was ending on that very spot he stood.

"I'm not leaving," she muttered, hardly audible over the sound of the A note that shook the very air. She walked over to Kaile's side in the whipping winds, putting her arm around his. He looked at her as she did so, pulling herself to him. They stood there together, watching the Black Sacrament being cast for the first time in many years.

"Ashaka arrovia finilla poderium!" he said. The mysterious words shuddered in the air, breaking the world like a mountain splitting into sharp shards. As Glasse said the words, his voice was unworldly, as if a god or a demon was speaking with the power to break worlds. "Ashaka arrovia finilla poderium!"

"This is it," Kaile said. "Not much longer now."

Davin hobbled over to their side, watching the storm as Glasse's words messed with the sound of the A ringing like a hurricane.

Suddenly, a light broke through the clouds above. It was a heavenly white that appeared in a circle at the epicenter of the swirling funnel high in the clouds. The light grew from a faint candle-like light to an overwhelming pillar of light that cast down onto Glasse like pure, ivory moonlight.

"Ashaka arrovia finilla poderium!" His words broke through the storm like a hammer pounding hot iron on an anvil.

Through the light, a bolt of pure light shot down from the heavens like ribbons of lightning. They crashed through the charcoal clouds, swirling winds, and surging storm. They flew straight down, weaving down into Glasse's fingertips. It appeared as if he were orchestrating the heavens above. The light streamed down into his fingertips as he yelled out in exhilaration at the power that coursed into his body.

"Oh no," Kaile moaned.

Seph squeezed his arm tight.

"It's happening!" Glasse screamed at the top of his lungs. "I'm becoming! I am one with the Ellydian! Grant me your power, goddess! Fill my body with your light!"

Suddenly, the clouds filled the hole that the white lightning emerged from, and it vanished as quickly as it came. The clouds floated back up slowly, still circling, but slowing and rising. The A note, that had swelled to fill the world around them, began to dwindle.

The winds quieted, pulling back to still air, and Glasse stood before them, humming with the A note, and an aura that held immense power within. His eye glowed with a white light, brimming with frightening, terrifying magic.

"I've done it," he said in a raspy voice. "I am one of the Lyres."

"Stay close to me," Kaile said, holding up his staff at the Synth. Before their eyes, the burns on Glasse's body slowly faded. The unburnt skin grew, creeping up his arms like growing moss, covering the black, burned tissue.

"I feel it," Glasse said. "It's deep inside of me. Raw,

unimaginable power. It was fate I become one of the Lyrian." His gaze turned to Kaile, Seph, and Davin. "And my enemies shall feel every ounce of it."

His hand motioned toward his staff, twenty yards away, as it shot through the air, up into his strong fingers.

The dark clouds still spun above him as he turned to face the three. "You spiteful, arrogant little brats. How dare you attack me! In my home! You're going to be an example for every other rat in this miserable land. The broken shall be rebuilt. The wretched shall be cleansed. The weak will be replaced by the strong! And you three will rot in the eternal damnation of the Nine Hells!"

He pointed his long staff at them. It rang with intense magic as he struck the B minor back into it, letting the A fade away.

Both Kaile and Seph shot fire from their staffs at the Synth, who with a wave of his free hand, sent their spells colliding to the side, far from him. Black fire dripped from the Synth's staff as the white light of his eye faded to its normal pupil.

"I'd like to say I hate killing young, promising Syncrons like you two..." A wry, evil smile crossed his face. "But that would be a lie..."

The black flames whipped around his staff as he angled it at them.

"I'm scared," Seph said to Kaile.

"Me too," he said, pulling her in tight.

"I don't want to die," she said. "I feel like I just got to live..."

"Me too..."

"Farewell," Glasse said. "Aladran has welcomed the strong again, and has outcast the..."

Glasse's voice broke as he said the last words. He fought to say another word, but his throat caught. He coughed, looking away, struggling to breathe.

"Wh—what's happening?" Seph asked.

Kaile smirked.

Glasse clawed at his throat, gasping for breath, dropping his staff as it clattered to the ground.

"Is he…" Seph asked.

Kaile's body relaxed as his shoulders dropped and his voice softened.

"He failed…"

Glasse dropped to his knees, suffocating.

"You won't want to watch this," Kaile said, not taking his gaze for one second away from the Synth.

"Yes. Yes I do," Seph said, her words firm.

From above, the white light appeared again in the epicenter of the swirling dark clouds. The light turned to ribbons of lightning once again, but this time when they shot onto Glasse, it wasn't his fingertips it yearned for. It poured into his eyes, into his nose and ears. The pure white energy filled his body, as his skin glowed a shaking, hot white light.

On his knees, his back arched, his arms went out wide and he screamed with the last bit of air in his lungs.

The white lightning that surged through him was so intense, Seph and Kaile had to shield their eyes at the surging light.

The lightning poured into him, and with one last pulse of shimmering light that cascaded down the pillar of light from the clouds to Glasse, the light exploded into him.

With a loud crash of thunder, the area Glasse was in erupted into an enormous explosion, and Kaile and Seph were thrown back from the impact. They were thrown onto their backs as a wet substance hit their skin.

Upon their backs, they, and Davin, all tried to gather their wits again. And once they came to, seconds later, they saw the light was gone. The clouds had returned to the sky, and Glasse had vanished. As Seph wiped the substance from her face with her arm, she looked to see her arm smeared with fresh blood. She panicked, as if she was searching for the location of her injury.

"It's all right, lass," Davin said, standing over her, grabbing her by the hand. She looked to see the dwarf's face was half-covered in the same fresh blood. "It's not you. You're not hurt, at least no more than you feel."

She looked at the blood that covered her arms, and then saw the same blood on Kaile's face. "Is this... is this... Glasse?"

Kaile picked something from her hair and held it out for her to see. It was a thin sliver of white, sharp at both ends, and had hanging flesh from it.

"Is that... a bone?" she asked with a quivering voice. "Ew!"

Davin cleared his throat as he looked at the bits of Glasse covering them and the road all around them. "I think it's safe to say... I think he's finally dead."

Chapter Thirty-Four

Soren heard muffled voices in his darkness. They echoed as if they were deep within an ancient, wet cave. They were calling his name. He was so deep in his darkness though, he thought, why leave? The safety and numbness of the darkness welcomed him, and he welcomed it.

But something kept pecking at his mind. Like a woodpecker hammering into the side of an oak tree, hungering for a juicy grub. The voice grew louder.

But what if they need me? What if she needs me? Rouse, Soren. You have to awaken from this darkness. The war isn't over yet, and Seph might need you.

With every fiber of his being, he fought off the cool darkness that sunk its claws into him. And the harder he fought, the more the pain returned.

"Soren! Soren! Wake up! You have to get up!" He heard Seph's voice, distant, yet reaching closer with each word.

He felt his body jerking, and the back of his head lifting from the icy ground to nestle into her arms. Soren opened his eyes, squinting, as the torchlight overwhelmed him and throbbed in his head.

"S—Seph," he managed to get her name out. He tried to smile, but the smeared blood on her face caused him to panic. "What—what happened?"

She rubbed his cheek with her hand. "We did it," she laughed. "And you're alive." She smiled wide with her lips and chin quivering. She dropped her head to his so their brows touched, and she sobbed.

Soren was overwhelmed.

He didn't know if it was the searing pain returning deep within his body, or the great relief that she was still alive. It was most certainly a mixture of both, and that's when his eyes wetted with tears.

"I—I thought you were dead," Seph said. "I thought I'd lost you."

He cleared his dry throat and feigned a fake laugh. "Can't get rid of me that easily."

She pulled her head back, wiping her tears with the back of her free hand. Soren saw Kaile and Davin standing over him, too. Kaile seemed larger and more powerful than he ever had to Soren. Davin, Soren immediately saw, was in desperate need of help. His body and face were covered in burns.

"Davin," Soren grimaced as he tried to stand.

"Normally, I'd say relax," Davin said down to Soren. "But we need to get out of here. We may have accomplished our mission, but we're soon gonna be overrun. Give 'em a hand, boy."

Kaile went behind Soren and, with both arms under Soren's armpits, lifted. Seph helped.

As Soren got to his feet, his entire body writhing in some of the worst pain he could imagine, he was astounded by how many people there were filling the streets—and every single one of them watched him, wide-eyed and many with mouths agape.

Soren was used to stares because of the scars on his face, but nothing like this.

"Glasse is dead, yes?" Soren asked them in a hushed voice.

"Yes," Kaile said. "The Synth is dead. He attempted the Black Sacrament in his desperation."

Soren gave a humph. "Of course he did. What a fool. Did he use an A?"

"He did," Kaile said with a raised eyebrow, holding Soren up as he staggered. "How'd you guess that?"

"He'd use an easier note to try to pull off the hardest spell," Soren said. "Like you said, he was desperate. Should've invested more and done a more honed note. He wasn't deserving, though. Not in my eyes, and not in the eyes of the Ellydian, obviously."

"It's him," a man said, pointing a finger out at Soren. He was two structures down and surrounded by dozens that were already flooding back into the streets. "It's the Scarred the king is looking fer!"

The man looked around with a baffled expression. All others around looked too stunned to respond.

"Get him!" the man shouted all around. "There's a reward! It's more than enough to spread around."

A couple of stronger men stirred from the crowd, plodding forward.

Suddenly an elderly woman shouted, "He fought off the Black Fog, ya fool!"

Murmurs erupted in the crowds that were all around them. Even the soldiers that protected Glasse were returning, and Soren looked over his shoulder to see Alicen peering over the broken glass of the home Glasse had intended to visit. Her face was streaming with tears.

"Kaile," Soren whispered. "Can you go find Garland and bring him to me? If he's still in there? I'd go, but I can barely stand."

Kaile nodded and ran off to the building.

The crowds bickered from within.

"But he's the Scarred the king wants…"

"He saved us!"

"…the reward!"

"We're only alive because of him!"

Soren groaned, his body still roaring in pain. Davin dropped to a knee again, grimacing and heaving breaths through clenched teeth. The burns on his body were awful, and Soren felt for the dwarf. Those burns would be slow to heal, and would surely leave permanent scars.

Soren was so inundated by his pain, and preoccupied with his companion, he hadn't noticed Seph standing beside him, shaking. Her small fists were balled, and she had the look of pure hate on her face, tears rolling down from the corners of her eyes.

"Seph?" Soren asked, but halfway through her name, she strode forward to the center of the square, halfway between the crowd and Soren.

The crowd hushed as she approached.

"Hey!" she shouted. "What in the goddess's name are you fighting about? You may not have seen it, but it wasn't us that brought the Black Fog here. It was Edward Glasse. You know, the Synth who works for the king? And it was the Scarred that saved your miserable, ungrateful asses!"

"It's true," a middle-aged woman behind said. "I saw the Syncron, er, um, Synth call the beast! It was dark magic, it was…"

"And you have the nerve to talk about a reward for what, handing him over to the king?" Seph said in a staggeringly powerful voice.

Even the soldiers that had been accompanying Glasse seemed dumbfounded as they looked at one another for what to do, and most ended up just staring at the ground or Soren, who could hardly stand on his own.

"What I say is true, whether you want to hear my words or not," Seph shouted in anger. "King Amón burned Erhil, not because of the Chimaera! All those people died because King Amón is evil!"

"Heretic!" some in the crowd shouted. But most listened to the young girl who'd help save their city.

"He burned Erhil and everyone in it, not because of the plague, or because of the Silver Sparrows, but because he enjoys it! He likes to watch children suffer and die. And you know what? He did the same thing to Tourmielle ten years ago!"

There were many gasps in the crowds as they watched.

"Better make this quick, lass," Davin said, looking to the north and the many torches that were being carried by soldiers down from the towers.

"The king killed my family," Seph said, still crying, but holding her composure, not letting her voice crack or quiver. "I don't ask you to join in our fight, but I do ask you. Listen to my words, and let those words fill every shack in Aladran. There's a war coming, and those who you think may care for you may be the worst, most evil of them all."

Around the corner of the building, Kaile appeared, dragging a kicking and screaming Garland beside him. Kaile grew tired of the fight quickly, tripping him and throwing him to the ground.

"There!" Seph said, pointing at Garland. "They are the ones sworn to protect you, and that bastard from Cascadia knew all about the murders in Erhil, and did nothing."

Garland scrambled to his knees. "Get her! Get them! Don't listen to her lies! Guards! Guards!"

The soldiers in the crowd still waited, thinking.

The sight of Garland sniveling was enough to send

strength trickling into Soren's legs to help Davin to his feet, and they both walked over toward Garland, who put his hands up together, praying to himself at the sight of Soren, rugged and beaten the way he was.

"Remember what happened here," Seph said as her parting words before she followed Soren. "The Scarred defeated the Black Fog! Tell the world what happened here!"

Soren walked up to Garland and grabbed him by the wrist tight, squeezing hard and causing Garland to wince in pain.

"You're coming with us," Soren said through gritted teeth.

"No, no," Garland cried. "Not again. I can't go with you."

"Alicen!" Soren said to her, still peering up over the broken glass only ten feet away. Her two girls were terror stricken behind her.

Alicen stood, pushing her children behind her as she stared with grief-filled eyes at him. "Soren…" she mouthed.

"You were my only friend," he said, loud enough he didn't care who heard. "I trusted you. Hell, I even thought I loved you for a moment. And you've broken what's left of this shriveled, dead heart."

"It's not broken," she sobbed. "You're good, Soren. I see that in you. I felt feelings for you, too."

"And you did what you did?" Soren asked. "Why?" He pulled Garland's wrist in, as Garland fought and begged to be set loose.

Kaile, Seph, and Davin all watched Soren and Alicen. They all listened silently, hurt by the emotion in Soren's voice.

"I didn't know," she said. Alicen forced her children back, and walked from inside the house, out the door, and stood only feet from Soren. Her face was covered in a thin layer of ash and dust, with clean streaks where the tears fell.

"Yes, you did," he said, his voice shaking. "You knew all along, and you still ratted them out."

"They said they'd give me a better life, and my girls too. I didn't know they were gonna burn the whole town. I thought the Silver Sparrows were evil. I thought I was helping."

"You still believe that lie now?" Soren shouted. "Is that what you tell yourself at night? There are dead children being picked apart by buzzards there now. There's no burials, no gravestones. Thousands are dead because you were only doing what you thought was *right*."

"I know what I did was wrong now," Alicen dropped to her knees before Soren, clutching him by the hand and pant leg. "I'd do anything to take it back. I'd do everything different. I would've left Erhil. I would've left with you. We could've been happy together. I could've made a good wife for you."

"You're just a worthless whore." Soren regretted saying the word immediately after, but it was too late to take back. He choked back his tears. "You gave that coin that Glasse gave you to Bael. You did everything they asked you to. You didn't care who you hurt. You just wanted gold. Well, Alicen, I hope you have enough now to last the rest of your miserable life."

"Soren, please," she cried as she tugged at him. "Forgive me! I don't think I can live with this without your help. I feel like I'm dying every second of every day. I can't stop crying. I can't stop thinking about them. They were my friends too. I loved them. I didn't know what they were gonna do." She dove her head into his lap. "Help me. Help me, please…"

He squeezed her hand gently, looking at the two girls within the house, absolutely terrified. Soren put his finger under her chin, guiding her gaze up to his. She stood, staring into his eyes, lips quivering, both hands clasping his arm as he slid the back of his fingers down her tear-soaked cheek.

"No," was all he said.

Her fingers released his arm in shock, and she was frozen in place. Her mouth moved, as if searching for the words, but nothing left her throat.

"C'mon," Soren said. "Let's get out of here."

Garland fought and yelled for help, but none came to his aid. Soren pulled Garland behind, as Kaile grabbed his other wrist. Seph helped Davin, still wincing in pain. As they walked into an alley on the far side of the house the children were in, a shadowy figure emerged two roads down.

Einrick... Soren knew.

"Why are you taking me with you?" Garland asked. "I didn't burn that city. I didn't even know that's what the king was planning."

In the roads behind, hundreds poured in to witness the devastation and destruction of the battle. Most wanted to hear about how Soren had driven the Black Fog away from those that were brave enough—or foolish enough—to watch.

"I need information," Soren said.

"Information, what information?" Garland moaned. "I told you what I know."

Soren tugged Garland's wrist and forced him to face Soren until their noses touched. "You know what I know?" Garland's pasty face sweated immediately. "I know you're full of shit. I know you didn't tell me everything. I know you're a liar, and you're going to tell me the fucking truth if you want to live."

Garland swallowed hard.

"Who gave you the Vellice dagger? And why did it come to my possession?"

Garland, still face to face with Soren, fought to look away from the intimating, menacing gaze of the Scarred, but Soren pulled him in close again. Soren gritted his teeth.

"I'm not fooling around," Soren unsheathed Firelight and held it up to Garland's neck. A bead of his blood poked free and trickled down the edge. "I have no qualms about killing you right here, right now, for what you've done. If not for all of Erhil, but for my friend Bael, who you let the Knight Wolf murder in cold blood."

"Soren..." Kaile muttered. "We have to go."

Soren waved him away. "Tell me now, or I'll slit your throat, and it better be the truth…"

Garland squeezed his eyes closed as tears squeaked out. Sweat poured down his brow and round cheeks. "If I tell you, will you let me go?"

"It won't hurt your chances…"

"Lord Belzaar…" Garland whimpered. "He… said I had to do something important with it."

"I knew it," Soren said. "You didn't trade for it. What? What did he tell you to do with it? One of the most prized possessions in all of Aladran. You just handed over to me to think I'd spare your life? Tell me! What did he want you to do with it? Where was it going?"

"You really don't know, do you?" Garland finally laughed, half-terrified, half-entertained.

"What? Know what?"

"You are as dumb as they say, aren't you?" Garland laughed. "You! You fool. It was meant to go to you!"

"What?" Soren said, shaking his head, pulling back.

"Lord Belzaar of Zatan gave it to me, and it was given to him by someone who said it was to go to you, and only you."

"Why? How?" Soren gasped. "Who gave it to him?"

"That I don't know," Garland said. "And that I'll swear to the goddess. Even if you beat me, I'll be forced to just make up a name."

"How?" Seph interrupted. "How did you know Soren was coming to get you? And that you'd be by the tree that you stashed it in?"

"You think I knew he was going to wake me in the middle of the night and drag me from my bed? You think I'd allow that to happen? Shit… I was planning on taking it to Erhil when Soren was there in the spring. Only the goddess knows how that all happened. But once I saw the scars on your face, I knew."

"Why didn't you tell me before?" Soren asked. "Why keep the secret?"

"You obviously don't know the code of the powerful in these lands, even after all this time. Secrets are the most sought-after commodity of them all. We all have them, and we all wish them to stay that way."

"So you were doing a favor to Lord Belzaar to keep a secret?" Seph asked.

Garland didn't respond, but his face twisted in disgust.

That was all the answer they needed.

"That good enough for you?" Garland asked. "Now let me go. I'm not going with you this time. I'll fight kicking and screaming the whole way."

Soren threw his fist into Garland's face, sending him falling stiff into Kaile's arms.

"Leave the rotten bastard here," Soren said.

Einrick ran to them with his hood covering his head and face, with only a sliver of his face showing.

"Come, we need to go!" Einrick said. "We need to get underground. Quick!"

He ushered them through the streets as the winter winds followed from behind. Soren was at the brink of crippling exhaustion, and Davin could barely walk when they finally found the place Einrick was leading them.

"Down here," he said, reaching into a break between two lines of stone in the ground behind a shanty house. He stuck his fingers through and pulled up the slab of stone, hinged on the bottom. As he pulled it up, stairs were revealed leading down into the darkness below the city. "Move, quickly!"

Kaile helped Davin in, and then Soren motioned for Seph to follow. He staggered down behind her, and Einrick entered last as he lowered the stone entrance. Just before he let the hinged door fall all the way down, a black cat snuck through just before it sealed shut.

Einrick sparked a torch alight.

"Follow me," he said. "We will make haste east, where we will enter back into the plains with the aid of Davin's spell, and you'll make your way back to Lady Drake."

They all nodded at the plan, all overwhelmed, but still driven by the adrenaline pumping through their veins to survive. They needed to get far from there, for the hounds would be after them soon. They all nodded, except Soren. Seph was the first to notice, and she cocked her head.

"Soren?" she asked. "What's wrong?"

Soren held his composure, for he knew what her response was going to be.

"You are going to Skylark," he said. "But I am not."

She didn't respond, but walked up to him and glared at him as the light of the torch glimmered on both their faces. The long scars down his face deepened in the shadow of the torchlight.

"I'm going into the desert. I'm going to find Lord Belzaar. I need to know the answer to this. And you need to get to Mihelik to train."

"I don't need Mihelik. I need you."

"Listen, Seph…"

Seph reached up and smacked him across the face, hard. It was hard enough, and quick enough, that his head fell to the side.

"No, you listen to me, you son of a bitch." Her brow was furrowed, her eyebrows angled down meanly, and her lips pulled back to show her teeth. Her lips quivered, but her words rang harshly. "I don't need anyone else. Don't tell me what I do and don't need. You're not my father. I don't need anyone to tell me what's best for me, or what's right, or what's wrong. You hear me? I need you! And you need me! Kaile can train me along the way, just like we've done. And guess what? We're still here. We're still alive. And I was a part of that, and so was

Kaile, and so was Davin. So if you don't like that, then too fucking bad!"

She slapped him again. "And that's for making me think you were dead back there…"

Soren didn't respond. He was too proud.

Fine. I guess we're all going to Zatan… together…

The End
Continued in Book III

Continue Reading

The story continues in Book 3:
The Fallen Apprentice

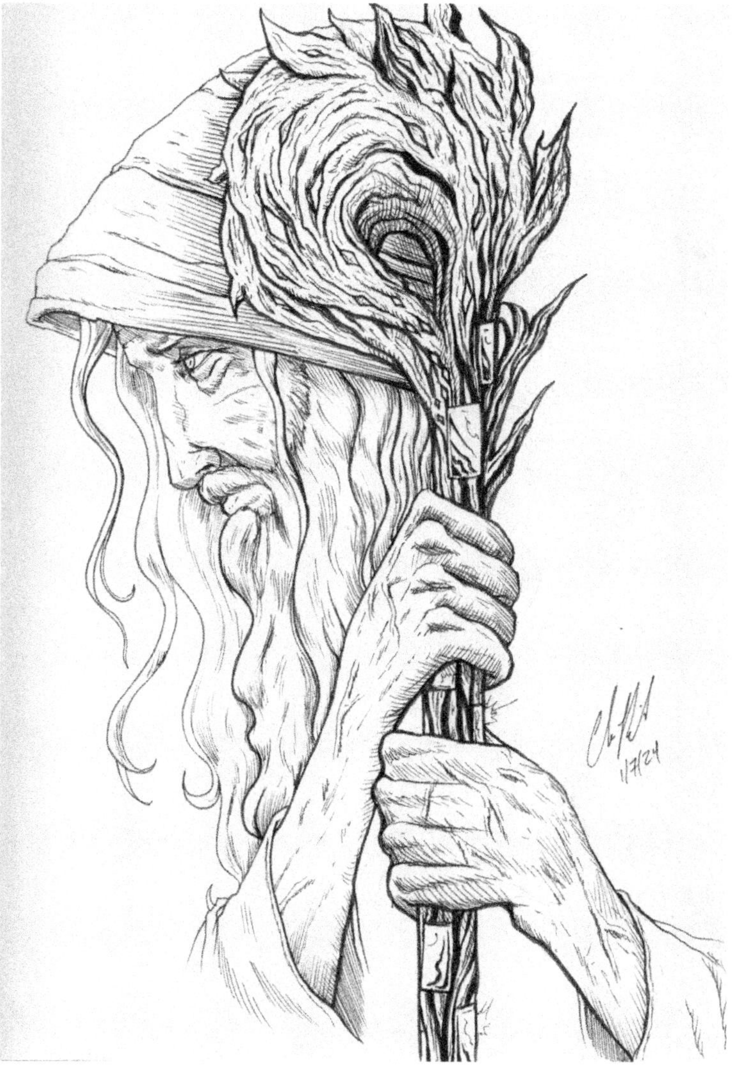

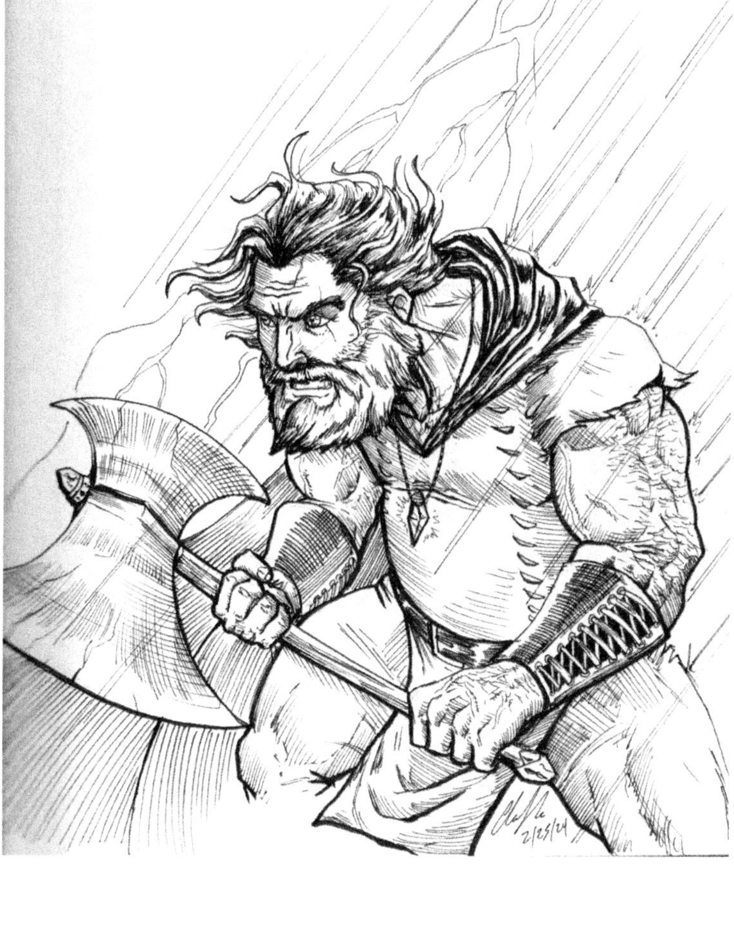

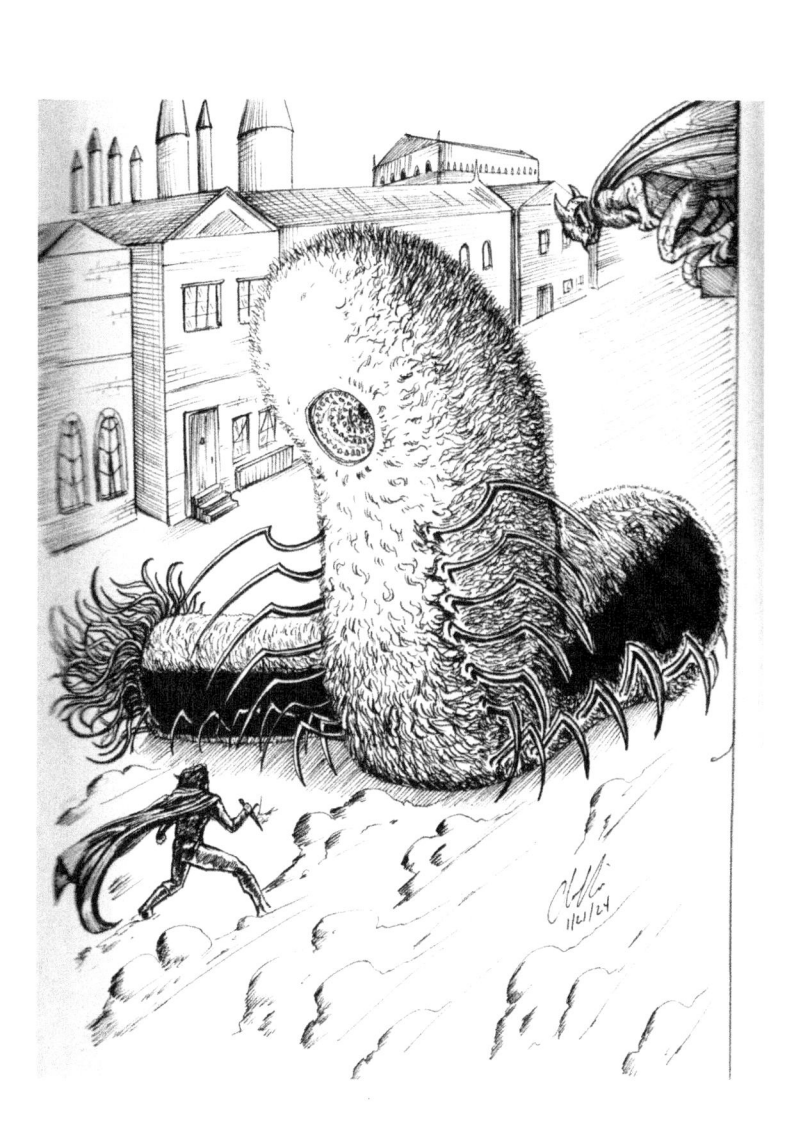

Pronunciation Guide

Aeol – A-ol
   Aladran – Ala-dran
   Alcarond Riberia – Alka-Rond Rye-beer-ia
   Arkakus – Ar-kackus
   Arnesto Piphenette – Piffin-ette
   Arnor – Are-nore
   Ayl - Ail
   Bael - Bale
   Cascadia – Cas-cad-ia
   Celestra - Selestra
   Cirella – Si-rella
   Dor - Door
   Doren – Dor-en
   Ellydian – Ellid-ien
   Erhil – Air-hill
   Garland Messemire –Mess-i-mere
   Guillead – Gil-ee-ad
   Ikarus – Ick-arus
   Kaile - Kale
   Larghos Sea – Lar-goes

PRONUNCIATION GUIDE

Londindam – Londin-daam
Lynthyn – Lin-thin
Lyre - Leer
Lyrian – Leer-ien
Malera Amón – Mal-er-ra A-maan
Mihelik – Mi-hay-lick
Myngorn Forest – Men-gorn
Roland Carvaise – Roland Car-Vase
Shivara - Sheevara
Solomn Roane – Solum Rone
Sundar – Sun-dar
Syncron – Sin-chron
Synth - Sinth
Tourmielle – Tour-me-el
Vellice - Vellis
Zatan – Za-tan
Zertaan – Zer-taan

Author Notes

The last four months have been a journey with this book. I'm not the fastest writer, and not the slowest. I'm often hailed by many as super fast and cranking out books, but I don't really enjoy that sentiment, because many writers I admire crank out a book a month. Crazy to many, including me.

This year, as I write this, in 2023, I finished the last half of Book 5 of Riders of Dark Dragons, wrote the Scarred, and now have completed the first draft of The Last Whistlewillow.

While Riders of Dark Dragons has become my most successful series, in terms of numbers of readers, and mostly great reviews, I feel as if Song of the Ellydian already has a special place in my heart, and I'm excited to see how people react to it.

In my eyes, Soren can be so flawed, so weighted down by his past and the failures that haunt him. But when it comes to a fight, who else would you want standing between you and an invincible monster?

In this book, I really focused on the dynamics between the characters, deepening the world, and pouring gravity into their

AUTHOR NOTES

cups. Writing the end of this book had tingles overwhelming my head and scalp at some of the scenes.

This is why I write.

Sure, I want to tell lots of stories for people to enjoy, get swept away to other lands, and forget about their troubles, but the feeling of creating something meaningful from nothing, beginning to love characters in your head, and can come alive on the screen and on paper really is a marvel of what we call life.

This year I turned 41, kind of a turning point in my life in a few ways, but it also casts a great spotlight of self-reflection on me. Ever since the Las Vegas writer's conference last November, I feel like my life is changing. I've turned off essentially all news, a lot of social media and other distractions. Although I still enjoy spending way too much time on YouTube… I'm trying to do what I should've done during the COVID lockdowns. I should have dug my head in the sand, focused on my worlds like Brandon Sanderson did, and created, not wallowed in for lack of a better term.

The future is bright, but many things in this world seek to distract us from our goals, from our capacities, and what we can accomplish in this life. You may disagree, and that is absolutely your right. We all have our own right. But for me, I'm going to focus on improving my life, helping others the best I can, and creating worlds that wouldn't be able to have legs if my brain didn't send signals down to my fingertips to click on letters on a keyboard to create words that glow on a screen in my lap.

This is book 17 in my journey. 20 is the big even I wish to hit soon. And hopefully that will be 2024.

Song of the Ellydian is planned to be a seven-book series, and in my head I plan to "write it" as two trilogies and an epic tomb last book. Although I won't break it up as such, perhaps if I release box sets of them, they may appear that way.

AUTHOR NOTES

I feel like writing this has been a little deep, but that's just where my head is at the moment as I drink my sixth cup of coffee sitting with my dogs as the sun has just come up.

So for my next trick, I'm going to make these author's notes... disappear!

Cheers, C.K.

About the Author

C.K. Rieke, though he constantly dreams of oceans and mountains, was born and lives in Kansas. Art and storytelling were his passions, beginning with "Where the Wild Things Are" and Shel Silverstein. That grew into a love of comic books and fantasy novels. He always dreamed of creating his own worlds through the brush and keyboard.

Throughout his college years, Rieke ventured into the realm of indie comics, illustrating and co-plotting stories that hinted at the epic narratives to come. But it wasn't until his early thirties, inspired by the works of fantasy luminaries, that he turned his hand to writing his own tales. The labor of love that was "The Road to Light," painstakingly crafted over two years, marked his debut into the literary world under the guidance of a revered editor.

Within the pages of his novels, Rieke spins tales of daring adventure and intricate character arcs that ensnare the heart. Yet, be warned, dear reader, for his pen is not without its blade—occasionally, beloved characters meet their untimely demise, prompting fans to pen letters of both torment and anguish.

C.K. Rieke is pronounced C.K. 'Ricky'.

Go to CKRieke.com and sign-up to join the Reader's Group for some free stuff and to get updated on new books!

www.CKRieke.com

Printed in Dunstable, United Kingdom